13 Days
AT
ANDERSONVILLE

The Trial of the Raiders

A Novel by
PHILLIP J. TICHENOR

Copyright © 2010
Phillip J. Tichenor

All Rights Reserved
Including the right of reproduction
in any form in whole or in part

This is a work of fiction based on an actual trial of prisoners, by other prisoners, at Camp Sumter (Andersonville) Prison in Georgia during the summer of 1864.

ISBN: 1449998119
ISBN-13: 9781449998110
Library of Congress Control Number: 2010901126

Cover photo: Reconstructed stockade wall at Andersonville, including the "deadline" rail fence which prisoners dared not cross for fear of being shot.

Author's Note

Perhaps no image of a military prison is etched more deeply in American history than Confederate Camp Sumter in Georgia, better known as Andersonville prison, during the American Civil War. Some 45,000 Union soldiers and sailors were confined there during the last 16 months of that conflict, and nearly 13,000 died from disease, infection, starvation, bad food and inadequate medical care.

Adding to the horrors of Andersonville was a gang of men known as Raiders, captured Union soldiers themselves, who for four months brutalized the camp with thievery, outright robbery, assault, and murder. Finally, between June 28 and July 6 of 1864, an uprising of other prisoners, supported by prison guards, led to capture and trial of the most notorious of these thugs. More than a dozen were tried by an unusual court martial made up of Union sergeants, themselves prisoners. Six Raider chiefs were convicted and hanged inside the stockade on July 11, 1864.

What remains a mystery is the trial itself. Since it was conducted outside the main stockade, it was not observed by the inmates at large. Various diaries and memoirs, and testimony at the later trial of Commandant Wirz, claim that a transcript of the trial was sent to the Confederate headquarters at Richmond, Virginia, for approval before the sentence could be carried out. However, to date, no transcript or other official record of this trial has been found. Similarly, there are no diaries or memoirs, known to this author after extensive inquiry, from inmates claiming participation in or direct observation of the trial. At least one fictional video version puts the trial *inside* the stockade, with thousands of inmates watching and shouting, but that scenario is contrary to all the available primary documents.

Some diaries reflect what writers *thought* was happening, but not a single one found is based on direct observation. One diary names a "Mike" who was said to have participated in the trial, but the same diary says nothing about what this man may have reported *about* the proceedings.

This is a fictional account of that trial and related events of the time. The names of the six convicted Raider chiefs—Collins, Curtis, Sarsfield, Muir, Delaney and Sullivan—are authentic, except for some question in the records and literature about whether Sullivan, or Curtis, was also known as Rickson. Captain Henry Wirz, General John H. Winder, Sergeant LeRoy Key and Judge Charles Mason were real persons, although words and actions attributed to them here are invented.

Coulee City, the home of Lucius McCordle, is a fictional town in the Midwest, then thought of as the frontier. Actions, words, and character descriptions of Sergeant Mahlon Blanchard, while fictional, are based partly on personalities of the era.

Author's Note

All other characters, including Lucius McCordle, Harry Nickels, and various stockade inmates and participants in the trial other than the six Raiders and Sergeant Key, are fictional.

During the time of the actual trial, Confederate General Jubal Early was on a semi-secret mission down the Shenandoah Valley en route to assaulting Washington D. C. That historic campaign is central to the plot of this novel. However, all personal actions and statements attributed to General Early here are fictional.

On the other hand, telegraphed military communiqués interspersed between chapters, from both the Confederate and Union Sides, are taken directly from the archival records, with one exception: the lost-and-later-found letter of June 13, 1864, from Lee to Early, which is a complete invention.

Acknowledgements

The author is indebted to Irving Fang, Hazel Dicken-Garcia, and Louis Tichenor for their thorough reading and critiques of earlier drafts of this work. He is equally grateful for the interest and patience of spouse Jo Tichenor and her support during the hours of research and drafting which this project entailed. The author alone, however, is totally responsible for the final version presented here.

The inspiration for this novel occurred while the author was deep into the study of Civil War-era newspapers of western Wisconsin and eastern Iowa for an earlier documented book about the life and civil war experiences of his great-grandfather, who had been a farmer and country lawyer, enlisted in the Union army, was captured in Virginia, and died in Andersonville Prison in August, 1864.

Like the real person in that book, ***Civil War P.O.W.: The Life and Death of a Farmer-Lawyer-Soldier,*** by Larry A. Jones and Phillip J. Tichenor, the lead character in this novel is a small-town lawyer from western Wisconsin who becomes a sergeant in the Union Army, is captured, and is sent to Andersonville prison. Personal experiences of the sergeant in this novel, however, bear little resemblance to the author's ancestor. Furthermore here is no evidence that the ancestor described in ***Civil War P.O.W.*** played any role in the actual trial of the Andersonville Raiders.

In writing this novel, the author had access to a wide segment of the extensive literature, primary and secondary, on the Civil War in general, and Andersonville prison in particular. This literature included a number of diaries and memoirs written by prisoners

Throughout this research, the author made extensive use of both microfilms and online materials that are made available by the National Archives. These materials include portions of military telegrams among various officers on both sides of the war, including Robert E. Lee and Ulysses S. Grant, which are interspersed between various chapters. These telegrams were found in *The War of the Rebellion (WOTR): A compilation of the official records of the Union and the Confederate Armies*. This material was made available on line by the Cornell University Library, whose cooperation is greatly appreciated.

In addition, the most-consulted historical sources about Andersonville were, for this novel, the following:

*Andersonville, The Last Depot, by William Marvel;
*800 Paces to Hell, by Dr. John W. Lynn;
*Images from the Storm, and Eye of the Storm, by Private Robert Knox Sneden and edited by Charles F. Bryan, Jr., James C. Kelly, and Nelson D. Lankford;
*Portals to Hell: Military Prisons of the Civil War, by Lonnie R. Speer;
*Tragedy of Andersonville, by General N. P. Chipman,
*The Life of Billy Yank, by Bell Irvin Wiley.
*The trial and death of Henry Wirz with other matters pertaining thereto. By S. W. Ashe.

ACKNOWLEDGEMENTS

*Several publications of the National Park Service's Andersonville National Historic Site, Georgia.

Prologue

October sunshine warmed the grassy path as the woman and child walked slowly and with apprehension up the slope in the rolling Georgia back country. Raucous crows ranted among the scrubby oaks, magnolias, and pines behind them, warning that in the clearing ahead lay the silent and rotting walls of a wooden stockade, remains of an institution many hoped to forget but nobody could. Weathered pine stakes once 20 feet long scattered like a ragged and remnant squad of delirious soldiers, momentarily surviving an apocalyptic battle but fated to succumb before the setting of today's sun. Here and there a few stood upright as if struggling for military discipline, their axe-hewn ends pointing stubbornly toward the blue sky. Others leaned askew while many more, broken and splintered off at the base, lay in the haphazard futility of corpses from a failed infantry assault, mutilated by legions of souvenir hunters who would take home or sell at curio shops these relic wooden slivers of an infamous human tragedy.

This was the main stockade of Camp Sumter.

A graying man in official uniform explained in sonorous tones that more than thirty thousand men lived in Camp Sumter and twelve thousand died between March of 1864 and April of 1865—some four years ago.

Most of you, he said, probably know this place as Andersonville. That, he added, comes from Anderson station, where the train squealed in with carloads of Union prisoners from the horrible War Between the States.

The 31-year-old woman, her red hair cascading down over her light shawl, led the nine-year old bronze-skinned girl away from the group and toward a sign that said North Gate.

Here, Aleysha, she said, is where Lucius did his lawyer work in that ugly trial. At least, so they tell me.

Aleysha saw out the corner of her eye a small group of African ancestry inside the stockade area, to the south of a little creek and a short way up the slope beyond. *I wonder if any of them are relatives of mine,* she thought. She turned back to the older woman and asked:

Aunt Maryanne, is this where Lucius died?

Maryanne sighed. Aleysha, you might say this is the place that killed him, but I don't believe he actually died here. We think he left here a living man, only to die at some other horrible place.

At least, that's what Mr. Harry Nickels said before he died. Maybe you were too young to remember Mr. Nickels? He was a prisoner here, too, but lived to come back to Wisconsin after the war, a very crippled and sick man.

What we do know is that the six brutes Lucius defended were all strung up, probably right over there.

She pointed to a spot not far from where the group of African-American visitors stood in fascination with the area before them.

Were they bad men?

Yes, Aleysha. Very bad. But Lucius always said, no matter how bad the criminal or how bad the crime, the defendant deserves the best defense he can get.

She hesitated, sighed, and added softly: That's why he worked so hard defending the man who killed your Pa.

Aleysha chewed her lip, and asked:

Aunt Maryanne…You started to tell me yesterday on that long train ride…but I fell asleep and don't remember if you said…was that why you and Lucius never got married?

And then the otherwise strong, composed woman from Wisconsin broke into tears and sobbed aloud, hugging the child.

Chapter 1.
The Secret Assault on Washington

At two o'clock in the morning of June 13, 1864, the flickering candle in the command tent darkly profiled the lanky frame of Jubal Early, his full, graying beard touching down to his field jacket. Darkness obscured the gold stars on his lapels, symbols that only a Major General could wear.

A mixed aroma of pork side meat, hard biscuits and heavy black coffee, cooked well before the usual hour, hung heavily in the damp air of this early Virginia morning. General Early's 8,000 Confederate infantrymen had eaten their meager breakfast and were now ready to march. That is, they were as ready as men could be when nearly half were without decent shoes or any footwear at all.

General Robert E. Lee's Bad Old Man, also known as Old Jube, was in an irritable mood. Three soldiers began dismantling his tent, and allowed one end of the heavy fabric to fall on Old Jube's head, knocking his cap askew. He swore bitterly at their clumsiness.

To Colonel Timothy Cranson, one of Early's staff officers, the General's bad temper was nothing new, even without the tent collapsing on his shaggy head. Contrary to what might have been expected, the successful but bloody repulse of Union forces at Cold Harbor ten days ago had not made General Early particularly pleasant. If anything, the long-legged but stooped Virginian, looking far older than his 48 years, grew increasingly irascible in proportion to his victories and those of the entire Army of Northern Virginia.

Orneriest cuss in the whole command, one of his officers said privately to Colonel Cranson, who agreed fully. Most men of the General's Corps hated him as a person. Yet when the cannons roared and bugles sounded, they fought for him with a ferocity matched by few other units on either side of this tragic war. Easier to face a line of smoking Yankee muskets than the wrath of this snappish commander.

Old Jube's eyes swept the scene before him. A long column of cannons, caissons, and meal wagons stretched out across the open field. A few bawling cows and steers—the mobile but inadequate fresh meat supply—milled around in the rear. Soldiers stood with muskets shouldered and backpacks strapped on, prepared for the march to Charlottesville, some 80 miles away at the upper end of the Shenandoah Valley. Horses, no happier than the soldiers to be aroused at this untimely hour, snorted and pawed. At command, they would push into their collars and pull wagons, cannons, and caissons along rutted and bumpy roads.

General Jube's sharp voice blared out across the field:

Get those goddammed horses moving, you dumb heads! We're doing 20 miles each day till we're back in the Shenandoah. We'll rid the Valley of that damned Yankee jackass Hunter if it's the last thing we do.

He watched a barefoot soldier hobbling along.

Cranson, Jube yelled. Telegraph those incompetent bastards at Richmond. Tell them to get off their asses with that shipment of shoes. Send them to Lynchburg and we'll pick them up next week.

Can't expect barefooted men to charge those well-shod Yankees over stubble, can ye?

It was as close to outright compassion for his men as Old Jube could manage.

Orders from unit commanders crackled in the still air. Drivers of caissons and supply wagons snapped their reins;

horse's heads dipped and rose in rhythm as the teams lurched forward. Freshly-greased wheels turned easily on their hubs, their only sound a crunching of well-worn sod under wooden wheels, soaked to stay tight and keep steel rims from slipping off and forcing a stop for hours of repair.

Columns of riflemen began streaming out, still hungry and worried more about meal wagons keeping up than caissons and cannons.

Shortly before the headquarters staff left, Colonel Cranson handed General Jubal Early a written message from General Robert E. Lee, stating officially what the famous Commander of the Army of Northern Virginia had told Jube to his face the previous day: Destroy Union General Hunter in the Shenandoah and, then cross the Potomac into Maryland and drive on Washington D.C. from the Northwest. But keep the plan secret.

Old Jube liked this plan. General Robert E. Lee was the only officer in the Army of the Confederate States of America that he truly respected.

As things stood, the Confederates had their backs to the wall. Even the horrible Union disaster at Cold Harbor on June 3 had not stopped the Federal advance. Instead of pressing directly toward Richmond, the rebel capital, General U. S. Grant had chosen to turn south. He would cross the James River with his massive forces and lay siege to Petersburg, south of Richmond.

Lee had told Early that a surprise attack on Washington would, one way or another, take the pressure off the beleaguered Confederate forces at Petersburg. When word of such an attack 110 miles to the north reached Grant, the Union General might well decide to send back to Washington a large segment of his forces—maybe 20,000 or 30,000 troops—and leave the remaining Union forces vulnerable to a devastating counterattack.

There was another possibility even more pleasing to General Lee. Grant might choose to launch a Cold Harbor-style frontal assault on the Confederate breastworks around Petersburg, so as to finish that job in a hurry before sending large units of his army back to Washington. Such an attack would almost certainly fail. It would be another enormous slaughter of bluecoats and a smashing victory for the South.

It was the kind of genius on Lee's part that Old Jube admired.

Since the written orders merely confirmed what General Lee had said in person a day earlier, Early had no further use for the note. He handed it back to Cranson, who jammed it into his haversack and mounted his horse, ready to ride west to Charlottesville alongside his commanding General.

That is, Cranson THOUGHT he stored the note this way. In fact, when he hurriedly pushed the note under the left side of his haversack's flap, without unbuckling it, he forced the piece of paper across and out the other side, allowing it to drift quietly and unseen, in the early morning shadows, to the ground. The Colonel wouldn't miss the note until later in the day, several miles away from Cold Harbor. He would then seriously consider suicide rather than tell his short-tempered General that it was lost.

Colonel Cranson knew well the story of how Union General McClellan's troops had found a copy of General Lee's secret battle plan shortly before the Battle of Antietam nearly two years earlier. Had McClellan taken full advantage of that discovery, odds were that he would have decimated Lee's Army of Northern Virginia and brought the Civil War to a quick end.

Now, though, Cranson figured this lost note could not possibly be found by Union soldiers. He decided to say nothing and hope he would never be asked for it. He was satisfied that the Union Army had gone south of Cold Harbor, across the James River, meaning none of Grant's units would ever come through this bivouac area.

By 3 a.m., General Jubal Early's Second Corps was gone. The only soldiers left were a guard detail in charge of some 250 Union soldiers captured during the Cold Harbor attack that General Grant had so unwisely ordered two weeks ago. Shortly after dawn, these guards marched their prisoners across the field General Early had vacated. This group's march would end a few days later in a hectic, start-and-stop train ride to Camp Sumter prison, also known as Andersonville.

Various scraps of paper lay scattered on the ground, and the prisoners snatched them up, hoping the clean spaces on those sheets could be used for writing to loved ones back home. Paper was hard to come by.

Telegram:
Headquarters Army of Northern Virginia   June 18, 1864
General J. A. Early   Lynchburg VA:

Grant is in front of Petersburg. Will be opposed there. Strike as quick as you can, and, if circumstances authorize, carry out the original plan, or move back to Petersburg without delay.
R. E. Lee[1]

---

[1] *The War of the Rebellion (WOTR) A compilation of the official records of the Union and Confederate Armies, Series 1, Vol. 37, Part I.   p. 766.*

Chapter 2.
Friday, June 24, 1864

Soft, cool rain splattered over the top of the boxcar, effectively washing the outside but without removing the stench. Mist mingled uneasily with heavy smoke billowing from the wide-topped stack of the ancient locomotive steaming, squealing and struggling to pull its load of Federal prisoners and underfed cows and pigs out of Macon, Georgia.

A lanky corporal, his head shaking listlessly, turned to his sergeant.

Lucius, what day is this, anyhow?

Lucius McCordle could hardly turn among the 60 or so men jammed into the rattling, jangling car that reeked of cattle and pigs. He regarded the question disdainfully, much as he would have as a lawyer a year ago in the hills and sweeping valleys of western Wisconsin.

It's Friday, June 24, 1864, Harry, he finally said, in an especially nasal tone aggravated by the stifling humidity of the cattle car.

Lucius always knew the day and date. He kept a diary in a small black book buttoned inside his shirt, one of many strict habits from his troubled courthouse days. It was a natural part of his orderliness, self-confidence and too-frequently-displayed brashness—traits from childhood that insured his being a Sergeant and not a Lieutenant or Captain along with most lawyers. Such traits seemed to work for others, but they had backfired on Lucius.

———

As if to forget the stink of the cattle car, Lucius pondered the events bringing him here. He barely remembered how his father Alex, and mother Kathleen came to America and settled in Coulee City, Wisconsin.

But he recalled well his 10 years of schooling and how he got into lawyer work. It was an escape from the drug business downstairs in the McCordle's dreary house.

Lucius never felt right about selling Calomel and Blue Mass pills to sick folks who were as likely to get worse as better from what he eventually learned was mercury.

He also thought being a lawyer would pay off if war came.

Oh, man, I was sure that getting away from the drug business and becoming a lawyer would get me Lieutenant or Captain bars. But it didn't happen. Shoot, as it turned out, I was probably lucky to make Sergeant.

Harry Nickels gazed at his corporal stripes, as if to convince himself that he had been a good soldier, but now fated to be a prisoner of the Rebels.

So they're takin' us to Camp Sumter, Lucius? Ain't that Andersonville?

That's what they say, old friend. Same place. Sumter is the camp, Andersonville's the town.

Hope it's as good as they told us, Harry muttered. I could use some good hot beans and bacon and barracks with half-way decent bunks. Could use a good warm woman, too.

Wonder if they ain't some lonesome rebel widows around here, the kind that gits excited by Yankee prisoners?

Friday, June 24, 1864

A big bearded fellow whose soiled private's stripe hardly showed on his tattered sleeve, growled. And just how you expectin' to get near rebel wimmen?

Don't b'lieve what they tell us, the bearded one continued. Them Rebs can't be trusted to tell when the moon comes up. Fergit the wimmen. They'll spit on us. And don't expect much for food, either.

Lucius grunted agreement. He doubted what the Confederate guard, a Corporal with broken teeth and a bad limp, told them a few hours earlier when the train stopped in a wooded area and the prisoners clambered out to do their bizness.

Y'all gonna be purty pleased when y' git to Camp Sumter, the Corporal had said. It's a new place. Has a grassy slope with a nice stream runnin' right through. Big shade trees. Keep the sun from burnin' yer purty white Yankee skin. An' y'all'll git good bread an' fresh beef from that big cook house they built there, jest fer the pris'ners. Eat better'n us out here guardin' trains. Mebbe even better'n the guards there.

He had grinned through his shattered and yellowed incisors, adding:

Y'all'll still be prisners, though.

Lucius pondered what this amiable chap had said. He took it with a grain of salt, but fully expected the newer Camp Sumter at Andersonville to be more tolerable than what he had heard about Libby prison up at Richmond. *Hadn't the rebel guards been quite decent since he and Harry were captured up at Cold Harbor? Maybe the horror story about Confederate prisons was a rumor planted by General Grant's officers, to scare Union soldiers out of allowing themselves to be captured.*

Yes, he had been taunted after his capture, by one or two men in butternut shirts, but for the most part they treated him as well as Union officers—and Sergeants like Lucius himself—treated their own men.

Well, Lucius thought, *these Rebs no doubt saw me as a tough Sergeant, better than many of their own.*

But tough? Hard to admit...but being a prisoner is almost a relief from the blood and horror of Cold Harbor. Still...how can I justify getting captured while most of my company were standing their ground, or taking ground, and dying for it? Well...who could avoid capture in that situation? I was the ONLY one to reach the breastworks, and my gun was unloaded. You can't reload on the run.

Some of these soldiers have taken bounties from men who don't want to fight and buy their way out. These damnable bounty hunters are likely to ask for capture, to save their own necks. Dregs of manhood, they are.

Guilt and humiliation were old demons tearing at Lucius' insides, making him wonder: *Am I TOO self-confident? Arrogant? Self-Righteous? Is that why I never was a highly successful lawyer? And now a Platoon Sergeant and not a Captain? But... isn't arrogance a virtue for officers?*

As a Sergeant in the II Corps of General Ulysses S. Grant's Army of the Potomac, Lucius in late May had charged ahead of his men across a hastily-built pontoon bridge spanning the North Anna River in Virginia. Other Union units crossed to the northwest. Lucius' officers assured him they were trapping some of General Robert E. Lee's ragtag Army of Northern Virginia soldiers in a pincer movement up against a loop in the river.

FRIDAY, JUNE 24, 1864

As a First Sergeant in his regiment, Lucius McCordle listened closely to what his officers said about strategy here. It was all part of a grand scheme to grind down and destroy the core of General Lee's Army of Northern Virginia, thereby opening Richmond to a Union takeover. Lee, they all thought, had retreated to the south, but foolishly left a few rear-guard units up against a river bend. These rebel troops, Grant's generals thought, could be assaulted from both sides, thanks to some existing bridges and a splendid pontoon bridge, installed rapidly by a Union engineer battalion.

After so many failed campaigns, the soldiers were in a good mood. Now, they thought collectively, we are on our way to rout Lee's army. Next, a quick march to the Confederate capital at Richmond will end the Civil War.

It was not to happen that way.

Lee had set a trap for General Grant which, if sprung, might have annihilated an entire Union corps of some 24,000 men in blue.

The shrewd Confederate commander had massed—not a rear-guard unit but his entire force of 30,000 troops—inside a huge inverted V of breastworks, hidden in trees and pointed directly at the river bend. This way, he could move his men quickly from left to right. He could swiftly attack either one of Grant's separated units with overpowering force, even though his total army strength was a third less than the Union's.

Grant came near getting caught in the trap. Unaware of the Confederate earthworks defining the V, he split his forces. Part of his command crossed the river northwest of Lee and a full Corps of 24,000 crossed to the southeast, thinking the bulk of Lee's Army was in full retreat toward Richmond. But when Union troops met heavy fire from barricaded rebel soldiers in the woods, Grant's officers finally saw the danger. To reinforce his brigade under attack on one side of the V, Grant's troops on the opposite side would need to cross the river twice—taking too long to save the beleaguered units.

So Grant pulled his troops back across the River, and sent them on another march south to cut off Lee's army at another point.

Lucius remembered, bitterly, when the troops got word to withdraw back across the river to where they had started. Disgust rippled through the Union ranks.

Out-generaled agin, a disgruntled trooper in blue grumbled. We just never git the big battle we're promised.

Well, General Grant says…

Fergit Genril Grant. He resembles Lee as much as a popple dog resembles a wolf hound.

Always d' same way, another agreed. We git outfoxed ever' time. Lookit Spots'vania. All that killin' and we ain't no closer to Richmond than before.

Lucius remained the loyal soldier and trusted Sergeant. He had the well-trained, life-long ability to look and act tough, steady, and true to his commanding officers. He had physical size and a voice low and gruff—when he wanted it that way. He couldn't tolerate other Sergeants—not to mention Lieutenants—whose yells in combat would shatter into stammering shrieks.

Aw, quit your complaining, he growled. That was a smart move, getting back to this side of the river. General Grant wants to win this war, as much as we do. Can't do that if half of us get our dammed heads blown off and the other half gets captured.

Murmurs and guffaws, only slightly muted, told him few soldiers agreed, much as they grudgingly respected him.

Friday, June 24, 1864

The grumbling shifted to another sore point: Only a few days earlier, an entire Union regiment had been taken out of the Army of the Potomac and mustered out of service. Their enlistment time was up, and they all scurried home.

Damn those bob-tail and rag-tag short-time skedaddlers, someone said.

Sullen disgust turned to bad temper the next morning, when the entire Union column set out southward, in a new plan to come at Richmond from the southeast.

For the next five days, Lucius' regiment marched, halted, and marched again, along dusty roads under a scorching sun. They ate and slept among ants, snakes, and a dozen other creatures. They exchanged fire with a few Confederate forces near Totopotomoy Creek.

Some soldiers called it Toty-Potato.

The big battle lay ahead, along a highway that ran through a well-known crossroads called Cold Harbor. As had happened so many times before, the campaign began with good news for the soldiers in blue: General Philip Sheridan's cavalry had captured the crossroad.

Lucius' men cheered. By god, we'll get those Rebs this time! Ol' General Phil should be runnin' this whole damned war!

For a while they forgot their withering fatigue from days of forced marching. They chanted On to Richmond.

Someone started singing John Brown's Body Lies A'mouldering in the Grave, to the tune of Battle Hymn of the Republic. The entire company joined in.

Lucius grimaced. He had seen such euphoria before and feared it would once again turn into despair. Still, he couldn't avoid feeling some of the excitement himself. *Aren't the Confederates running out of men? And aren't they unable to properly feed or equip the men they have left? More than half the secesh men captured lately have been barefoot, ragged, emaciated, or all three.*

The news from Cold Harbor buoyed spirits and energized the march for two more hours. Inevitably, though, it slowed to weary trudging. Muskets slid from sore shoulders to hands. Gun butts fell to the ground to be dragged until Lucius or a squad Sergeant yelled at the men to look sharp.

A dull murmur of doubt and wonderment rippled through the rapidly tiring company.

Say, what is this place Cold Harbor? We that near the ocean are we? We gonna see icebergs or somethin'?

Naw, Cold Harbor, that's a place where you sleep without no stove or fire.

No, by gum, that ain't right either. It's a place where you stay without getting fed.

That so? Sounds like ever' place we spend nights, don't it?

Hey, I hear Sheridan's men whupped the Rebs with those repeating carbines. Why ain't we got guns like that?

Oh, ain't you heard? Lincoln can't find the money to buy them for infantry. Just for the high-falootin' calvary.

Now see here, you're s'posed to say CAValry!

Oh, quit talkin' like a school marm. Gawd, I hope they give us cooked beef tonight.

Don't bet on it. You seen any cook wagons lately? And the cows walkin' behind? Bet they's still five miles back.

Say, you think they'll be able to find this Cold Harbor place?

Well, 'ol Phil Sheridan found it. He prob'ly just followed his nose. You can smell a rebel house a mile off.

Friday, June 24, 1864

Well, good thing he found it, one way or 'nother. Way I hear it, we ain't got good maps, and no one knows how to read 'em.

Lucius knew the truth of this last statement. *Our company's maps can't be trusted. Bridges are marked in the wrong places; distances along roads aren't right; hills, valleys, gullies, and river bends never seem to be quite where the maps said they would be. Officers argue to beat hell over how long the stretch is between different places, and where to find high ground for artillery.*

General Grant's II Corps, including Lucius' regiment, alternately marched south, west, back east, and then west again until, late in the evening of June 1, 1864, they were still some distance from the Cold Harbor crossroads.

Orders came down to march all night and be ready for battle next day. So march they did, late through the night and into the early hours. They shuffled and stumbled into the battle site shortly after 6 o'clock the morning of June 2, to join the rest of the Union forces. The blue coats strung out along a front stretching from the Bethesda Church to the Chickahominy River.

Grant had intended to assault the Confederate line that same day, but the run-down condition of the II Corps led him to postpone, first until evening and then until 4:30 the following morning, June 3. This delay gave Lee's units time to protect their riflemen and cannons with earthworks and deep trenches that charging Union soldiers would need to cross. Grant's troops would be clay pigeons in Lee's shooting gallery.

That evening a private scrawled on a scrap of paper:

If I die, I want my old watche sent to Grampa and my knife to my litle brother Edwin. Tell Ma that tonite I am singing just before the batle Mother. Tell Maggie I remember how prity she is and how I luuved her leters and may God Bless her and all my family and her family. Most affectionately to all who know me, I am, Derrick Holmes.

Pvt. Holmes opened the small, bone-handled jackknife that would go to Brother Edwin. He sliced the lining inside his battle coat and crammed the note inside the opening. With a needle from his knapsack, he sewed the lining back together. Crudely, but effectively.

Bugles blared at 3:30 a.m. The cooking wagons had hot potatoes, bacon, and hard tack ready a half-hour later. Glum troopers lined up for rations.

The soldiers had not slept well. They had marched several days without enough water or food. A day of rest hardly put them in fighting condition. They expected, accurately, that thousands of them would be wounded, killed or captured.

Cannons began booming before daybreak and, with the first glimmer of sun—mostly at their backs—the order to attack came down from General Grant. Captain Arthur Kenaston, Lucius' company commander, ordered all men to fix bayonets. Lieutenants gave points of attack to their platoons. Clouds of white and gray cannon smoke hung over the open swamp, spreading the acrid odor of gunpowder.

Cannonading stopped. Bugles blared and the attack began.

Men in blue shouted hoarsely as they charged, and the Confederates across the open swamp let loose their bloodcurdling yell. Lucius was both terrified and excited with the

Friday, June 24, 1864

battle drama. When Captain Kenaston led the charge with his headquarters squad directly toward a Confederate breastwork, Lucius sprinted along.

It was sheer obedience, born of hard discipline.

He pointed his rifle, on the run, at a cannon crew. He pulled the trigger and missed. Reloading without stopping was impossible. He saw the puffs of smoke from Confederate muskets behind the breastworks and saw the back of Captain Kenaston's skull disappear in a splash of crimson. It wasn't the first death Lucius had seen near him—only the first company commander to go down this way.

A Private shouted, *This's hell on fire!* Then he, too, dropped in screaming agony.

Lucius ran on, yelling as if crazed, until he reached and leaped over a breastwork where three rebel riflemen stood with empty muskets. A butt came down on the side of Lucius' head and all went black.

———

A grave detail three days later found the note on the bloated body of Pvt. Derrick Holmes. The 18-year-old had made it almost half-way to the Confederate line when he went down with a bullet in his lungs, his body tangled with five others in the open field. Some might have been saved, but the attempt of General Grant to negotiate a temporary cease-fire with General Lee had failed. The two generals disagreed over protocol.

General Grant never received a precise accounting of casualties in this battle, but total Union losses in the Cold Harbor area since late May were well over 10,000.

———

When Lucius regained consciousness, he felt blood oozing from a swelling lump above his right ear. His head throbbed. He was prostrate in a shallow ditch a few rods behind the Confederate gun battery that he had charged some time before. Two unshaven men, one in gray and one in butternut and holding Lucius' Springfield rifle, analyzed him:

Purty neat, ain't he? He an officer?

Naw, a sargint. See, his stripes is all muddied up. How'd he git this far? Jest lucky?

The one in butternut spoke directly to Lucius:

Yer saved by the stars, Sargint. We done shot up your men all the way up the line. Y'all did damned well to make it to us. And lucky we was all reloadin' and jest conked you on the haid.

Yer General Grant, he's a butcher, ain't he? How could he order a charge like that aginst all our guns?

The soldier half lifted Lucius to his feet, and pushed him to an area some 20 rods back of the earthworks where nearly two dozen other Union soldiers, including a Lieutenant from another company, lay in the dirt. Several were wounded and all had the look of the wholly beaten.

Lucius saw the familiar face of a friend from boyhood. Corporal Harry Nickels grunted and Lucius McCordle nodded without words.

This was June 3. For the next 21 days, Lucius and a pack of other Federal prisoners captured by the Confederates at Cold Harbor would move from place to place, often for only a night or two, and then move again. There were rumors they would go to the place they all feared—Libby prison at Richmond. But with Richmond more or less under siege, the Confederates stopped sending prisoners there, partly on the theory that a sudden Union takeover would free thousands of men to return to the Union ranks.

FRIDAY, JUNE 24, 1864

So uncertain were the Confederates that they marched or transported Union prisoners by rail, back and forth over the same terrain before deciding where to stop. Feeding captives was tough; Confederate Army commanders had to scratch to feed their own troops.

Nearly a dozen days after their capture, the prisoners marched through the fields where Confederate General Ewell's Corps, much of it taken over by General Jubal Early, had recuperated after the bloody repulse of Grant's troops at Cold Harbor. Debris lay scattered on the trampled sod and dirt. Corporal Nickels along with several others picked up scraps of dirty, wrinkled paper.

Just might be good enough to write a line home, one prisoner said. The Confederate guards had no objection. They, too, kept their eyes open for paper, as did soldiers in all battlefields of this war.

At a small hamlet of rickety shacks in northern Georgia, guards on two train cars ordered the prisoners off, lined them up, and marched them down a street. A gathering of women, old men and children gawked at the Yankees. Lucius McCordle kept his head high to avoid direct eye contact. Harry Nickels, more adventuresome, looked directly into the soft eyes of a young woman while her companions shouted with mischief:

Hey, won't y'all look at these here Yankees! My, they don't look like nothin' to be feared, do they?

Say, now, thar's a purty one, the fellow with the red hair. Why, tear that blue suit off him and he's same as one of our'n!

Laughter and giggles.

Waal, now, I didn't mean…. Say, there's a cute one. Can I take him home?

More giggles. Guards ordered the prisoners to face front and march forward.

Steam shrouded the rusted locomotive as it whistled, wheezed, and screeched to a stop at Anderson Station.

Prisoners stumbled out of the cattle car and guards marched them to the stockade, where they stopped briefly outside to be listed. Their next stop was the North Gate Enclosure. Guards divided them into squads and put a sergeant in charge of each. Lucius had a squad of 90, mostly men he didn't know and never would.

A heavy stench filled the air.

Yow, smells like they left hawg carcasses out to rot.

Hawgs, hell. That's plain human turds.

Turds that rotted, you mean.

Sweet as a roasted maggot, ain't it?

Then the gates swung open, the new arrivals walked into the main stockade and quickly learned the last speaker was right. Crudely, but with precise accuracy.

Among the stunned new occupants at Andersonville stockade, one spoke for all:

My Gawd.

Lucius and his fellow prisoners huddled inside the gate. They were dulled with weariness yet staggered by their new surroundings. Ashen-faced men in filthy rags crowded near them and gawked. A burly man, unshaven for months, with hair and beard matted with old sweat and greasy food remnants, leered at them.

Welcome, boys! What good things you fresh fish has brung us, eh?

This giant wore better garments than most of the surrounding woebegone men. His blue coat was as yet untorn. His boots were the best of any in sight. His sartorial conspicuousness was offset by his foul smell. Huge sweat circles spread under his enormous arm pits. Rank mucus drooled from his mouth of dirty, broken teeth and onto his matted beard.

He moved close to Lucius, who didn't budge, but thought: *He smells like an old billy goat.*

Lucius' physical size and unflinching stance temporarily fended off the goon, who turned abruptly to the shorter Harry Nickels and grunted.

I'll have this.

He grabbed Harry's knapsack, a signal for more brutes behind him to charge the new arrivals. They grabbed nearly all hand-carried possessions—blankets, cups, fry pans, tent pieces, sacks—from the new prisoners.

Lucius barked out in the gruffest voice he could manage:

Detail, stand at attention!

It worked—temporarily. A body of military men where all form of discipline had disappeared now reacted more or less instinctively to Lucius' authoritative and throaty call for order.

But only briefly.

The lull gave Harry Nickels time to grab his knapsack from the thug, who had gotten caught in the milling mob, tripped and fell.

Bleary-eyed, jaded prisoners stood by, taking it all in. These almost-daily arrivals were a diversion that some bored inmates purposely came to see.

Raiders, one said, after the thugs left. They's our welcomin' committee. Lower than snakes and meaner than pimps.

Another added: And you got to meet the biggest of 'em. That was Mosby. First time I ever saw him leave without getting what he come after.

―――

Lucius shrugged. His knapsack remained where he had lashed it tight to his shoulder. *Like any prison*, he thought. *Nobody running things and discipline goes to hell.*

But as he turned away, another prisoner bumped him from behind. Lucius lost his balance and fell to the ground.

He put his right hand in the muck and pushed himself to one knee. He raised the hand to within a foot of his nose and had his first close-up whiff of the foulest earth in Georgia.

Still in a crouch, he slowly looked up and across the prison area. Hundreds of tents and crude huts—shebangs—scattered across the sloping stockade ground, not in any arrangement of rows and without clearly defined walk paths between them. Simply helter-skelter.

There was one wooden structure inside the stockade. It was the sutler's shack, where prisoners could buy various tools, food and water—if they had money.

Harry Nickels took a deep sniff of the awful air.

Smells sweet, don't it, he said as he wrinkled his nose. Sweet as a smoking candle made outa rotten wax.

Chapter 3.
Saturday, June 25, 1864

I'm not sure whether I should write to Maryanne. I don't know if what I write would reach her, or if she would deign to read it if it did. Anyway, I could never tell her the truth about this place, even though she respects and expects the truth, however unpleasant. One prisoner called this an ant hill of men swarming around and going nowhere. But that isn't quite right. Ants have purpose. Kick off the top of an ant hill, uncover all their eggs, and what happens? Ants scurry around and it looks like total confusion. But keep watching and you see every last egg picked up by some ant that knows exactly what to do and where to go and pretty soon all the eggs are out of sight and protected. These miserable men should be as orderly as ants! Truly, it's even wrong to call them pigs. Put a bunch of hogs in a pen and they find one corner where they do all their defecating. These men act more like cows—or maybe bulls. Dump wherever they are and foul up the whole yard. So don't call these men pigs—bull-headed is more like it. Make a stench so thick you can actually see it. Men haven't washed or changed clothes for as long as they been here. But...here I am, blaming the men and not those damned Rebels who built this place. No, I'm blaming both armies for training men to kill but not how to live where things are tough. Here, it's just like Camp Lagoon.

What a damnable place that was, just a mile from Coulee City in that swampy field near the big river. How often did I try to get those soldiers to practice clean living, like doing their jobs in latrines instead of in fields? And what would they say? Just, Cripes, Sergeant, ain't no privacy in them latrines. They say that if you're captured, do your damndest to escape. We're no better than Achilles at Troy, leading men into war with grandiose battle plans but no thought of how to live in captivity or get home after fighting stops.

(Diary of Lucius McCordle, Saturday, June 25, 1864.)

The north gate creaked open late Saturday morning and a steaming food wagon, driven by a pair of slave men, trundled into the compound. Half a thousand prisoners rushed toward the wagon in full disarray. They hadn't eaten for two days.

A guard fired his musket into the air, and a Confederate Lieutenant shouted:

Nobody gets rations until their Sargints draw them. Get your buckets, Sargints, and draw for your men.

Confusion reigned. Lucius grabbed a bucket from the wagon and lined up behind other Sergeants, to collect rations for his starving squad. The gruel today was rice, a few pieces of chicken, uncooked corn meal and chunks of salt pork.

It smelled bad.

Saturday, June 25, 1864

His men held out their cups, bowls, or whatever containers they could get their hands on, and Lucius ladled out their rations. These new prisoners were dismayed.

Wouldn't feed this slop to my hawgs.

Ain't much of it, neither.

Yup, know what you mean. I'm hungry enough to eat the ears off a mule.

Man, you boys sure complain mightily, just like all the fresh fish. Do it some more, maybe Cap'n Wirz will run bring you a sugar titty[2].

Lucius slurped up most of his gruel and a short time later bent over from the pangs of diarrhea.

They say diarrhea and dysentery kill more boys than rebel guns do. If this keeps up, I'll be in those numbers. How can anyone survive in this squalid place?

There were no barracks at all, simply a mass, disorganized conglomeration of the sorriest shelters one could imagine. As a Sergeant, Lucius would need to somehow manage his squad of 90. Their first job was to set up shebangs, as these pitiful huts were called. And, he needed one of his own.

Harry Nickels offered to help.

He disappeared for nearly an hour, then reappeared with a grin and an armful of booty. It included a pair of actual tent halves clipped together, two stakes, and a strong cord to make an A-shaped tent. He proudly displayed three long, thin, and crooked sticks.

Makes a wonderful good cooking stack, he said.

Lucius eyed him quizzically.

---

2   A 19th century pacifier for infants, made by soaking a tightly-wound rag in sugar water.

Where did you get these things?

Well...at the sutler shack, over there. The sutler, he's a crook, but he's got lots of stuff. He even has food that's fit to eat.

You have money for all this?

Well, yeh, but it won't last long with those prices. Worst of it is, he wanted four dollars. I had five in Union money and for change he gives me a worthless rebel shin plaster[3].

Lucius wasn't sure whether to be impressed or suspicious. He asked:

Where can we set up our shebang?

Our caboose, you mean? Well, up there a piece.

Harry nodded to the north.

They're dragging out a boy that died last night. He was in a caboose by himself. I put my name on it.

How'd you do that?

I drove a stake and warned every damned boy who came by to stay away. Or, bejabers, I'd knock him down.

See, the boy who died, his shebang was blankets, kinda rotted. Then I got me some canvas tent pieces from the sutler, last ones he had, or so he says. But we still keep the dead boy's blankets, case we need them.

So we're vultures, Harry? Watch for a boy to die and pray we get his goods before anyone else?

Sure do; they tell me it's the first thing yuh learn here.

That night, the Sergeant and the Corporal slept in their newly-built shebang, cloaked in the lingering death smell of the former occupant.

Around 1 a.m. they awoke to shouting and commotion, maybe five or six rods away.

Now get out of here! Hey! They's a thief here!

---

3   Confederate paper money.

Saturday, June 25, 1864

Then came a scream of pain, another, and more yelling. Thudding sounds of fists and clubs landing on soft flesh. The sound of heavy-footed running. Grunts and groans from struck victims. Muttering and more shouts and commotion.

Raiders, Lucius murmured. *Why the aitch haven't the guards taken care of them?*

Not bothering US, are they? Harry asked sleepily.

Not so far. My back is still sore from that clubbing.

A new chorus of shouts and yells erupted, this time with a tone of vengeance.

Come on, boys! We're the Regulators, and we ain't about to let them damned Raiders get away with this!

Lusty yells of support, sounds of a melee that lasted ten minutes, then receded. Now came boastful statements of revenge:

Well, we got some of it back.

Yeah, busted some of their bones, too. Glad I had a chance to use this club.

Me, too. Didja see the way I smacked that hooligan acrost the kisser?

No—guess not. I was fightin' off this big one with the red rag around his neck. If I'd had me a club, I'd a whacked him so hard he'd be in hell pumping thunder.

Any of our'n get hurt?

Well, Tommy, here, got smashed purty bad. Tommy?

Hey, he fell down. Let's tote him to the hospital.

More murmurs and sounds of shuffling feet and a wounded man being carried….somewhere.

By gawd, I reckon he's dead.

Well, on to the hospital. They can tell whether he's breathin' or not.

Hell, that's about all they CAN do. Ever hear anyone come back from the hospital?

Nope. It's just the first step to the Promised Land. Anyone knows that.

Lucius went back to sleep.

It rained a few hours later. Lucius woke up hearing water trickling down the slope. He felt the ground beneath the rags under him.

It was still dry, thanks to Harry Nickels. He had carefully dug a trench three or four inches deep around the upslope perimeter of the shebang.

Harry had done the same thing on the marches in Virginia. He knew where to get things, and how to use them.

Like a good supply Corporal, Lucius thought. *Give him room to work and don't ask too many damned questions.*

Harry and Lucius had kept each other reasonably healthy during the frenetic marches and box car rides since being captured. Harry used his well-honed scrounging skills to find cooking gear, fuel, food and whatever else survival required. Lucius cooked their meager rations. He had a knack for making them almost edible.

Confederate guards watched with curious admiration.

Some a'them Yankees is as clever as usn's, one underfed guard in gray opined.

These two clever Yankees had been friends since childhood. Their friendship had survived the fact that each had, at different times, been in love with Maryanne Callander. That common experience was, in curious ways, both bond and bother.

———

Lucius carefully set up the tripod sticks to hold their cooking pot, half full of corn meal and salt pork. If he boiled the food—such as it was—they'd be less likely to get sick from it.

It's a good thing Pa ran an apothecary, and Ma kept needling me that well-cooked food keeps you healthy. And I picked up a few notions from that Sanitation Commission agent, at Camp Lagoon, near Coulee City. That fellow went on and on about what good latrines meant for soldier health.

Trouble is, no one paid much attention, and soldiers got sick by the dozens. Nobody wanted to learn. The camp lieutenants could scarcely teach a dog to bark.

So, to Lucius, boiling or frying food was the only sure way to get a hot meal. Beans, mush, and salt pork stew ladled out by meal wagons—Union or Confederate—were often cold or undercooked.

What he and Harry did miss from those wagons was coffee. Coffee in the morning, coffee at noon, coffee with the evening meal.

Coffee perks them up, officers would say. Gets them ready for the morning battle.

And since it was made with boiled water, coffee was the healthiest drink they could get.

Before the day was over, Lucius found himself cooking for four Sumter prisoners, including Harry Nickels and Burtrum Claxton, a black prisoner, dockworker, and barber from Erie, Ohio. In the stockade, his barber talents were highly prized.

Lucius would admit only to himself that his friendship toward Burtrum was owed to his memory of Maryanne Callander. The worse the turmoil among starving and dying colored people, the more agonizing his memories of this woman.

Headquarters of the Army of Northern Virginia June 26, 1864

His Excellency Jefferson Davis, President Confederate States

...General Hunter has escaped Early, and will make good his retreat...I fear he has not been much punished....If circumstances favor, I should...recommend his (Early's) crossing the Potomac. I think I can maintain our lines here against General Grant...At this time, as far as I can learn, all the troops in the control of the United States are being sent to Grant, and little or no opposition could be made by those at Washington....

Very respectfully, Your Excellency's obedient servant.

                R. E. Lee, General [4]

---

4   WOTR, Series 1, Vol. 37, Part 1, p.766.

Chapter 4.
Sunday, June 26, 1864

Weather hot. Found a place to set up our shelter. Up the hill from the creek, jammed in between men from Pennsylvania. One relieves himself just outside his tent. Tried to turn and sleep the other way, to keep my nose away from it. He seems sick, might not make it another day.

My Irish parents knew being poor, but this would turn them sick. Pa would first want to get calomel and other nostrums to all these poor boys, like he did for anyone who came sick to his apothecary in Coulee City. But that's not what we need here. Good, well-cooked food would be more like it.

(Entry in diary of Lucius McCordle, June 26, 1864)

———

Late Sunday morning, the ration wagon, with bins of smelly pork, bags of corn meal, and iron kettles of hot gruel slopping over the sides, bumped and clattered into the north end of the compound. Lucius quickly got in line with a bucket and drew rations for his 90 men. Neither the corn meal nor the salt pork had been cooked.

He sniffed the salt pork and shook his head.

Same as yesterday. Isn't right. Listen, boys. Make sure you cook this stuff long enough, or it's going to kick up your innards something awful.

One man in his charge nodded. Others grumbled loudly, that they were without cooking equipment and had no way of scrounging up any today, if ever. One spoke their collective mind:

Might as well of shot us before we got here. Helluva lot easier than bein' poisoned by this stuff. 'Tain't food. It's pig slop, or worse.

Lucius doled out the rations to the men, then took his own to his little cooking tripod.

He needed water. He looked toward the south end of the compound, toward the foul creek.

Drink that stuff and we'd kick the bucket inside a week, he growled to the listless men around him. Unless we boil it first.

Lucius was one of few who thought that boiling water, or simply being sanitary, had anything to do with avoiding sickness.

He looked around and saw a crudely dug well about 20 feet away. The owners of the well and two nearby shebangs glared at him, suspiciously. One of the group strolled toward Lucius, and made an offer:

A pail of this here water and a piece of corn bread comes to a dollar.

Lucius had precious little money left, after bribing Confederate guards on the train.

No thanks, he told the would-be merchant.

He wondered where Harry Nickels was.

A moment later, Harry appeared with a bucket of water. Now where did you…?

Lucius, you ask me no questions and I tell you no lies.

This was vintage Harry Nickels at work.

I never know quite how to take Harry. He's an old friend from boyhood days, but he once courted Maryanne Callander and—so she told me—promised to marry her. But he lied, after leading her to think he was an officer when he was just a private in the militia across the state. That's a problem with close friends. You hate to ask them what you really need to know, so as to not end the friendship. All you can do is wait for them to blurt it out, and hope they aren't giving you a lot of humbuggery.

Lucius dumped most of the raw corn meal into the one metal pot they owned—and protected—and stirred in some water. The fire grew and Lucius in a crouch suspended the pot precariously from its wire handle, on a long stick. He stirred the meal with his left until it formed sticky, pasty, dough.

He sprinkled the remaining dry meal on the bottom of a metal plate, and dumped the mixture on it.

Keeps the dough from sticking to the pan, he explained.

Harry had seen Lucius do this repeatedly on marches. He could do it himself, though not as well.

Lucius propped the plate over the fire at an angle and allowed it to cook until the dough was light brown. Next, he split two sticks and carefully inserted the lightly-cooked but now stable dough into the stick ends. He held the sticks over the fire and baked the dough to a dark brown.

He had hardly finished his baking when another commotion erupted several shebangs away, toward the westward side of the compound.

A scream. Get your goddam selves outta here! Hey! That's my eggs. Look out! Aww! Now you broke them all. Thief! Thief! There they go! Took my blanket! I paid for those eggs at the sutler's, too!

More voices joined in as men scurried in multiple directions—some toward, some safely away from the action.

Cuss that Curtis and his bunch! Damn them!

Stop them! Those bastards!

Some dozen men ran, stumbled and charged into the fleeing thieves, who dropped the blankets but turned to face their pursuers. Two thugs brandished crude but dangerous knives, taunting:

Come on boys, see what happens. One more step and we slice your nuts out!

The pursuers stopped and bunched together a few yards short of the thieves. A spokesman for the pursuers yelled lustily:

We're the Regulators and we've had enough of you cussed devils! Just wait. Your goddammed days are numbered!

Except for the occasional forays by the Raider gangs, an eerie and uneasy tranquility shrouded the stockade. Life hovered in the miasma of smoke and putridity that grew thicker in the moist morning air as one trudged down the slope toward the sinks.

Lucius strolled the opposite way, north and up the slope, bumping men or shanties nearly every other step. The shebangs, crowded together in helter-skelter fashion, almost defied a man's attempt to get inside.

Amid one cluster of shelters, five men sprawled around a blanket in a game of Faro, with a deck so badly worn and torn that after a single deal its owner knew with considerable accuracy which hands held which cards. Some men muttered and some spoke clearly, either way communicating at once the boredom, anxieties and fatalism they all shared.

Where'd you get these damn cards, Jared? Some whorehouse?

Yer right; he probably talked some floozy into playing double or nothing.

Yup. And he got nothing, 'cept the cards back.

Aw, quit griping, you boys! Clean cards is as scarce around here as clean shirts and under drawers.

Hey! Baker! Ain't that yer name? Don't cover them cards you's a layin' down. Tryin' to hide somethin?

Hide what? I ain't got nothin' you birds can't see.

Yah…that's for dammed certain. And even 'f you got it, whatcha gonna do with it in this place?

Waa…aal…you might find one of the girls in here…

Aww…go on…ain't no womenfolk in this place.

No? Y'mean you ain't heard? Just watch the ones who never pee standing…

Hey! You got nothin' better than women to jabber about? Why not go find out when the prisoner exchange happens?

Hell, let me tell you. That exchange ain't never going to happen. Grant and Lincoln don't give a damn about us. They's just lettin' us rot.

Ha, ha! While you birds was flappin' your big mouths, I just won! Push that money here. It's all mine.

They completely ignored Lucius, who wound his way through the dog tents and bough-covered shebangs, on to places where men stretched out on dirty blankets, covered only by Georgia sky. Ahead of him a bewhiskered man, his left sleeve tattered and dangling, worked on his knees with a short-handled spade he had traded for his watch and a metal spoon.

What I wouldn't give for a night with my Molly, he muttered.

And Lucius McCordle continued to suffer silently over his own missing love.

Sure, men jabber about women. That's all they think about. Including me. I loved Maryanne Callander even though I couldn't get all worked up about her effort with that Underground Railroad. Thought too much like a lawyer, I guess, and how the laws stood. How could you fight slavery in court, after the Dred Scott decision in 1857 that said slaves have no rights at all? If she had been arrested for violating the Fugitive Slave Act, would I have had the gumption to defend her in court? Even now, I'm not sure. We were both lucky that Wisconsin sheriffs looked the other way when escaped slaves came through our area.

Suddenly a hirsute man bellowed in triumph: Water! And sure enough, Lucius saw the oozing liquid in mud about five feet below the surrounding soil surface. With luck, the man would catch enough water for his own use, and more to sell.

———

A private from Michigan discovered about midnight that his shebang partner was stiff in death.

Help me get this boy's corpse outa here, he called to no one in particular. He's just layin' here a'rotting 'neath the pale old moon.

———

A step farther, two men lay under a lean-to shelter of crooked poles with a roof of pine boughs, oblivious to the death scene. One was either asleep or in a coma. The other, a sickly man in his late thirties, struggled with a pencil and a paper and, seeing Lucius, asked:

Hey, kin you write good?

Tolerably well, Lucius answered.

Sunday, June 26, 1864

Mebbe you kin write for me a note to my daughter…well, to my wife, but it's mostly to my daughter Henrietta. She's just 7 years old. I call her 'Henny, and I got some things to say to her.

Lucius squatted, took the pencil, and struggled to hold the ragged and torn sheet of paper where he could write on it.

Here, on this, the man said, his shaking hand giving Lucius a flat but splintered piece of board.

Now here's what I want to say to Henny.

Dear daughter, don't let no one say your Pa is dead, 'cause he ain't. I'm a live one, lying here under the warm and peaceful Georgia skies. Henny, I wish I could tell you just how nice the nights are here, when the moon comes up and the crickets chirp and the night birds call. And the owls hoot. Oh, Henny I think all the time of you and your wonderful Ma, and hope you're taking care of Mabel and feeding her well so she'll give you lots of milk, and feed the pigs good so you got meat for the winter, and read the Bible ever day and thank the Lord God for your good health and pray to him that your Pa will come home any day now and this war will be over and the whole country will be a happy place. Little girls like you can put on your bonnets and play ring round the rosie and laugh and sing 'cause there won't never be no more wars like this one. Lord bless you, and that is all for now. Your loving Father, Ambrose.

Lucius wrote as much of this as he could on the tattered sheet of paper, using both sides.

He was about to ask whether he could take the letter to the guards, but saw the man had fallen asleep…or simply passed out.

As Lucius looked around, a man squatting beside a shelter about six feet away spoke to him.

Just put the letter down next to him, Sergeant.

See, it won't go nowhere. He asked three others to write this letter for him this past week. He ain't yet told anyone where to send it, 'cause he don't know.

Poor chap. The fever's got to him and he's tetched some. He ain't got but a few days, we figger. But he gets so much good out of dictatin' that letter, I wouldna stopped him or you, no how.

I wish that Copperhead[5] editor in Wisconsin Buck Sewall, who hated President Lincoln and the Union, could see these pitiful men. Looking at how these Rebels treat prisoners might change his Secesh[6] mindedness. And what I never understood was why my lovely Maryanne would work for a newspaper like Sewalls, when she was so opposed to slavery that she helped escapees from the plantations find their way north, through Coulee City, and on to Canada.

Maybe I should have stayed with Pa's drug business, instead of becoming a poor lawyer for poor folks in Coulee City, doing title work and civil cases that hardly kept me alive, and didn't give me enough reputation to make lieutenant, or even captain. I'd know more about keeping these wretches alive. Here I am, a lawyer who has no court to hear the grievances of these men. (Entry in Lucius McCordle's diary, June 26, 1964)

---

5   "Copperhead" was a derisive term for a Northern person who opposed the Union Army's attempt to defeat the Confederate Army and abolish slavery.

6   A term for favoring secession by the Southern States.

Chapter 5.
<u>Monday, June 27, 1864</u>

Dear Maryanne: You'll probably never get this letter, because they only let a prisoner write one, and I already sent one to Pa and Ma. But yesterday I helped a sickly man pen a few lines to his daughter. The poor fellow knew the letter would go nowhere. But just as that made him feel good, maybe I'll feel better writing to you, a letter you may never see. I wish we had married, and I know why we didn't. You were working hard to transport escaped slaves through Coulee City and up to Canada, and I was no help. May the Lord forgive me for that.

But I wish you to understand why I was defense lawyer for the drunkard who killed Amos, the Colored barber in Coulee City, and a man whose family you knew and greatly respected. As I know you recollect, Amos was trying to keep the mob from finding that editor Buck Sewall and tarring and feathering and maybe even stretching his neck for being a traitor in print. Amos was a hero and got killed for his effort. But Maryanne, the barrel factory worker who clubbed him to death deserved a fair trial. That is my code of honor, and I couldn't violate that anymore than you could violate your promise to help Colored folks escape slavery. I told you this the day you came to my cramped little law shack to talk me out of defending the barrel worker, but you left then, saying

you wondered how we could live together without thinking the same way about slavery. Yes, I know I worried more about saving the union than about freeing slaves. I knew and feared that our marriage would never happen. I still hope and pray it will, but the future is not in our hands.
Your affectionate marriage partner in waiting, Lucius.

(Entry in Lucius McCordle's diary, June 27, 1864).

A Confederate guard yelled in Lucius' direction.

All Sargints, 'specially new ones, fall in at the northwest corner.

A curious Lucius complied quickly. He looked for Harry Nickels to keep watch over their shebang and precious cooking equipment. Harry was nowhere in sight.

Probably scrounging more food, Lucius thought.

He shrugged and made his way among the milling men toward the far corner of the compound. He couldn't take a step without bumping into somebody.

He saw another Sergeant who looked as if he'd been there longer.

Lucius asked:

How many men in this place, do you know?

Prit' near thirty thousand, they say.

Thirty thousand? On what, 20 acres?

Less. About 16 now, maybe 10 more in a few days, when they expand to the north.

Lucius and his new acquaintance joined dozens of other Sergeants near the northwest corner.

Captain Wirz, the camp commandant, sat glumly atop his horse. His first words quickly and crudely betrayed his mid-European background.

All you sergeants. Follow the guards out into the woods. We want you to get some clubs for your men. We are going to get rid of these bad people, once and for all.

His w sounded like v and his th was more like a t or d.

He sounds German, Lucius said to no one in particular.

Swiss, I think, another Sergeant said. He's a brute. They say he had a prisoner shot the other day, just for walking up to the deadline.

The deadline?

Yeah, that's those scantling boards strung around the edge, a few feet in from the wall. We ain't s'posed to go near them, or they shoot.

So you cross that line, you're dead, see?

Wirz wheeled his horse around. The gate opened and the Confederate guards led Lucius and about 20 others out and into the nearby rolling hills where a few trees remained, surrounded by hundreds of stumps of earlier cuttings taken partly for shelters, but mostly for cooking fuel.

Wary guards handed axes to a half dozen of the men and told them to cut some small trees and shape the limbs into clubs.

The same Sergeant moved close to Lucius and whispered.

They's talk of a big escape being planned. See that well hole we passed? There's another one near it, but covered by a shebang. The ones who use it, they're digging a tunnel every night. Lotsa men helping them. They's others diggin', same way.

When those tunnels is dug, they'll be mizzling outa here, you just watch.

Maybe you think ol' Wirz is helping us finish off these Raiders because he has a big heart? Don't b'lieve it. He thinks if the Raiders ain't put down, there'll be a big panic and three or four thousand men will riot and just smash right through the gate. Hell, if they did, those puny Reb guards and their rusty old muskets wouldn't stand a chance.

Sure, some of us would die, but we're dying anyway. Musta been 80 or so drug out to the dead pit just yesterday.

Well, suppose there *was* a breakout, Lucius said. What would we do then? They've got cannons and dogs, and the men here are all half-starved. How far would anyone get looking for food and water here in Rebel country?

Yah, maybe not far, but like I say, we's dead anyhow.

A rebel guard yelled at them to quit talking, and set to cutting wood for clubs.

Chapter 6.
<u>Tuesday, June 28, 1864</u>

Every morning a different rumor swept through Camp Sumter. Prisoner exchange. Better food. No food. New barracks. Rescue by Union cavalry. An escape tunnel.

Today the rumor was different and definite, and its tellers were giddy with delight.

The Raiders' days are over!

Lucius with his tripod cooked a handful of corn meal saved from yesterday. He hadn't seen Harry Nickels since the middle of the night, when he remembered the Corporal crawling out to get some night air.

A Pennsylvania artilleryman ambled slowly toward Lucius, put his right hand to the left side of his mouth and said quietly:

The Raiders is gonna be rounded up, but don't say too much, 'cause the Regulators wanna surprise them.

Who are the Regulators?

You don' know? That's a police force, of prisoners like me and you. Led by a Sergeant from Illinois, name of Leroy Key. He has a funny moniker, Limber Jim. Wagon man, once, I guess. Knows what he's doing. Got a good crowd of toughies. Mostly new boys from out west, they ain't starved to death yet. He's workin' out a plan with Wirz and the prison guards. You just watch.

Lucius looked around for the missing Harry Nickels.

Maybe Harry is just out scrounging for things to make life bearable. Like eggs or fresh vegetables from the sutler. Dang, but he's a resourceful fellow! He knows how to find things, how to listen to folks, how to figure out what's in their heads. He talks and sounds like a nutty, back country bonehead. But he isn't, and I should be the first to get wise to that.

Small groups of prisoners milled about, murmuring in low voices, quieting to a hush whenever a stranger approached.

Farther south, near the east deadline and just north of the fetid sink area, Lucius spotted Harry Nickels winding his way up the slope through the irregular rows of the pitiful shebangs. It didn't look right.

Harry turned his head frequently and almost furtively, his face showing traces of fear—uncharacteristic for Harry. Then, suddenly, he began chatting rapidly with a small group of other prisoners.

His glaze of fear disappeared and he quickly became his usual contented, amiable self. He seemed well-acquainted with the group, none of whom Lucius had met in their brief time at Andersonville.

What is going on? Did Harry finally bite off more than he could chew?

A now-suspicious Lucius looked down, his eyes shifting idly over the interior of the shebang he and Harry shared. Near the middle, between their sleeping spaces, rested the familiar burlap sack that held most of their valued possessions—their cooking utensils, an extra pair of trousers, a watch, two jackknives, diary books, a pen, a dried-up ink pot, a crumpled hat, a bag holding their meager supply of coins and other Union money. It was *very* meager now, since Harry had spent most of this money at the Sutler shack.

Each of the two men checked this sack regularly, starting the moment they arrived here. When Lucius walked about, Harry guarded the shebang, and vice-versa. This morning, Lucius was the guard, not because it was his turn, but because Harry was nowhere around.

As his eyes focused, Lucius saw the sack bulging more than usual. He dropped to his knees in the soft earth and looked inside. Wrapped in a dirty rag was a pair of knives, made from flat metal strips—probably broken saw metal—that someone had laboriously sharpened and made into crude cutting tools. Or weapons. Things that neither Harry nor Lucius had when they first entered this hell hole.

And Harry Nickels still hadn't returned to the shebang. *Well, he's a friendly cuss; maybe chatting with a bunch of men he couldn't have known for more than a couple days, or even less.*

The stockade was alive but quieting noticeably. Men moved quickly, often looking cautiously in every direction. When they clustered, their voices dropped to a whisper. Excitement rippled quietly through the air.

―――

Sergeant Albert Simmons from Iowa was short and stout, with a pugnacious look. He and Lucius had been crowded together in the same smelly cattle car and, as the only two sergeants there, more or less took charge.

Once in the stockade, it didn't take them long to find out how much they had in common.

Albert, Lucius began.

Jus' call me Jed, Albert answered.

Jed? Where'd you get that moniker?

Waal, fact is, it's short for Judge.

You were a judge? Lucius asked.

Naw, my old man called me Judge at first, sort of a humbuggery, if you know what I mean. Then my brothers thought that sounded too high-falutin' and shortened it to Jedge, and finally to just Jed. And it stuck.

But...back to your Pa. He really wanted you to be a judge?

Nope. It was all family teasing. He called his real sons things like Sonny, and Counselor, even Palaverer...

His real sons?

Yeah. See, my old man isn't my real Pa. So I don't call him that. To me, he's Pater.

Pater?

Yah. A word I picked up from the pile of books he threw at me.

He really threw them?

Figure of speech, man. He wasn't exactly mean, just treated me different than Sonny. But getting back to you, Lucius. You're Irish, aren't you? And Catholic? I thought so. My family was, too, as much as I know about them. Ward was the family name. Lived in Cornwall with the Cornish until Cromwell's brutes drove them out. Isn't that a good one? Cromwell in Cornwall.

Silly joke, Lucius mumbled.

Oh, I s'pose so. Well, my real Pa got killed in the lead mines when I was three, my Ma died a year later, and the Simmons family took me in when I turned five.

A lawyer's family?

Yup. Percy Simmons—that's Pater's name. He brought us to America and set up his law office in Dubuque.

His two sons Reginald and Barton—that's Sonny and Counselor—they're his favorites. Went to law schools out East, they did.

So did you go to law school? Lucius asked.

Nope. You didn't neither, I bet.

No...that's why we're both Sergeants and not officers, I guess. My Pa had this apothecary...

Well, Pater told me not everyone needs law school, Albert continued, already disinterested in Lucius' family.

So I had a stint one year being flunky on a river boat, throwing out the Captain's slop buckets and things like that. But then Pater said I could join Simmons & Sons, Esquire, and work into the family business. That's when he started calling me Jedge, and then the family, like I told you, shortened it to Jed.

So Pater, you call him, was really talking you down? Lucius asked.

Y'know, I was never sure of that. Anyway, he told me to read the books in his office, watch how he handled cases. And you know something? I can out-argue any one of those fancy men from Eastern law schools. Schools don't teach you how to stand your ground in front of judge and jury.

So should I call you Jed?

Sure. Everybody does. Other sergeants know the story, and they used to ask me about military law, same way as for you I expect. Like, does our Major break army rules when he holds up our pay? Are we getting the food we should?

So would you take that to the Major?

Jed (Albert) grinned: Would you?

Well, I've had my ups and downs with officers…

Oh, have I ever had ups and downs, especially with a Colonel named Mahlon Blanchard who had been a fast-talking lawyer and then a judge who tried to get the legislature to create a special district for him, with Coulee City in the middle, until the state Supreme Court put a stop to his shenanigans…

No, Jed continued, I play it careful, you know what I mean? I'd ask the company Captain if the Corps was getting all its rations. See? Company officers always gripe about the higher brass, never their immediate superiors. They can get away with that, because a Captain knows his Major hates their Colonel too. That way the Major quietly agrees with the Captain but never lets on too plainly.

So I'd hear just enough from the Captain to tell other sergeants I was looking out for 'em. They'd think I really talked with the Major, when it was only the Captain...

So how well did you know your Captain?

Too well for his own good, Jed said. Not to mention mine. He was spending time with another man's wife, evenings, when we were drilling, back in Camp Franklin. That's in Dubuque.

Albert Jed Simmons spat a stream of dark tobacco juice.

Where'd you get the chew? Lucius asked.

Jed removed his kepi, with the curled horn of his infantry regiment still intact just above the sweaty line over the visor. He wiped the prematurely balding crown of his head, then replaced the cap quickly. He had been sunburned once on his bare scalp, and that was enough.

Chaw'in tobacco? Oh, I found some...

Lucius saw new threads in the sole edges of Jed's boots.

You've been fixing your shoes, Albert...I mean, Jed? How'd you manage that?

Jed pulled in his fleshy lower jaw, wrinkling his chin. He gazed around carefully, as if he were telling his platoon things he didn't want officers to hear.

Got them sewed up by a man south of the sink, he said. Good cobbler, though I dunno where he got his big needles.

Then lowering his voice still more, Jed added:

Some claim this cobbler's one of the leading Raiders. Name is Sorsfield, something like that.

Lucius shrugged. He still didn't take the Raider talk all that seriously. *Left to themselves, soldiers in a prison camp can be their own worst enemies, often vultures among their own kind—unless they've been well disciplined. And they haven't been, or they wouldn't tolerate living like pigs in a sty, as they do here. Oh, Lord, how I tried to get them to use latrines at Camp Lagoon, back near Coulee City. But they wouldn't do it, going instead out to the fields. Latrines weren't private, they'd mutter.*

Lucius turned to walk away from Jed, heading south.

Where you going? Jed asked, still in low voice.

To the sink. Gotta answer nature's call.

Don't go there, Lucius. Too close to the Raiders' she-bangs, where they stash their loot. Might get your head bashed in. 'Specially if they figger you're sizing them up for the Regulators.

Lucius looked down that way.

You think something's really going to happen?

Damn sure it is. You hear about this man who just got beat up? Dowell, or Doud, his name is. Got attacked and fought back hard. Some Raider bastard mashed his face so bad, a rebel guard got sympathetic. Even took him out to see Wirz.

To see Wirz? I heard nobody ever gets to meet him.

Well, Doud was cut up awful bad, but he still had his wits. Word is that when Wirz saw him, he decided it was time we use these clubs he had us get from the woods.

Anyway, Jed continued, LeRoy Key is in charge. A sergeant, some Illinois outfit. Seems he just might have this whole thing in hand.

Everyone calls Wirz a heartless bastard, Lucius said. Think he's changed?

Why? Jed answered. Just because he wants to rein in these scalawags? Naw, his heart hasn't got any bigger. What he fears is a great big riot. Ten or twenty thousand prisoners might rush the gates and bust out. He wouldn't have guns or cannons enough to stop us.

So, if we had a breakout, Jed continued, Winder would have Wirz shot. Then Winder would be worried about his own neck, too.

And who is Winder?

General Winder. Wirz answers to him.

So, between Key and his Regulators and Wirz' men, Jed added, they're going to hogtie those Raiders and put them on trial. It's going to happen soon.

Jed turned to leave, but now Lucius caught his sleeve.

If you knew there's gonna be a roundup of these scalawags in the air, why'd you go down their way? To get your shoe sewed? Or to set up a lawyering job?

Jed was irked. He looked around again. Spies, he knew, might be anywhere among this teeming mass.

Say, Lucius, he said, are you accusing me of huckstering? Fact is, I'd heard this Sarsfield could fix shoes. Then, too, he knew I was a lawyer, and, well, he maybe did figger he might need one some time. The others, they all think they're kings of the mountain, that everybody's too scared to stand up to them.

Lucius was suspicious.

We just got here a couple days ago, he said. How'd you find those birds so fast?

Just listened, Jed answered. Heard this one could sew shoes, like I said. So went to see him. Talked some, let them know I'm new here. His gang prob'ly thought he was signing me up.

Lucius frowned: So did you let them think that?

Dammit, Lucius, Jed muttered under his breath, why are you spattering mud over me? You don't trust me, do you? Fact is, I DID allow Sarsfield to think I was serious about joining them. It seemed like the only way I could get my britches out of there without losing them.

Well, Lucius said, I must say I wonder how, in this hog barn, this Raider—Sarsfield, you say?—could find out that a new prisoner, like you or me, was a lawyer?

Lucius, Jed answered, there's not much these birds don't know. They got spies everywhere. They got you marked, too, in case you don't know.

But Sarsfield, Jed continued, is the only one who isn't cocksure he can beat off anyone who tries to collar him. Well—maybe this sailor guy Muir, too…

One of the Raiders is a sailor?

Well, Muir says he is. Only been here a few weeks, just long enough to fall in with Sarsfield and Collins. Sullen cuss, has eyes like dead mice in a pan of sour gravy. But mean, too…he'd stick a knife through you with as little compunction as stabbing a toad.

So these Raiders, are tough buggers? They must eat well.

You can be damned sure of that.

And how do they get this food? Just steal it?

Sure, they swipe potatoes and ration meat and every damned thing. They've stolen so much money they go and buy what they can't pillage.

Starving men will sell food?

Some do—but these brutes buy stuff from guards, too, don't forget.

Huh. So, are they leery about these Regulators?

Maybe, maybe not. When they see a tough crowd, they usually just go and recruit them. Do away with the opposition and get stronger at the same time.

Lucius asked: Do they fight among themselves?

Aw, they've prob'ly bashed in heads of a couple hoodlums they didn't trust. And then, they aren't sure about this man Key. Some Raiders think he's just another rowdy leader hoping to wreck the competition and run things HIS way.

And what do you think?

Jed hesitated.

Odds are, he said, Key is serious about stopping the stealing and murder. If it worked, he'd be top dog, something he'd likely enjoy. And...the fact the Raider hoodlums down there let me go may be a sign they ain't too sure about Key. Besides, it made a difference when we boys from the west come here. Wisconsin and Illinois and Iowa, I really think we're tougher.

Jed, did anyone see you over there? Wondering if you aren't part of that crowd?

Jeezus, I hope not... I made it a point to stop at the Sink, so it would look like I was just back from taking a good dump.

Lucius, inside himself, continued to stir his doubts.

Yes, that's probably what Jed hoped. But I'm still unsure. Did Jed really go over there to get his shoes fixed, or was he thinking of maybe joining them? Or...was he sizing them up for the Regulators? Either way, he learned a lot in a short while about that crowd, just like Harry did.

But I have to be on guard with him, just as I learned back in Coulee City to be wary of Judge—a real judge—Mahlon Blanchard. That man had one of the sharpest thinking caps in the territory. After the state Supreme Court cut down his scheme to become a district judge, he wheedled a commission as Colonel, and organized a volunteer Regiment. So when the shooting started, he became a local hero. And then he flummoxed me out of getting a commission because I wouldn't take a bribe.

Chapter 7.
WEDNESDAY, **J**UNE 29, 1864

In early afternoon, the roundup of the Raiders began.

Small groups of men with clubs formed north of the creek and sink and moved southward. Sergeant LeRoy Key bellowed orders. Other teams arose from shebangs in the center, not far from Lucius. A platoon of jittery Confederate guards appeared from the north gate, nervously fumbling the hammers on their muskets and hoping the prisoners would actually take on the Raiders and not the guards themselves.

This time, the guards had no need to fear the mass of prisoners. The Regulators had one thing in mind: Get the Raiders. Dig them out, root and branch.

And this they did, although it was far from a clean, disciplined application of law and order. It was, rather, unleashed fury from small packs of men who now had clubs, leadership, and help from Captain Wirz' Confederate guards, edgy as they were, to exact revenge.

At first, groups of Raider men in the south end stood and waved, defiantly, cheerfully challenging and cursing with every profanity imaginable the approaching guards and Regulators.

Such threats had worked before, without fail.

But not this time.

Regulator men in numbers answered taunt with taunt. The two groups clashed, not in one single epic battle, but in scores of violent, noisy, swirling melees, mostly on the slope south of the putrid sink area.

Down went the Raiders' outlandish huts festooned with colorful blankets and banners, swiped over the past months from other prisoners too weak or cowed to resist.

Most fights didn't last long. Clubs landed with soft thuds, followed by yells of pain. Confederate guards used the butt ends of their muskets. A few Raiders, well versed in close-in fighting, landed telling blows on their attackers.

Outa here, you bast... one Raider started to yell before a splintered board smacked full against his mouth. Blood and bits of broken teeth flew from his shattered jaw.

Come get me, 'f you think you can... another started, his words cut off by a wildly swung pine club that knocked him silly.

Skirmishes erupted around the various huts where Raider groups had stashed their booty. Key's men subdued a dozen, then 30 or 40. They rounded up and herded the bloodied thugs into the small enclosure surrounding the North entrance gate.

The captured men, some bleeding and others so stunned they had to be dragged or even carried, now stood in a huddle just past the open inner gate. They stood bloodily in full view of hundreds of triumphant prisoners who loudly wished them the damnation of Hell and the curses of God in Heaven.

All the known gang leaders were there, in ropes or chains—Mosby, Sullivan, Curtis, Muir, Delaney, and Sarsfield.

Lucius took no part in the roundup. Except for what Jed Simmons told him, he hardly knew who LeRoy Key was and had little inclination to seek him out.

Whatever his motives, right now Key is the most popular fellow in this part of Georgia. But...why did the Raiders run the prison for so long?

Poor discipline. These sorry Union prisoner-soldiers for months had no idea how to organize a police force. More interested in whiskey than milk, better at sowing wild oats than wheat. They came out of our training camps slack, slovenly, and shiftless.

Like my mentor in Coulee City, Lawyer Eldon Ashton, used to say: Let villains run the town for years and then when they do something really horrid, a mob strings them up without a fair trial. That's what will happen now; these raiders won't get any *kind of trial. Summary justice is no justice at all.*

———

With most of the Raiders corralled and the rest on the run, prisoners by the thousands crowded around the North Gate enclosure and shouted lusty threats at the captives. Two days earlier these men had been meek, fearful and quiescent. Now, with the tide turned, they were full of bravado.

They shouted at the captured raiders with gusto:

Hey, hang onto yer necks, you fellers in there! They're going to get a good stretching!

Hope you bastards liked all that stuff you stole! Too bad you ain't going to get to use it!

Say boys, how about we just cut their balls out? They ain't gonna need 'em now!

Raucous laughter.

Sure, and then scatter their brains all over this filthy ground.

Anyhows, you dirty buggers are gonna swing, and that's a dead sure thing!

Ha, ha! That's a good one.

Don't worry if you can't sleep tonight, you fellers. 'Fore long, you're goin' to have a nice snug berth in Georgia sod.

Say, I hear you boys got big hearts? Hell, that's good! Worms in your graves'll feed well on 'em!

Three of the more famous Raider men—Patrick Delaney, John Sullivan (also known as Terry or Cary), and Andy Muir—stood with their hands and feet tied.

Charles Curtis suffered even more. Key tied the thug's hands together, pushed them down over his knees and then ran a stick through the inside arch of his knees and above his arms. Another Regulator tied a dirty rag around Curtis' head and inside his mouth.

When untied that evening, Curtis wouldn't be able to stand or walk until next morning.

Now that's buckin' and gaggin' where it does some good, one of Key's men said with satisfaction.

Willie (Mosby) Collins and Andy Muir sat uncomfortably with their hands and legs in irons.

Collins shouted:

Just wait, you sons of bitches! No one winds us up and gets away with it. Yer all marked! Yer guts and cocks will spill all over this place. Just you wait! The Irish always win in the end!

Sarsfield, being more rational than Collins, decided to keep quiet, sensing that tough talk now might simply speed his walk to the noose.

Lucius worried.

It's one thing for vigilantes to subdue and round up these suspected hooligans. But will they live to trial time? With the mood for revenge getting mean and nasty, the odds are high for a quick lynching.

Then Lucius saw something else he feared.

Standing in the enclosure among the captive Raiders was his childhood friend and shebang mate.

Corporal Harry Nickels, head down in a slouch, his torn Union pants and shirt muddy and shredded, slumped on the ground, his hands tied.

Lucius heard faintly the approaching Jed Simmons:

Lucius, you look like you've seen a ghost. This roundup gettin' too much for yuh?

Oh, my god, Jed. See that boy back there, slumping behind the one in stocks, his hands tied behind him? That's Harry Nickels, a Corporal from my company. Chum from our days as children. We share a shebang. I wonder....

So did he fall in with the Raiders? Jed asked.

I don't know exactly what he HAS done. But I'm worried. He found a bunch of things for cooking, and I never knew where he got them.

Maybe you don't know the man as well as you thought?

Lucius shrugged, then said, sharply: Well, Jed, you spent some time the last day or so moseying around those Raider men. Did you see Harry when you were over there polishing their apples?

No, dammit. Look, Lucius, can you get this through your head? I went over there to get my shoes fixed, nothing more, nothing less.

Lucius decided not to push his suspicions about Jed any further—for now.

The boys are yelling pretty loud, Lucius said. If they had their way, they'd string the brutes up right now. That's what worries me about Harry.

Well, I guess you're right to worry, Jed said. I've been listening, and it seems Wirz is worried about the same thing. Right now it's in this Sergeant Key's hands. Let's see what he says.

Sergeant Key raised his lanky, strong and sinewy frame on a rickety potato box, waved for quiet, and spoke:

Well, boys, we've got the worst devils now, and they's more to catch, scattered from hell to breakfast around the stockade. But some we maybe rounded up by mistake, so we're going to let them out.

A loud groan of No-o-o-o! erupted. One ragged, rope-bearded man wearing a badly-stained kepi, shouted from a raspy throat:

It's took all year to stop these devils so we can't turn 'em loose now!

Agreement roared from the crowd.

Sergeant Key held up his hand.

We've hooked the main ones, he growled. Now, let me tell you what's gonna happen.

The worst of these critters will be tried by court martial. It'll be fair. The court will be made up of prisoners. Mostly Sergeants who only been here a short time. Wirz wants men who ain't already made up their minds.

Cap'n Wirz got permission from General Winder to do this, Key continued. If the court decides to hang anyone, they first have to get permission from Richmond.

A ragged man with a shaggy, dirty beard bellowed:

They gonna hang?

That'll be up to the court.

We don't need no court. Let's stretch their necks now.

No. This will be a regular trial, fair and just.

But we can't try a couple hundred, Key added. They's too many in here. So any boy who doesn't have one solid witness to testify against him is gonna be turned loose. Now.

Loud objections roared from the crowd, but Key's decision—actually made for him by a Confederate guard lieutenant—carried the day.

Key motioned to his men to bring him one of the captives, a small, pathetic, woebegone fellow with a hang-dog look. Blood flowed under the right side of his soiled cap, from a club wound behind the ear.

All right. Who will testify against this man? Key asked.

Many murmured, some shouted, but none offered witness.

One prisoner yelled: He's well fed, damn him! Only a Raider could get enough grub to fill out his guts that well!

Key persisted. Anyone see him jump anybody? Or steal something?

Hearing no more, Key said, What's your name?

His voice shaking, the bedraggled man said, Chester Murphy, Seventeenth Indiana.

Okay, Chester, skedaddle the hell out of here.

Chester Murphy headed for the exit, but fifty or more prisoners quickly lined up in two rows starting at the exit and running in a serpentine line down the north slope and toward the swamp and sink.

When he saw he had a gauntlet to run, Chester wailed, put his hands over his head, and bawled:

Christ boys, I'm bloodied now, don't hit me more.

Throaty voices answered him:

You ain't half as goddam bloody as yer goin' to be.

Yer guts'll be jelly, yuh damned shit-ass.

The gauntlet men deliberately ended their line at the swampy, smelly sink.

One of Key's men pushed Chester into the line, and he broke into a run. Flailing clubs and sticks, and some bare fists, pummeled the sorry private from Indiana. He fell several times, but managed to get up and run again. The last man in the gauntlet line decided to not raise his club and, instead, held out a foot, tripping the hapless Chester. He sprawled in the mud, his broken right arm bent grotesquely under his chest.

Chester's screams brought only taunts from men in the line.

After Chester, the Regulators released dozens more captives the same way. Some took more blows than others, but none got through the line unhurt. Three men had broken arms or wrists and two had broken legs. One had a skull fracture that would lead to his death two days later.

Much but not all of the wild clubbing, kicking, and punching along the gauntlet line was from vengeful prisoners, some who were themselves victims of Raider assaults. Others were men who simply couldn't resist the fun and exhilaration that allowed them to forget worrying whether they would live another day.

So Key knows what he's doing; by letting the gauntlet boys batter those men, the mob is getting its vengeance out of its system. Makes mob lynching of the leaders less likely just now.

The last captive through the gauntlet was Corporal Harry Nickels, new in the prison and not recognized by most of the gauntlet men. He suffered a bleeding forehead and a badly bruised and cut left arm that fended off the worst blows.

After the gauntlet run, Confederate guards and Regulator men under Key corralled the remaining thirty or so suspected Raiders—including the notorious six leaders. All ended up in the enclosure of the North Gate but now out of sight of the thousands of wretches in the inner stockade.

Well, brutal as the gauntlet was, Captain Wirz and Sergeant Key avoided a lynching. But it was hell for Harry. Now just how—and why—did he get mixed up with that bunch?

No matter how close we were as young sprouts, there were always things about Harry I didn't know. Like, what did he tell Maryanne when he finally skipped out on her? Was he really planning to marry her? She told me he did—and that he lied to her, saying he was a lieutenant. But the way he prattles on, how could she have believed that? Wagon shop men like Harry don't often get to be officers. Not that they aren't up to the job. It just doesn't happen.

―――

Since his capture, Lucius had heard little from the outside, about the war and fortunes of the Union and Confederate armies. New prisoners spoke mostly of confusion in the ranks and stalemate on the front lines. Many said little, for lack of pride in what they had done, or how little they had done, in the hours that led to their capture.

―――

Dear Maryanne: I must keep writing these letters to you even though you'll never see them, because scribbling these things down does me good, or at least gets things off my chest. Oh, how it thrilled me to meet you in the tea house that time, and I still see you sitting there on the Queen Anne chair, wearing that gorgeous blue and white frock and—in spite of our not getting on well up to then—you smiled at me. I can never forget that smile, because it said so much about what might be. Then there was that ride on your Pa's stable horses back in the oak woods. I asked you to marry me and you said you would—but first, we would have to see eye to eye on the slavery question. So is that why we never married?

Your affectionate husband-in-waiting, Lucius

(Entry in Lucius McCordle's diary, June 29, 1864)

Headquarters Petersburg
His Excellency Jefferson Davis
President Confederate States June 29 1864

Mr. President...I still think it is our policy to draw the attention of the enemy to his own territory. It may force Grant to attack me or weaken his forces. It will also, I think, oblige Hunter to cross the Potomac or expose himself to attack...there will be time to shape Early's course or terminate it when he reaches the Potomac, as circumstances require...

With great respect, your obedient servant. R. E. Lee General[7]

---

7   WOTR, Series 1, Vol. 37, Part 1, p. 769.

Chapter 8.
6 a.m. Thursday, June 30, 1864

Lucius had slept very little. A badly battered Harry Nickels kept turning and moaning, unable to sleep. His left arm was more than bruised. The swelling told Lucius that it had been fractured, but the bones had not separated. Lucius had found some rags and tied a crude splint on the arm.

The splint made sleeping even more difficult.

At some time, Harry's got to tell me what he's been up to in the past two days. But let him sleep first.

———

As the sun climbed above the east stockade wall, Lucius heard shouts, screams, and exultant yells from Regulators rounding up more Raiders, mostly marginal ruffians who had escaped the previous day's onslaught by losing themselves among the thousands north of the sink.

Lucius was satisfied that such thugs were apprehended but worried: *How on earth can these men be defended if there is, in fact, a trial? Should I offer to defend them? How can anyone possibly put together a decent court here? Or a courts martial? Would anyone have an army courts-martial manual here? Pretty damned unlikely.*

———

Harry stirred with a groan from his painful, turbulent sleep.

Lucius avoided asking his suffering friend how he was doing.

How about some grub, Harry? Make you feel better, I bet.

Harry grunted. Lucius didn't wait for words, but cooked gruel from his carefully-protected bag of flour, and dumped in some salt pork that hadn't yet rotted. An emaciated fellow in a nearby shebang complimented Lucius on the nice smell he was making and asked if he could have a taste.

Not this time, Lucius answered quickly. Saving it for my wounded friend, here.

That bastard's a friend of yers? Wull, I seen him yestaday. He's a goddam Raider, he is. Got banged up by the boys in the line. Serves 'im right.

Lucius glared back at the sickly speaker.

*In fact, I don't know whether he got mixed up with the Raiders, or not. But the last thing I ought to do now is admit that to somebody like this. I've already been suspicious of Jed, and he's the only other one here I can count as a friend. Well, possibly a **former** friend.*

Lucius answered: They let him go because nobody spoke against him, remember? He's new to this place, like me. I'd say he got rounded up by mistake, so let me feed him. If there's some left, I'll grant you a bite.

Lucius hoped this man didn't see the bulging sack in the center of the shebang.

Harry Nickels was now awake, and Lucius carefully spooned him some gruel with salt pork. Harry ate some slowly, then rose, stood to check his balance and walked a few shaky steps. The grumbling but sickly fellow in the next shebang also rose and ambled off in a different direction.

Lucius confronted Harry, but in a low voice.

Harry, how the hell did you manage to get rounded up? You sure as shootin' must have been down there when the Regulators went to work. What the dickens happened, anyway?

See, Lucius, Harry began, I was over there all right, but just for trading.

For trading? You must be hornswoggling me, Lucius said.

Nope. Doncha know how I always find where good things are? Hell, they's got a store down there better than the Sutler's shack.

Stolen and robbed stuff, you mean.

They told me they got it all on trade.

And you believed them, Harry?

Not all of it, but I wanted to find out who they were.

Why? Why the hell....?

See, they was what all the boys here was talkin' about since we got here, so I was curious.

Curious? Or just too damned nosey for your own good? Or maybe trying to get something out of them for yourself?

Goldarn it, Lucius, I found them friendly. We traded some stuff; that's where I got that food first day, remember? And did you see the stuff I brought here when you were away?

Yes...I saw it and wondered why...

Lucius, hard up as we are, those are tools we need to stay alive...

To stay alive? Or to get us killed when someone sees it's stuff from the Raider huts? Harry, did you go off half cocked down there? Are you touched in the head?

They got to braggin' about themselves, Harry said, so I listened. I learnt lots of things about them.

Were he not so beaten up, I would rip him apart.

So what did they tell you?

Just about anything yuh might want to know.

Such as?

Well, I found out a few things about these leaders. Let's see what I remember...

Take this top man, they call Mosby. His name is Willie Collins. Says he's English by birth but Irish by blood. Came here with a big family when he was a lad, grew quick, worked in the knitting mills, and headed up a gang in the back alleys of Philadelphia. Claims when he was grown up he saved some poor little boys from starvation.

He tells that he liked enlisting so well he did it three or four times. Signed up, took the bounty of more than a hundred dollars, and then deserted and went somewhere else and enlisted again. Some say Mosby fought at the second Bull Run, first fight of the war. Got shot in the leg there, I guess, but not too bad, though he limps some. Claims he was a hero at Gettysburg, with the Penns'vania infantry.

Got promoted to corporal up there. Guess he got captured near the Rapidan River, in Virginie. Some say he deserted and helped himself get captured. Funny any man in his right mind would do that, 'specially if he really *was* a corporal. Been here since March.

He's a big critter, must be six feet tall. Got light hair, like most of the Irish. He's a tough one, and seems to run the whole Raider camp. I didn't talk straight *to* him, I'm tellin' you what others said. But I saw him quite a bit. He's got the fanciest duds in the whole stockade, and he was eatin' and drinkin' damned good over there.

So you say he's the head man? Lucius asked.

Seems to be. Even runs the singing and carousing. Puts on a big show at night, till it gets late and they go out on raids.

Then there's this Curtis, if I got the name right. Heard some call him Rickson. Or was it Erickson? Naw, that'd be Norwegian. Anyway, he don't stand as high as Collins, but he's a tough bunch of bone and muscle. Brutish and talks nasty. Says he's a Canadian, but came down to Rhode Island and did carpenter work there. He signed up for the bounty, like Mosby. Then got himself captured.

Curtis is one mean sonofabitch. Some say he's a Navy man, but I dunno. He's like most of these birds, prob'ly enlisted to get a bounty and deserted at least once. He's quite young, maybe 21 right now, had a lot of John Barleycorn and fist fighting with everybody in town, to hear him tell it. He likes to tell how he cracks jaws and ribs with one swing of his big, hard fists. Has a grin like a monster, scary even to the other Raiders. Been here since winter, got to know the stockade well and helps Collins run the place.

I heard someone say there's a couple of shoemakers over there, Lucius said. Anything to that?

At least one, Harry said. He shifted his weight under the shebang, trying to get comfortable. His arm throbbed. Geez, I need some whiskey, he mumbled.

Sorry, just drank the last six bottles, Lucius answered.

Don't get smart, Lucius, Harry muttered. I wasn't humbuggin'. I got a small bottle, see, right here...from this Sarsfield. Oh, hell, it ain't here. Musta got broke in the fracas yesterday.

You traded for liquor? What did you give him in exchange?

Lucius…I'm telling you a lot here…but like I always tell you, ask me no questions…well, not too many…and I tell you no lies.

Damn! How could this old friend, in a just a few days, get snarled up in the sticky scum that's been fermenting for months up that south slope? And he's not telling what I want most to know: Was he a partner in Raider crime? After just a few days here? He's being secretive, just like back in Coulee City.

Harry breathed heavily and continued, this time about the Raider John Sarsfield.

Sarsfield is a first-rate shoe maker and fixer, Harry said. 'F yuh don't b'lieve it, look what he done to my shoes.

Harry tried to point to a foot with his left hand, immediately grimaced from the pain, and then used his right hand to slowly ease the left arm back to rest on his stomach.

How about that! Harry and Albert the Jedge both had shoes fixed by that hoodlum. What a business he must have had! I wonder: Did Sarsfield talk to the one about the other?

Another Irishman, Harry continued. Sarsfield hasn't been here all that long, maybe six weeks. Like Collins and Curtis, the way all of them enlisted twice or more for bounty money. Sign up, take the money, desert to another place and enlist all over again. That's how they do it.

Well, that's nothing new, Lucius said. Happens all over the country.

Yah, Harry continued, from what he told me, he wanted to desert one more time, but couldn't make it before his New York infantry went into the Wilderness. That's where he got captured. On purpose, way it sounded to me.

Sarsfield's a shortie, no taller than lots of wimmen. But another tough nut, I tell you.

Harry hesitated, wondering what to say next.

6 A.M. THURSDAY, JUNE 30, 1864

This Harry is a great observer of people. Seems to see them once and remember everything about them and what they say. Or at least, what he wants to tell you. I remember more than once, when I took a case to court in Coulee City, I would call on Harry to find out the dirty stuff about people I was opposing in court. He even knew more than I did about shenanigans of other lawyers.

The raiders, Harry continued, seem to be jealous of Sarsfield, 'f you know what I mean. First weeks here, he went on parole outside the stockade, 'cause Winder used him to repair a bunch of Confederate boots.

Lucius asked: Winder actually put him to work?

Harry should have worked for Buck Sewall, our feisty Copperhead editor in Coulee City. He has a good sense of how people take advantage of each other. And, maybe Sewall did call on him, more than I or other people realized.

Well, Sarsfield sure bragged about it, Harry said. Then another Raider pretended to do shoes, too, and tried to get paroled. But Winder musta figgered he was fixing to skedaddle, so it didn't work for that boy.

And who was that? Lucius asked.

Name's Delaney, a tiring Harry answered. He's been in and out of the Army, once in the Pennsy'vania Infantry, another time in some artillery brigade. Did stone mason work a few years back.

Delaney claims he has a wife and family somewhere, Harry continued, but doesn't seem eager to get back to them. Acts as if he's almost relieved to be here rather than trying to feed a scolding wife and snot-nosed urchins. Pretty hard sort of man, mean as any of them.

You'd think these mean bastards would make good fighting men, wouldn't you? But no, seems every one of them asked to get captured.

So Curtis is a sailor? Lucius asked.

Curtis claims that, but the real sailor in that bunch is a boy named Munn, or Meeyor, or something like that, Harry answered. Another Irishman. He got captured when the Rebs made a midnight raid on a ship with a funny name. Water Witch. Someone made a joke of it, said it was beewitched, way he said it. Meeyor didn't think that was funny and offered to tear out that boy's guts. Looked like he was goin' to pitch into him...

You saw the Raiders fight among themselves? Lucius asked.

No, not really...but Meeyor looked hell-bent to smash the boy's brains. What I did hear, though, was Meeyor bragging how he fought off and knifed some Rebels before they pinned him down. So maybe I shouldn't call him a deserter...

Harry, Lucius said, you sure picked up a lot about these criminals in a very short time. That's a real smart way you have, of watching people.

Sore as he was, Harry Nickels looked at Lucius with a self-conscious but satisfied grin.

Hell, Lucius, all I had to do was listen. They's bragging and puffing all the time and telling things on each other. Some of it may be so, some just plain balderdash. I'm telling you what I heard, for what it's worth.

Anyway, Meeyor crows about all the fights he got into back in Dublin. He's the snarlyest one a'the whole shootin' match. Maybe he was in prison, I don't know. Someone said he's a good Catholic, sees the priest whenever he can. Others said he had things to confess. I wouldn't know.

With that, Harry Nickels slumped to the ground and drifted off into a fitful doze.

So did Harry in fact become one of them? Did he go out on raids? Hmm. For all his smartness he was stupid enough to be in the wrong place when the Raider roundup began.

Now say, there's another possibility...what're the chances he was working for Sergeant Key? Naw...that would be too complicated. More likely, Harry was just being Harry.

Later, when his old friend was awake, Lucius asked him if he saw a Raider named Cary.

Sort of a tiny man, Lucius said.

Let's see...Harry said. I didn't talk to him, but there's one named Terry Sullivan, another guy from Ireland. And, well, yeah, some maybe did call him Cary. He's in the same tent with Mosby, and it seems the two of them go back to New York, where they signed up for the bounty. Some say he—this Terry—lived in Canada, but got kicked out.

Lucius asked: Why is that? Big as Canada is, they wouldn't worry about one more bastard, would they?

I don't know, Harry answered. But this Terry is a gambler, spends a lot of time with cards and dice. Talks real dirty, the way small toughies often do. Got a great big chip on his shoulder.

Harry was spent. He turned over in pain and went back to a troubled sleep.

Chapter 9.
8 a.m., Thursday, June 30, 1864

Lucius tried without success to rest in the doubtful shade of the shebang, or caboose, as Harry preferred to call it. Harry was feverish, but had gone back to sleep. Lucius picked up his dog-eared journal and began to scribble.

Harry had said little more about his time around the Raiders, and Lucius didn't press him.

I suppose I should be thankful my troubled old friend is still alive, and not outside the stockade with the ones to be court martialed.

Jed Simmons yelled:

Lucius! On your feet! They want all us new Sergeants this morning at the North Gate.

What for?

It's about the trial. They know you and I are lawyers. Maybe they want our advice. What do you know about the military code?

Not too much, Lucius said. I served on one or two trials. Privates who got drunk, went on French leave, that sort of thing. We'd put them under lock for a couple of days, and that was about all.

But holy Christmas, Lucius added, remembering his battered shanty mate.

Harry Nickels is in bad shape. He won't be able to feed himself. How can I leave him?

Lucius turned back to his shebang and asked Harry: Are you all right for a couple of hours?

Yeah, Harry answered, give me a cup of water and those dried beans.

This Lucius was able to do. He found the now stale water in his canteen hidden under the blankets—alongside the mysterious stuff Harry said he had gotten in trade from the Raiders. The beans, which he had intended to cook today, he gave raw to Harry.

Then he joined Jed, who was waiting next to the North Gate.

Some 50 Sergeants gathered in the enclosure, where the captive prisoners were first corralled but now sat, stood, or lay in some grotesque punitive posture outside.

Captain Wirz, next to a man who looked stunningly familiar to Lucius, addressed the Sergeants in his usual accented and broken English.

We are going to give these men a fair trial. It will be handled by you men, you Sergeants who got here a few days ago. We have picked one Sergeant already to head up the court martial. He is Sergeant Blanchard, from Missouri, a man who was a judge.

Lucius was stunned.

What? Mahlon C. Blanchard? Indeed, can this be him? Once a judge in Wisconsin, then a Colonel, then cashiered from the army for stealing and selling rations? And now a Sergeant from a Missouri outfit? The same stocky, long-bodied man? Well, he isn't quite so well-groomed and his hair is starting to turn gray. His mustache is bulkier... Yet it's that same pugnacious nose and chin thrust forward. Same swagger. By god, it IS him!

Wirz continued in his Germanic drawl, making w sound like v and they like say.

General Winder, Wirz said, after the trial will send the transcript to Richmond, so they can tell whether any punishment you wish on these men is authorized.

8 A.M., Thursday, June 30, 1864

Wirz then proceeded to pick the jury by lot. He put some 50 slips of paper in a hat, 12 with red marks. The Sergeants one after another reached in the hat—held high by a Confederate soldier—and when 12 had marked slips, the drawing ended.

These Sergeants made up the jury.

———

Lucius could hardly believe what he was seeing and hearing. Indeed, standing there was Mahlon Blanchard, the last person he might have expected to find in a prisoner-of-war camp full of enlisted men.

How did this pompous and loquacious ass, a cashiered Colonel in the Union Army, end up here in Andersonville? And as a Sergeant, no less!

Lucius, now thoroughly discombobulated, had mixed reactions to drawing a blank slip.

I don't relish being in this court-martial, or whatever it is. And having Judge/Colonel/Sergeant Blanchard running things would make it worse. But...these men deserve a decent defense...just as Harry Nickels would if he hadn't been sent back to the stockade.

Wirz had more to say.

The court president, Wirz said, has picked one Sergeant to be prosecuting attorney with a helper, and two to be defense lawyers. He nodded to Blanchard, who stood up quickly and announced in his familiar baritone:

We have some former counselors here. Sergeant Warrick Breck from Pennsylvania will handle the prosecution. He will be assisted by Sergeant Delano Richman, from Illinois.

For the defense, Wirz said, we hope there will be a volunteer or two. There are more lawyers among you Sergeants. Any of you wish to do the defense?

Oh, Lord! If I volunteer, I would once more deal with this arrogant ass who killed my chances for an officership. Does he know I am in the crowd? Is he still smarting from the trouble I caused him? Probably so, with a grudge against me. After I cost him his Army job, he left town without giving me so much as a parting kick. And that's probably only because he didn't get the chance. Now, if I volunteer, he might try to get back at me. If I do well and actually make these birds look innocent, I wouldn't survive a day in the stockade.

The task seemed hopeless—yet necessary, as Lucius thought again about the rights of the accused.

He grabbed Albert Simmons and said: Jed, if I volunteer, will you too?

Simmons rubbed his jaw, grimaced, and then said: Well, I wouldn't do it alone, but if you take on being chief defense counsel, I'll back you up.

With that, Lucius raised his hand and said, I'll be the defense counsel and Sergeant Simmons here will be my assistant.

Your name? Wirz asked.

Sergeant Lucius McCordle, Wisconsin Volunteers. I will be assisted by Sergeant Albert Simmons, Iowa infantry.

Jed raised his hand and nodded.

A murmur went through the group. Sergeant Blanchard gave Lucius a quizzical glance, looked down, and said nothing.

Now, Lucius found the task was upon him.

How in damnation can anyone put together a defense for these brutes? How can we do anything but act out a formality?

8 a.m., Thursday, June 30, 1864

...But then, they say this is to be a fair trial. And yes, it will be out of the stockade, and out of the hearing of the 20-some thousand prisoners inside. So will that really make it fair? Will Blanchard as judge—excuse me, Court President—make it any fairer? I doubt it.

And suppose the court does find them innocent? I wouldn't live for two minutes if I went inside that stockade after successfully defending them.

The Sergeants not selected for any part of the court martial were excused, but warned they might be called on if any of the named jury members became too sick to serve.

Most of the selected Sergeants were happy to be out of the stockade for a few days. They could temporarily enjoy their slight but noticeable separation from the filth, rank odor, and turmoil inside, and the chance to get first crack at the ration wagon that would stop for them before going into the stockade.

For Lucius, the bewilderment of an impossible defense job, complicated by a nemesis from the past, was enough to give him a headache. He longed for some of that liquor Harry had said he traded with the Raiders, but lost in the clamor of the roundup.

Chapter 10.
9 a.m. Friday, July 1, 1864

Sergeant Blanchard relished his job as trial court president. This cashiered Colonel in the Union Army found restoration of his pride and stature in being the top judicial officer in this peculiar trial of prisoners by other prisoners. He reverted to his demeanor of better, pre-military days, as a somber but firm judge who could be warmly good-natured when and if he so chose.

He wore proudly a blue shirt that still showed minimal wear and tear. Crossed cannons sewn on that shirt proclaimed his service in a Missouri artillery regiment. He remained neater than nearly anyone else in the compound, including the Confederate guard officers.

Blanchard's first act was to call a meeting of the four attorneys—Lucius and Jed Simmons, for the defense, and Warrick Breck and Delano Richman, for the prosecution.

Blanchard spoke with clarity and authority.

Well, men, you heard the Captain. This is going to be a fair trial. We'll set up court just outside the enclosure. Witnesses come in one at a time. That way, we don't have a big audience. If we held court out in the stockade, there'd be so much yelling and pandemonium, we wouldn't be able to think.

Now, even this way, it won't be easy. We have no court martial book of rules, just a tattered old Georgia law book that isn't much help. But I was a judge before the war, so I know how things are supposed to run. Besides, we are soldiers and we all know how courts martial work, or most of us do, anyway, so we'll do the best we can.

Sergeant Breck, you and Sergeant Richman write up the charges and have them to me by this evening.

Sergeants McCordle and Simmons, you've got the rest of today and maybe tomorrow morning to talk with your clients, if I may call them that. There looks to be many of them, so you might want to meet with them as a bunch. But—however you do it—it's up to you.

Breck, a tall but round-shouldered and slightly stooped infantryman, stated his plan of prosecution, easily and confidently.

I'll write it up, but I can tell you right now what the charges are against those ringleaders.

There are six of them. Names are Collins, Curtis, Sullivan, Delaney, Sarsfield and Muir. I'm charging them with pilferage, grand theft, insurrection, murder, and inciting others to do the same. If they're found guilty—and I'm sure they will be—I'll recommend death by hanging.

Blanchard was unimpressed.

You're charging just the six? How about the other dozen or two we have out here?

Breck answered: Well, main thing is to try and convict the six top men. See what the testimony is. Make an example of them. We'll put out a call for anyone who wants to testify to come forward. There'll be lots of witnesses waiting at the gate, you can be sure.

Blanchard scowled. Shit. You've got that rag-tag bunch of scalawags and you're going to bide your time till some trooper raises a howl about them? By gosh, Sergeant, it behooves you to do better than that. Seems to me better to go whole hog and charge them all.

Breck hesitated. We can charge them later, depending on evidence.

9 A.M. FRIDAY, JULY 1, 1864

The Court President shook his head. Well, whatever you decide, go ahead, Sergeant Breck. We'll keep an eye on the witnesses' statements, and make sure it isn't just all hearsay. That's about all we need to do, the way I see it, isn't that right, Sergeant McCordle?

Just as I feared, Lucius thought. *Nobody's really taking the defense seriously, including Jed Simmons. Blanchard didn't even address him, assuming he felt the same way. This is going too fast.*

Yet...Breck is smart just charging the six ringleaders. If everyone got convicted, they'd have a mass hanging. It left a bad taste in the country when they had that mass hanging of Indians in Minnesota. They could never have that large a hanging here. There's bound to be friends of a few who would put up a right good fuss, if not an open fight. Then there's another thing. If it ever got out we stretched 40 necks here, the ones of us who live to go home probably wouldn't want to defend what we did.

Lucius spoke slowly and carefully.

Well, how much time do we have, Judge Blanchard?

How's this for a shot across his bow? If he hasn't remembered me by now, calling him Judge should improve his memory wonderfully.

It will take us, Lucius continued, several days to interview the defendants—even if it's only the six—and then the witnesses.

Blanchard answered briskly.

First of all, you'll call me Court President, not Judge. Secondly, we don't have time to kill. Everybody wants this to be fair, but fast. Speedy trial, that's what justice calls for, isn't it? No, the trial starts tomorrow afternoon. Wirz doesn't want this to drag out, now that he's got Richmond approving it. So we're going to move fast.

Funny...he doesn't seem to remember me.

Lucius beckoned Jed Simmons to where they could talk privately.

Jed, I have something to shock the pants off you. This Sergeant Mahlon Blanchard? I know him from way back.

The Hell you say!

No, for sure. I know him, all too well. He was a judge and big name in politics in Wisconsin a few years ago. Then he was made a Colonel in the militia.

He was a COLONEL?

Yes, a Colonel! How and why all this has happened, I don't know and it doesn't matter now. But I'm guessing he took resignation to avoid a court martial, then enlisted in Missouri as a Sergeant. Probably knew better than try for an officership, because he'd soon be found out.

So is he an old chum of yours?

Hell, no! He hates my guts because I was in the Democratic Party and, frankly, blabbered too much about him to the editor of a Copperhead paper, before the war started.

Then, in '63, there was this trial where I defended a man—a barrel-maker—who killed a Colored barber...

You defended a man who WHAT??

Who killed a Colored barber who was trying to protect this same Copperhead editor from a mob...

A Copperhead editor? Hell, Jed said, we have one of those in Dubuque, and they sent him to jail in '62, but no mob ever went after him. Even though another editor suggested stringing the man up from a lamp post! After three months in jail in Washington, they let him out and he's back publishing. That's Iowa politics.

Lucius scowled at the interruption, not knowing what to say next.

Then Jed's brow furled and he asked: So this trial you're talking about, Lucius, was in Blanchard's court...?

No, different judge. By this time, in '63, Blanchard was the regimental Colonel at our local camp. One of his soldiers witnessed the killing. Blanchard tried to bribe me to keep this guy off the stand...

Jed interrupted:

A Colonel...and former judge...tried to BRIBE you? Jeezus, how?

By offering me a commission, to run the camp hospital...

Huh. And you turned him down?

Danged right I did.

But...why did he try to buy you off?

Well, see, Colonel Blanchard had been selling rations and putting the money in his pocket. Or, so my soldier witness thought. Blanchard obviously feared what the man...a drunken rowdy and bounty hunter, I expect... might say in court.

As I said, I was defending the barrel maker, who was charged with killing Amos McGurdy, the Colored barber. I had interviewed the soldier and thought his testimony would help my client.

I refused the bribe. The soldier, in court, sure enough, spilled the beans about Colonel Blanchard stealing and selling army rations. It made a big story for Buck Sewall, the Copperhead editor who hated Lincoln, the Union Army, and Blanchard as well.

So as they say in Iowa, Jed said, you got yourself into wonderful pig slop.

Yes, Lucius answered, and here's the irony: Buck Sewall is the same man Amos had tried to protect from lynching, and got killed for his effort!

Okay, Jed said, so the soldier testified about his Colonel selling rations. Wow! How did that bear on the trial?

It didn't. I tried to stop him because that was irrelevant to the case, but it was too late. Word was out now about Blanchard. And, then, a short time later, Blanchard was gone. I later heard the Washington brass forced him to resign his commission. I never knew where he went.

Jed scowled.

So if he got kicked out, how did that keep you from being a lieutenant?

Well, the judge...Blanchard...had many friends among lawyers who were already militia officers, and, well, I never got nominated. The officer who replaced him, and most of the officers under him, saw Blanchard's ruin as entirely my fault. Fact is, Blanchard was popular with most of his officers and troops. Except the platoons who came up short on rations. But they were passed off as worthless scum—which many, like my witness, seemed to be.

Jed scrunched up his mouth.

So you're saying Blanchard is one hell of a horse's ass?

Lucius twisted his mouth, thought a moment, and said: Well, he is and was, but he can also turn on the charm and be one amiable fellow. Knows how to put you at ease. If he wants to.

Lucius chuckled as he remembered: First time I tried a case before him, I and the jury men and the other attorney all lined up at the same trough in the Gentleman's Room. That was embarrassing for many, especially when Judge Blanchard himself marches in. So what does he say? He bellows out: Well boys, when a man has to piss, he has to piss!

And just like that, Lucius concluded, everyone saw what a great fellow he was.

Jed grinned and shook his head. Funny thing. I can't quite imagine you, Lucius, making an enemy of a judge. Especially one like that. But from what you say, it sounds like he must have a wonderful mix of enemies and friends—and also a way of coming back when he's whipped. In fact, I gotta say, Lucius, this Blanchard seems square-toed and plain-spoken. I'd expect him to be a good judge, and I'm…ha, ha…a good Jedge of that myself!

Save your bad jokery, Lucius said.

Lucius shifted to more pressing matters.

We've got to talk with these six accused leaders, he said. They're the ones with necks at risk. Whatever they've done, this court must hear their side. Otherwise, we're just going along with a charade.

Jed gazed dully on Lucius for a moment, then cocked his head to one side, looked down.

We both know the whole point of this, Lucius, don't we? It's to hang these men and, that way, wet things down in the stockade. Things are so bad, with all the hollering and fighting; somethin's gotta be done.

This irritated Lucius.

So, you're saying, he answered, that we just sit on our hind ends, let this trial run its rag-tag course and wait for the verdict? Is that what you mean?

Well, Jed answered, we don't know for sure it WILL be all that rag tag. Anyway, our job is to make sure witnesses are REALLY SURE they saw what they claim—or if it did in fact happen to them as they said it—and that's about all we need bother about.

Hell, Lucius, who can doubt those good-for-nothings are guilty? Bounty jumpers, deserters, rogues, swindlers, pimps, rowdies…that's what they are. They're mean bastards.

They'll hang for sure. Ravens and vultures out in the pines can't wait to shove their beaks into their rotten guts.

Lucius frowned. Jed, I've wondered about you ever since seeing that stitching Sarsfield did on your shoes.

Why…what are you wondering about? I needed shoes fixed, and like I keep telling you, that's what I got…

And you got a hell of a lot more, Lucius interrupted. You had a big confab with them and now you're convinced they need to be pushed off a bucket with their necks tied to an oak tree limb. Were you a spy for the Regulators, or something?

Jed Simmons reddened.

Dammit, he said, I went there on my own—I told you that. And just because I think they deserve hanging doesn't mean I want them lynched.

Lucius answered: Yah? Now, say here: Did you think that way before you went to Sarsfield to get your shoes sewed up? He did what you wanted…and now you've got him hanging before the trial begins?

Waal, in Dubuque, I'd take myself off the case, Jed said. But this ain't Dubuque, pardon my English. Don't forget, Lucius, after that little visit and shoe fix, I could see inside the brains of our clients…if that's what they are…quite well.

Lucius scratched his itching head. *Probably have lice already. And I have gut cramps from this horrible food. Hope I can make it through this trial.*

Jed, Lucius said, maybe you can see inside those mangy heads and maybe you can't. But dammit, if we're decent lawyers, we've got to try defending hard enough to at least save their necks.

Why? Jed asked. If we make an honest attempt, and fail, why shouldn't they hang?

Because killing criminals, even insane ones, is inhuman, Lucius answered.

So you mean we should claim they're out of their minds? Insane?

Well, why not argue that? They remind me of a crazed maniac back in Wisconsin hills I once defended...

Crazed? How did you know that? You an insanity expert?

Wait till I tell you, Jed. This maniac...yes, that's what he was...shot and killed a well-liked youngster who was out hunting squirrels. This broth of a boy had blundered unbeknownst near the cave where the crazy galoot lived. When a Sheriff's posse got there days later, they found the crazy man had the corpses of two river prostitutes in the cave.

Holy Jeezus. And nobody had missed them?

Jed, Lucius answered, where've you been? You think anyone in a river town is going to tell the sheriff that two floozies have gone missing?

Anyway, you're sidetracking the story. The posse boys wanted to hang the brute then and there, and so did a mob that gathered in town. But the sheriff was a big man of wonderful persuasive powers. He kept the mob at bay, saying there would be a trial.

I offered to defend the hermit, because I remembered an older lawyer saying you judge a civilization by how it treats its most odious members. Other attorneys, though, probably didn't agree. They were glad it was me, not them, who took the case. Anyway, I got the jury to believe the man was tetched in the head, and the judge sentenced him to an asylum down state. They sneaked that sorry beast of a man out of town at midnight, before the mob had another chance at him.

So you used the insanity defense, Jed said. Ordinarily, that works only when a man kills his wife's lover. And not because the jury really believes the man is loonier than a bed bug. It's because killing the bastard who cuckolded you is the one cause for murder that people really think is justified.

Well...this gets us nowhere, Lucius said. So...how should we meet with these accused men? One at a time, or in a group?

Hm-m-m. If we see them all at once, Mosby, no doubt, will do all the talking. That might give us time to plan some kind of defense.

Yeah, but...the other way, we hear each one's slant on what happened. See if they point fingers at each other.

Should we give them a chance to do that?

Maybe; what do you think?

Well—if, say, Delaney claims he was threatened by Mosby or Curtis...

Not likely, Lucius said. They may be bad, but they're not stupid. But, let's see them one at a time.

Fine and dandy, Jed said, and added: You know what, Lucius? After all I've said, and knowing your fracas in the past with our Court President, I'm sort of looking forward to this. Yessir, by dang, this so-called fair trial might be more fun than watchin' a mad hound dog go after a porcupine.

Yes, Lucius said without humor. We should enjoy ourselves hugely.

---

9 A.M. Friday, July 1, 1864

The two sergeant-attorneys decided to see Willie Collins, Muir, and Delaney first, this afternoon. It wouldn't be easy. The six head henchmen sat in stocks, scattered around in the corridor between the inner, stockade and the recently-added outer wall, near the North Gate. A bit farther away, to the south, were the two dozen Raider accomplices.

Lucius asked Lieutenant Horatio Granbury of the Confederate guards to find a place where they could meet with the six leaders, one at a time and out of hearing of others.

The Lieutenant was eager as anyone to move this trial along quickly. He had thought it unwise to let prisoners judge the fate of their own kind, and believed Captain Wirz shared the same view. But if General Winder and Richmond said that was the way to do it, that was the way it would happen.

In the Confederate officers' minds, catastrophe was always just around the corner. A massive breakout would create pandemonium and the whole Guard detail would be court-martialed, the Lieutenant worried. He might end up before a firing squad.

Captain Wirz had told the guard officers to point their cannons directly toward the stockade. If at any time it looked as if a throng of prisoners were charging one of the gates, Wirz ordered, the cannon crews should fire grapeshot directly at them. Anything to prevent the more than 20,000 prisoners from finding their way to the Union lines and replenish the cursed U. S. Grant's divisions.

Lieutenant Granbury had another worry: returning to civilian life and having it known that he had cannonaded a stockade full of sick and starving prisoners. Especially if the South lost, an outcome that seemed increasingly likely.

Which one do you want first? Lieutenant Granbury asked Lucius. We'll put him in the stocks outside, around the northwest corner.

Let's start with Willie Collins. The one they call Mosby.

Two guards walked the husky but limping Collins, biggest man among the accused leaders, to the remote stock. He was stooped over, carrying the 15-pound ball connected to his ankle with a two-foot chain. This forced him to lean over uncomfortably as he shuffled, slowly and awkwardly. The guards plunked him on his posterior and clamped his hands into the two holes of the stock, at about chest height.

After hours in various kinds of physical restraint, Collins six-foot stature was hardly recognizable. He was bare-headed. His stolen but trademark wide-brimmed hat—grabbed from a hapless Massachusetts Private some weeks ago—was now in the hands of one of the Regulators. His tunic, looking quite new and fresh before his capture, was now soiled and bloody. His red hair and beard remained caked with mud that his hands, first tied behind his back and now held in stocks, couldn't rub out.

Dried blood covered his left ear and streaked down to the corner of his mouth. His lips were swollen and dark blue from the pummeling by angry, vengeful men. A dark, bloodied right knee gaped through a hole in his trousers, torn apart when the captors forced him face down on the ground, and tied his hands behind him. They had dragged him from the south end, through the sink and marsh area, and up the hill to the North Gate.

Like any lawyer at first meeting, Lucius asked about his bloodied client's health.

Collins, looks like your scars will heal. But your left knee looks awful. And that limp. Did that happen when they clubbed you, and dragged you through the muck?

Collins breathed heavily.

Nope. That's a war wound. But...if you're so danged worried about my health, why the aitch don't you git me out of this stock. You can't do that? And you're my defense lawyer? What's your name?

Sergeant Lucius McCordle, 56th Wisconsin. Lawyer in civilian life.

Collins nodded, as if to say he didn't really need to learn Lucius' name anew, just confirm it.

Lucius caught his meaning.

Why? You think you know me from somewhere?

Yeah. Before they went after us I was figgering out who all the new Irish were that came in last week. Had you spotted pretty quick.

So you check up on the Irish. Were you born in Ireland?

Nope. England. But I'm a hundred percent Irish, I can tell you that.

Catholic?

Well....let's say I was born into a good Catholic family, and I saw lots of priests in my lifetime. And, yeah, I know Father Whelan here.

So what about the wound—the limp?

Up at Manassas, second battle there. Took a bullet that made me so slow I got captured. I was lucky, though. The bullet went right through and I din't lose the leg.

I got away from the Rebs, joined up again and stood my ground at Gettysburg, by god. And now these sonsabitches wanna hang me for trying to look after my boys here.

Lucius said: So you're a battle hero? You can tell that to the court. Might help. Just don't call them bad names. Anyway, Collins. I heard someone say that—before this war—you once saved a young lad from going a bad way. How did that go again?

Huh, you heard that? By golly, that's somethin'. Well, yeah, I promised a priest in Philadelphia—Father Dunbar, he was—I would help save this kid from the thieves, the bad people, the ones who wanted to do messy things to him.

And did you?

In a way. I knocked those buggers in the head and took the kid away.

Back to school?

Hull, no. I got him and some others to work for me.

Collins looked at Lucius and chuckled. And I taught them how to make do.

Make do?

Make do with what he could find or figger out. If they ain't a knife around, make one. All yuh need is a file and an old saw blade.

So you taught this kid how to make knives?

Damned right. And knife using. They'd hold that under a peddler's nose until….

Yes, Lucius thought to himself, *he recruited young boys for his gang, same way he hornswoggled boys into his gang here. The court will see that right away. What's the right thing to do here? Should I tell him right now that all this is humbuggery? If I do, I probably won't learn all the horrible stuff on his mind. But if I don't warn him and he goes on like this at the trial, the President of the court, if he's competent, will tell me I'm not doing my job. Unless he, too, figures this trial is just a sham.*

What did you tell the priest in Philadelphia about all this?

That I saved the urchins. He could ask them, if he didn't believe me. The little buggers, I mean.

Did he?

Sure as hell. And the boys told him what a wonderful man I was.

He believed them?

He wanted to. That was the thing about Father Dunbar. He did good because he wanted other people to be good. He wanted so bad for me to be good, I almost got good just to please him.

So did you, the way he wanted?

For almost two weeks.

And then?

And then I got hungry and run into the others, just as hungry as I was.

You were how old?

Fifteen, maybe sixteen.

Well….you can tell this to the court…but emphasize the part about…

Empha…what? Sargint, talk in plain English.

Sure. Play up the idea that the Priest wanted you to help poor kids do the right thing, and that you did the best you could.

Will that save my neck?

Not sure. But it won't hurt. Let the court know you have a good-hearted side. Just don't brag about how you taught the lad to make weapons. That kind of talk would send you straight to the noose.

Collins grinned maliciously.

They'll never hang us. There's too many of my friends in there. They try to put up a rope somewhere, my boys'll pitch into 'em and rip it down, right quick. At least, there'll be a wunnerful fight there, I'll tell ya. You see, Sargint, I wasn't just a gun toter. I wuz made a corp'ral. That put me in charge of 10 or 12 riflemen. I got a way of getting' men to do what I want them to.

Yes...including going on night raids for booty. This scalawag may be less interested in saving his neck than in looking tough when he faces the court martial.

———

Lucius changed the subject.

Collins, you had a whole storehouse down there in your shebang. Everything under the sun. Like your own Sutler shack.

Holy Chri....They told me you wuz going to defend me. An' here you are, making me look like a thief...

We are defense attorneys, for all of you. But we've got to find out what was going on at that South End of the Stockade. If we don't, how the hell can we do you any good? Last thing you want is for your lawyer to get surprised by something you knew all the time. See how that is?

Yup...okay...well, it was like a Sutler shack, in a way. But that sutler over in the stockade, he's just in it for himself.

And you?

Collins tried to look around—not easy, in the stocks—and his manner changed. He rolled his eyes, conspiratorially.

Doncha see? Say, Sargint, may I call you Lucius? That's OK? Swell. Well, anyways, I was getting together things we'd need for the big breakout.

The breakout?

Ever'body's been talking about the breakout, where you bin? You got mush in your ears or something', you ain't heard that? Sure, I'll tell you what I know, but I woulda figgered you knew SOMETHING that goes on around here!

Now look, Collins. I've only been here a few days, and all I hear, you know goddam well, is talk about the Raiders. Especially you. They want to string you up and fry your testicles.

My what?

Tear your balls out…kill you.

Well, now, that means we had them scared. See, if the pris'ners hadn't been afraid of us, Wirz woulda known our plan.

Your plan?

Sure, it was going fine until this Sargint Key turned on us. I offered to get him in on the plan, but he wouldn't go along. He just wanted to be the big hero himself. Shoulda knifed him when I had the chance.

So just what was your plan?

Not what you think. Wirz thought we wuz goin' to make a tunnel, or storm the north gate. So that's why some of our guys started diggin' a tunnel and then, well, we kinda let it slip, on purpose, to some of the guards. That made Wirz go wild, thinkin' they wuz goin' to be a big bunch crawling outa here like moles.

Huh. And you think that kept him off your trail, do you? But you still haven't imparted your scheme to us.

I ain't what?

Lucius was tiring.

Jed interrupted. You ain't told us what you aimed to do.

Well, let me ask you smart fellers. Whut's the sickest part of this place?

Jed answered. The sickest? Everybody's sick, or nearly. But I guess the puke and dump are the worst down at your end of the stockade. Makes us wonder why you picked that spot on the South slope for your shebangs, so close to that stinking sink.

Hell, we did that to keep others from botherin' us. But yer gettin' off the track. The sickest places here are the dead pen and the hospital—which it really ain't, just a place outside the stockade for livin' under the same kind of rotten blankets you have inside.

Lucius interrupted: Well, what ABOUT the dead pen and the hospital?

We had it all figgered out, Collins answered. We would get a coupla skinny guys to play possum and lay in the dead pen to be carried out. Another bunch would play sick and get admitted to the hospital.

You really mean that, or are you just bamboozling us?

No, that was it, no humbug. But you ain't let me explain it yet. That's where all our stuff comes in. The bunch playing dead and sick, they'd have their pockets fulla stuff to eat and a few knives and then…

Collins squirmed, in obvious pain. Christ, men, can't you get them to set me loose for a coupla minutes? My legs're paining me. Here we're talkin' about saving my life and I can't even think…

Lucius ignored the complaint.

Collins, you must be crazy. Maybe one or two—or a few—could sneak out that way. But how the dickens would you get any number out? The Court will think this was just a weak-minded ploy for a few of you.

Sargint, you just ain't thinkin' about this at all. See, the hospital gate is the least they…the guards and Wirz….worry about 'cause it's all sick people out there. So our boys get into the hospital and when it's dark they slip back, force the South gate open, give the signal, and men pour out like gravy out a bowl.

Lucius shook his head.

Maybe we should let this man say all this before the court martial. They'll think he's really crazy and then we can claim total insanity as a defense. In fact, I don't think he really is balanced. How the devil did he make Corporal? Probably was good with a gun and knew how to scare others into doing whatever he wanted.

He asked Collins:

Do you think that will help you in this court martial?

Ain't it worth a good try? We wuz really workin' for the boys, wuzn't we?

Sounds mighty doubtful, the way I see it. In fact, it would probably be better if you didn't testify at all. The prosecuting attorneys would tear you apart.

Collins was not through.

Y'know, Sargint, yer as ornery as a bear with a sore hind end. Lemme tell you a thing or two, now. I heerd soon's you got here, t'other day, you was one a' them fossilized Democrats that hated Lincoln. Yezzir, I heard it more'n once. Word about one a' yer kind gits around quick.

See, Sargint, boys who went to the fightin' and were so unlucky as to get captured, they don't cotton to that. Yuh hear it allatime, the Democrats, that's a treason breedin' party.

Collins, Lucius asked, why in tarnation are you saying all this?

Think about it Sargint. You come up with a good plan to defend me, or I start yellin' what a rebel-lover you are.

Collins' evil contrariness reminded Lucius of hateful clients from the past: *Like the Coulee City brewery worker, whose claim of self-defense for an assault charge didn't fly in spite of a witness who said the straw boss had struck the first blow. After the judge sentenced the worker to the county jail for six months, he threatened me with a good thrashing for not paying the witness to give the judge a better story.*

Lucius out of sheer habit wondered about the health of this defendant. So by releasing Collins now and replacing him with the next accused Raider, he got Collins' out of the stocks for a time. This allowed him to stretch his legs and walk, even if only a short distance and carrying a 16-pound ball on a chain.

They might well end up hanging him, but meantime I'll do my best to make sure he gets some kind of humane treatment. But is that possible? NOBODY in this stockade is treated like a human being!

Collins had one more thing to say, and he said it with a snarl.

Yer getting' me so riled up, Sergeant, I kin tell this make-believe court something about you and your pal, this Nickels boy, something even you don't know yet.

Lucius was stunned.

What did Harry do... tell the Raiders old stories about Maryanne? What on earth...?

So he asked Collins: What's this about Nickels?

Collins smirked. I ain't tellin', not now anyways. You talk to Sarsfield, he kin give it to you straight. And Collins would say no more.

Chapter 11.
2 p.m., Friday, July 1, 1864

Andrew (or Andy) Muir was next. This young roughneck had not been beaten as badly as Collins. He had a certain amount of sartorial splendor about him. His Federal Navy blouse looked as if it might even have been washed once or twice since his capture.

Lucius looked at Muir thoughtfully for a moment. A man of modest height but bulging muscles, this fellow looked every bit the tough thug—but a thug who knew how to keep his garments in good order in the most harrowing conditions.

Navy training does that to a person. Better than the Army can do.

Muir, Lucius asked, someone said you've only been here, what? Has it been a month?

Less than that, Muir answered. The Rebs captured the Water Witch June 3, middle of the night. Happened when I was sleepin' below deck. 'F they'd had boys like me on deck, wou'nt never of happened. T'ree days later, I was at this godforsaken place.

So how'd you get mixed up with the Raiders so quickly?

Muir shrugged, trying to shift his weight in the stocks.

Jeez, you believe it too, don't you? The only thing I did was pick the wrong place to build me a hut to live in. I knew they was other sailors here but, see, it was confusing when I got here. This man they call Curtis—later claims his name is really Rickson—said he was a sailor once, too, and offered to protect me.

So did he?

Well, I believed Curtis and shared his tent. He give me some good food the first couple of days, and then...

And then what?

Then things got mixed up. I went out with him one night and he got to hollering and arguing with someone from Indiana. Curtis claimed this boy had stolen his hat and Curtis wanted it back. The boy was small and the one with him was so puny they wasn't any argument at all. So Curtis just took the hat, easy like, and told the boy if he had any sense he'd pay rent for the hat.

Pay rent?

Sure. He was usin' something he didn't own, didn't he? But then the boy started blubbering he didn't have any money, and Curtis saw something in the moonlight, grabbed it up, and by golly, it was some potatoes in a piece of gunny bag. Curtis said that would cover the rent of his hat, so we left.

How did the Indiana boy take that?

Oh, he kept on like a cryin' baby. You know, Curtis is a big man, not quite like Willie Collins, but bigger than me. So I din't expect nobody to bother us when we left, seein' they was no fight at the time.

Well, then a bunch of Iowa boys yelled at us, but then I seen some of our own boys watching and they yelled back. One of the Iowa boys came running after us and tried to jump me. I turned and walloped him. Curtis told me I done good.

After that, I helped Curtis pick up some other things...

Pick up other things?

Sure...like some money he took off a coupla fresh fish. With money, we could buy a few things.

You mean from the sutler shack?

Some of that, but also from bigger boys we din't want to tangle with, at least not without our whole bunch behind us. After a few days of that kind of thing, Curtis told me to hand over some of the stuff I got on my own. Got me dammed mad, he did.

Muir, they're saying you have a gang of your own. Is that so?

Muir chuckled. Have I got a gang? Put it this way. They's a bunch of friendly boys I spend a lot of time with now, other'n Curtis. We pertect each other from the scum around the stockade, y' know what I mean?

So you've been staying away from Curtis?

What I'm gettin' at, here, is that I blame my whole problem on Curtis. He got me into this. I can tell the court all of this, and more. That should help, shouldn't it?

Lucius pondered a moment.

You might tell the jurymen how Curtis talked you into doing outrageous things, Lucius said. But if anybody saw you jump some weak little boy fresh in the stockade, you aren't going to be believed. In fact, if you say those words fresh fish, the jurymen will probably hold it against you.

So I'm asking you directly, Lucius continued. Did you ever kill anybody?

Naw...except maybe that Rebel I walloped in the fight on the Water Witch. But here in the stockade? Nope...and anybody who says I did is a liar.

Next question: Did you ever take something from a dead boy?

Muir looked off to one side, then back to Lucius.

Well...I maybe once or twice saw a body in the dead pen had a better shirt than I got...But everybody does that, don't you see?

Muir…let's go back to where the Rebs captured you on that Union ship. Tell me more about that.

Shure. It was the Water Witch, like I just mentioned. Nice tub with side paddle wheels. Cost the Union a half million dollars, it did. Why they put such a dumb Captain on it, I'll never know. He anchored where the Rebs could find us easy in the middle of the night.

But boy, we made those Rebs pay for their attack! We killed a bunch of 'em before they finally whipped us. Why, myself, I knocked two of them overboard, would of done more if our weakling Captain hadn't surrendered.

Jed Simmons asked: Sure you aren't bragging some? I've heard that maybe 50 or so from that steamer—Water Witch is the name?—are here in the stockade. Know any who can say how hard you fought?

Andy Muir thought for a moment.

Naw…I know a few, but they wou'n't be no help. It was dark as a stack of cats that night, except for the lightning that showed the Rebs where we was. I was below, sleeping, and was first to wake up. I run up topside—din't have no gun—and grabbed a big wooden belaying pin, used it like a club to knock these two guys over the side.

He grinned.

One of 'em, you could hear his skull crack before he toppled over.

You knocked two Rebel soldiers over the side of the ship? Jed asked.

Shure did, and prob'ly no one else saw it, 'cuz the other seamen were still in their bunks and the officers was startin' to give up. So sure, I'll tell this court martial how hard I fought those sneaky Rebs. If they hadn't been so many, I coulda whipped 'em with mittens on.

Fine, Lucius said. And if you want to testify against Curtis, that's your choice. Do so if you wish; I can't promise it will help. But if you do, I'm not your attorney any more. Then you're working for the prosecution and I will come after you to tear down your story.

———

After the guards took Muir away, Jed asked:

Lucius, this Muir didn't mention your friend Nickels, like Collins did. Shouldn't we have brought this up with Muir? Find out what was going on with Nickels?

Lucius reddened.

Jed, I have no damned idea whether I should have or not. Hell, YOU went back there to get your shoes fixed, you know these bastards better than I do. Why didn't YOU ask him?

Then Lucius softened.

Okay, yes, I thought about it. And yes, I know Harry spent a night or two with those scamps. He gave me a rundown on them. And maybe he spilled his guts to them. But what the hell did he say, that Collins could use to blackmail me? I don't know but I can't imagine anything.

Think of it, Lucius continued. A man on trial for his life, in a place like this, coming up with a lame threat like that? Sounds like a trick Collins learned in the alleys behind breweries.

———

Next, the defense lawyers asked for Patrick Delaney, a muscular fellow of average height, wearing a handsome Hardee hat which, to Lucius, looked suspiciously like one worn by soldiers of Wisconsin's Iron Brigade. Both brims still spread wide, and the top held its crease.

Lucius asked. Your full name is Patrick Delaney?

Yez kin call me that. Many does.

Not your real name?

Who cares whut my real moniker is? I'm called here as Delaney, so let that be it.

Well...if something happened to you here, and nobody knew your right name...how would they know who to write to?

Who'd care to write about me? I've got a wife and little kids back...let's say in Penns'vania, and when things went bad for me, I come to the 'clusion they's better not knowin' whut really hoppened.

Lucius stared at the well-contoured Hardee Hat.

Delaney, how did you manage to hang onto that hat during the roundup? And keep it from getting mussed up?

Delaney chuckled. Fact is, yerz wanna know, a boy took it and I bought it back.

You...BOUGHT it back?

Sure. I knew this roundup was gonna happen. Collins... or who yez might call Mosby...had a good idea. 'Keep yer money,' he sez. 'Yez might be needin' it if this Key bunch tries getting' tough with us.'

Curtis and Collins had this big arg'ment, yez see, about whether Key wanted to capture us, or join us, or just take over our bizness. And we figgered that ever'one has a price. So I had money, and after they rounded us up, I give this boy a couple greenbacks and I got my hat back.

Delaney continued: Funny thing is, Collins lost his hat, too, but din't have no chance to get it back. I guess they took his money when they swiped his hat.

So someone in the Regulators is working for himself, taking money from captured Raiders. No one thought to gather up the Prisoners' money, mark it, and hold it until the trial is over. Well, not too surprising; corruption is everywhere.

How'd you get this hat, in the first place?

Like I said, ever'body's got d'er price, so I bought it from this Wisconsin boy.

Delaney, be honest. Did you do any really hard fighting in the Union Army, before you were captured?

Dammed fer sure I did. Bristoe Station, up in Virginia. Last October. Geez, I'd only been in the army a month. Wuz wishin' I'z back in...well, I'm not a sayin' where, mind you... doin' stone work and takin' care of that sweet woman and wee ones.

But now I wuz put in the Eighty-third Penns'vania, I wuz. Went straight to Virginia. Rebels tried to whack us on our retreat one day, but we turned and mauled 'em good. 'Course, some things didn't go right. I got shot in me arm, fell off to one side, and, first thing, yez see, I'm captured.

Delaney, did you rob anyone here in the stockade, or kill anyone?

Patrick Delaney looked away for a moment, then slowly turned back toward Lucius McCordle and answered, evenly and matter-of-factly:

I'm an Irishman, like you, I iz, so I'm talkin' facts. When I wuz cuttin' up and fittin' stones back home, I did what I must to feed me brood. An' did good work, cause I learned it from me Pappy, who wuz the best stonecutter in Connemara,

But if t'ey hired some kraut eater an' he give me trouble, I whacked him. When they send me to dis place, I figger out how to get by. They want to shoot me or hang me for that, well, that is whut they'll do.

Tis a small thing in this war, to die for tryin' to live.

Delaney, Lucius said, you'll maybe get a chance to speak in your own behalf. What can you say to the court here—these twelve Union Army Sergeants—that might make them think kindly toward you? Can you mention any good you've done here in the stockade?

A slight smile crossed Delaney's young but hardened face, his slightly-bulging left eye softening slightly.

Yezzir, they's a couple things. I never kilt nobody for no reason. And I helped many a man with bad shoes. Now Johnny Sarsfield, he taught me shoe-fixin' and I got good at it, I did. He even borried me a coupla needles an' some string, so's I could sew up the soles on lotsa boots for fellas. I din't charge 'em much either, but yez know, bizness is bizness. If I had a bit nicer hutch than some others, it's cuz I earned it wit' me good work.

Yes...he probably did fix some boots...for his followers so they could run well when they were out on midnight raids with him in the lead. Yet, this could be some help for him.

Well, Delaney, be sure to say that to the court when and if you get a chance. Just remember, you're talking to a bunch of company and battalion Sergeants who don't easily believe a Private who gets in trouble.

Wull, as I told yez, dey can do wit' me body as t'ey wish. I'll be grievin' for anyone I might uv hurt, but if I got punishment comin', I take it like a man. I makes me confession to Father Whelan. He's a good priest, he is.

Bulky Charles Curtis was not quite able to walk to the stocks. He had sat for hours, bucked and gagged. This physically devastating treatment—hands tied around the hunched up knees, stick shoved above the arms and under the knees, feet tied back, mouth gagged with a dirty rag—would ordinarily leave a man unable to walk for some time after being released.

Two Confederate soldiers, one emaciated and missing multiple teeth—signs of scurvy—struggled to help and half-carry Curtis to the northwest corner of the stockade. He crumpled to the ground, apparently so weakened that when Jed nodded to the guards, they returned his nod and strode off, leaving Curtis out of the stocks. With the 16-pound ball chained to his ankle, he wasn't going to go far.

Yet, Curtis was not as physically shattered as the hapless Confederate soldiers who had just dragged him in. His muscular body, well fed in recent months, had withstood the torture of the buck-and-gag treatment incredibly well. No scurvy or dysentery had visited this man. He slowly pulled himself to a sitting position, his back against the outside of the stockade wall. As he did so, the more able of the two guards shuffled nervously some 35 or 40 feet to the north, his rifle now at cross-arms position and, maybe or maybe not, properly loaded and ready to fire.

The Sergeant-attorneys, too, were wary.

Don't look too comfortable, Curtis, Jed said quietly, or they'll cram you into those stocks like they did others.

Curtis grunted, wiping some streaks of mud from the sky-blue Union pants he had swiped from some hapless recent arrival. His flowing thick hair parted between his eyes and bushy eyebrows, revealing a stubbly face clean-shaven just three days ago. His once-handsome dark blue shirt hung awkwardly on his heavy body, one shoulder torn away by a

Regulator who had tried, without complete success, to rip off the Corporal stripes that Private Curtis had never been awarded.

Jed Simmons had some immediate advice for this particular prisoner:

We're told that your friend Collins was the only Corporal among you Raiders. Better get rid of those stripes before the trial…however you can. They're proof you're a thief.

Curtis, unlike the others, used few words and chose them carefully.

You call me a Raider, eh? And you're my defense attorneys?

Lucius and Jed nodded.

Curtis said, I ain't a Raider. I'm a trader. And a dammed good one. I got these stripes in a fair trade.

Lucius asked: Just what is your full name?

Which one you want? Curtis asked. Back in New Brunswick, I was Charles Curtis. Left there as a boy. Rode a ship down to Providence. Joined the Navy. Used my uncle's name, William Raleigh Rickson. Didn't like the Navy. Left it. Enlisted in an artillery battalion a year ago. Then took back my old name Curtis. Didn't want them to find me on no Navy deserter list. What else you want to know?

Did you get a bounty for enlisting? Jed asked.

Sure, Curtis answered. 'S'way it works. Took a rich boy's place. Why not? Anyone signs up without bounty pay is stupid. And I ain't stupid.

See here, Curtis, Lucius said, our job is to advise you how to defend yourself.

Defend? Curtis nearly shouted. Against what? This silly trial? Any one votes to hang us Irish, they don't dare go back. Into the stockade, I mean. They'll get torn apart, right quick.

I got friends there. Those asses that bucked and gagged me? THEY better worry. I got them marked.

Curtis grunted again, then continued:

That boy, Key. Y' think he wanted any more than take over our business? Will, too, you let him. I made one mistake. Should have conked him when I had the chance.

McCordle: Don't be so sure about your friends. The stockade is all riled up. Remember? Dozens of your chums got banged up in the gauntlet line.

Simmons. That's right. They were mad enough to fry your hide, right then and there.

Curtis: Miserable pair, you two. Yer telling me I got no chance. Okay. I got a dammed good defense. You two ever heard of Robin Hood?

Jed looked at Lucius and rolled his eyes.

Curtis continued: Sure, we picked up some things. Blanket here, extra shirt there. Now and then some extra bread. Stuff the fresh fish didn't need. Gave it to poor boys din't have decent clothes. You go find them. The boys we helped, I mean. They'll tell how much good we done 'em.

We've got to warn you, Lucius said. Lot of people try the Robin Hood defense, but no one really makes it work. Especially since you're a private who others would call a deserter.

Jed then asked: Is there one specific man you helped the way you say? Who will testify for you?

Sure, Curtis answered.. Name of Dick Hartman. New Jersey infantry. He walked around mostly bare assed 'til I give him a pair of extra trousers a fish didn't need. Then there's one named Tread... Treadwhistle, something like that.

Stockade's a big place, Jed Simmons said. Supposing we can get back in there, where do we find these two?

Don't need to go back in, Curtis answered. Both these boys got rounded up, and kept, out here.

Wait, Lucius said. Those men are on trial, too...and we're supposed to defend them. But if one accused person says he helped another accused person...that won't be very convincing to the court. Isn't there someone else, someone who didn't get rounded up?

Sure, Curtis said, more than one. But I don't know their names, or where they sleep. One they call Whipper, or something. Most times, though, I just hand out stuff to boys who need it. Jus' to show how much I helped.

Which boys? Jed asked.

Goddammed easy to answer that, Curtis said. I did some good for a nigger boy from Penn's'vania. If I 'member correckly, ain't that what this war is for? Freein' the niggers so they can live better, and free? Ain't that what Old Abe meant in that Prockalmation?

Yes, of course, Jed answered...that all slaves in the Confederate states are free...

But they ain't going to be free, really, till the war is over, right? Curtis said. So in the meantime, it's the Irish, like us, who takes their side and helps them out.

YOU help them out? Lucius asked. How?

Curtis: See? You ain't been here long enough to re'lize what we've been doing for the niggers. They're like neighbors, see? There's most a hunderd of 'em, and they're all bunched together on the South End, close to us Irish traders.

McCordle: So...you seriously mean you jokers are Irish traders?

Curtis: That's right. We're traders, doing business. Enyone kin tell you, place like this needs smart traders.

We're so good at it we have stuff left over, so we give it to the Blacks.

Simmons: Stuff such as?

Curtis: Oh, such as sweet potatoes, an egg now and then, good blankets, salt…and you kin see what a difference it makes. White boys from New York or Vermont, they die all the time, don't they? But ask anyone about the Colored boys. What's the last time a Black body was thrown into the dead pile? It don't happen often, thanks to the Irish looking out for 'em.

McCordle: You keep calling yourselves The Irish. Why?

Curtis: Aw, come on, Sergeant, you know what I mean. If we's all English, even Norwegian, Key and his bunch wun't be hounding us this way.

Simmons: I don't know if being English matters, but that court won't give a hoot or a holler for your Robin Hood defense. Frankly, Curtis, they'll say you've got too much hair on your face and too little nobleness in your soul to be a savior of the poor.

Curtis made no mention of Harry Nickels, and neither Lucius McCordle nor Jed Simmons asked him about that visit by Lucius' old friend at the Raiders' lair.

―――

Okay, bring in…Sullivan, that's your name?

Lucius wasn't sure what to call this short but stout fellow, smallest of the accused Raiders.

You can call me Cary, whutever yoush want. Yoush can even call me Sharpshooter Shullivan, 'f yer like. I'uzh one helluva good shot, knew how to take care of myshelf.

His words were mushy, from a mouth still oozing blood after the bashing 24 hours ago.

So don't worry about me and thish shilly trial, Sullivan said. They shust want to take away the schtuff they shold or traded us. After they shteal it all, have their trial....hell, they might even shend us to a diff'rent prison. That wou'n't bother me none.

Sullivan's blue eyes squinted sharply at Lucius McCordle and Jed Simmons. His light skin was almost obscured by the heavy, dark red beard—red from both whisker color and dried blood that pasted a layer of gruesome masculinity on his small frame.

Simmons: Sullivan, why did you join the Raiders?

Sullivan: What makesh you shay I choined them? THEY choined ME...well, me and Mosby. Lishen. Shomeone like me, they know how to get by. They shee me and how I do shings, they get chealous, you shee.

McCordle: Where did you meet Curtis?

Sullivan paused.

I tellsh you what. Why don't you two chust go to hell? I don't need your help. They're getting' back at us, that'sh all. Ain't noshing you can do 'bout it. Let 'em buck and gag us, like they already did Curtis. Or shoot us. Would they hang us? From what? The pigeon roosts?

Sullivan's head sagged.

I'm ready to die. Jush shut your moush and let me be.

But, y' know, we might not die after all. Listen. Did yer boy Harry...ain't that his name? Din't he tell you how we's now got a ticket out of thish place? You ain't chalked with Sarsfield, have yuh? Well, when yuh do, yuh'll learn a few things.

And with this second mysterious reference to Lucius' long-time friend, the once-feisty but diminutive former working man from upstate New York would say no more. Heavy lids fell over his blue eyes. He slumped, a dejected bundle of flesh and bones, defeated, resigned—yet oddly proud in his resignation.

―――

Holy moley, Jed muttered. Looks like Harry Nickels figures in this mess in some curious way. Let's get Sarsfield here, and find out what the hell this is all about.

You should know about Sarsfield, Lucius said to Jed Simmons. You said he fixed your shoes, remember?

Yes... he did, and by god if you don't quit badgering me about that, I'm going to knock your block off, an annoyed Jed answered. Then he added:

Let's get done with him, as quick as possible. We need to spend the rest of the night figuring out our defense strategy. If we have any. And find out what's going on with your friend Harry Nickels.

Lucius simply nodded.

Barely taller than the little Cary/John/Terry Sullivan, John (his assumed name) Sarsfield seemed the most physically uncomfortable of all accused Raider chieftains. From his short body, his hands were high in the stocks, in a forced stretch.

At 23, he was only a year older than Muir and younger than Sullivan or Collins, although with his rough-hewn crooked nose, broken in pre-army street brawls, he could have passed for 30. He wasn't as badly beaten in the round-up as Collins or Sullivan, but more than Muir or Delaney. An enormous welt showed through the snagged hair and encrusted, dark, blood on his forehead, witness to a stunning whack that knocked him out yesterday. His upper jaw showed a bloody gap where two teeth were freshly missing.

Sarsfield was well known in the stockade and hated as much as any of the other five known leaders. As one fearful shebang dweller just north of the foul sink area said in mighty understatement, He ain't exactly the salt of the earth, no matter how good he is at fixin' shoes.

Somehow, Sarsfield had kept his colorful Zouave jacket, with its dark red curlicue trim, from being torn off by the Regulators. It was his prized trophy, yanked from the back of a sickly youngster in a midnight raid. It marked him a few days ago as a tough thug leader and now labeled him as a murderer. No captor now wanted to wear or be seen with that particular tell-tale garment.

Sarsfield blurted at Jed Simmons: Huh, so you're my lawyer? Think you can do as good a job defending me as I did fixing your goddammed shoes?

Jed shifted, uncomfortably. Our job, he said, is to see you get a fair trial.

So that's all there is to it? Sarsfield snarled. I done you a good turn and you ain't really gonna get me off?

He didn't wait for an answer, but spat out a combative challenge:

They can't hang me, cuz I know too much.

Too much? About what? Lucius asked.

About something that can mean the Rebs takin' over Washington, Sarsfield sneered. And Grant's whole army getting all torn up by Lee. Now wouldn't that be the cat's ass?

A perplexed Lucius asked: What the aitch are you talking about?

Sarsfield's eyes shifted quickly, from side to side, gleaming with inspired conspiracy and feigned confidentiality. It was as if what he was about to reveal was vital to survival of all humanity and known only to him.

General Jubilee Early—you know who I mean?

Lucius answered slowly: Well, yes…Jubal Early, pretty well-known rebel General…what about him?

Well, this Jubilee Early, Lee sent him off from Cold Harbor June 13 on a secret campaign. Get my hands outa these stocks and I'll tell you all about it. And you'll see this is one big fat new hawg in yer slop!

Lucius settled back on the crude bench, cupped his hands around his left knee and gazed quizzically, first at Jed Simmons, then back at Sarsfield.

Jeezus. This creepy devil has something up his sleeve, and Jed didn't hear it when Sarsfield fixed his shoes. Or did he? Huh.

We can't get you out of the stocks, Lucius said. If we tell the guards what you're telling us, Lucius continued, they would likely put the buck and gag on you. Or, maybe just call you crazy. If they believe you, they'll want to know how you know that. And maybe shoot whoever let it out.

Fact is, Lucius added, throwing up his hands, this sounds like something you made up.

The conspiratorial gleam only brightened in Sarsfield's puffed and reddened eyes, peering out sharply under the heavy, swollen bruise that nearly obscured his left eyebrow. He scowled at Lucius and said:

Sargint, you'se a questionin' my veracity, ain't you?

Your…what?

My veracity. My telling the truth. You don't think I know words like that? Fact is, I studied the law for a while, case you ain't heard. So I can talk yer way when I got a mind to.

Anyway, what I'm talkin' about is down in pen and ink on a piece of paper, and me's the only one knows. 'Cept, a'course, a boy who has the other part of it, and he's scared as all hell what to do with it.

Lucius and Jed sat quietly, wondering what would come next.

Lissen, Sarsfield continued, this kin save the goddam Union, if I kin git the word out to General Grant. All you do is get me hands loose so I can stand up, and promise to keep me neck from getting' stretched.

Sarsfield, Jed Simmons said, you may think you've got something big to hold over this court martial, but I firmly believe you are plumb full of bull shit.

A look of feigned shock crossed Sarsfield's face.

You just don't believe me, do you? Here I fixed your goddam shoes up good, and you say sumpin' like that, Sarsfield said with a pout. Okay, yer gonna be a horse's back end.

Sarsfield turned away from Jed and toward Lucius, and said: Well, anyway, let me give you boys some facts.

This here letter is signed by Robert E. Lee himself. It tells Old Joobie to take his army up the Shenandoah Valley and whip the Union boys up there—way the Rebs usually do, you know. Then they keep goin' north and cross the Potomac and come at Washington from the northwest.

Lee figures that if Early gets at Washington, Grant would have to pull his army out of Petersburg and go back north to save the Capital. Ain't that somethin' to pickle your behind? Might cost Grant and Lincoln the whole goddammed war.

Aw, come on now, man, Jed said. They'll say you're batty as a bedbug. How in the name of heaven and hell would— did—this prisoner—get such a letter?

This prisoner, Sarsfield answered, found that paper in a Rebel campin' place, after Early and his boys left.

Sarsfield, Lucius asked, how did you come to know all this?

Sarsfield grinned. Well, one night, kinda late, we happened to meet this nice boy and asked, gentle like, nice and friendly, if he didn't want to maybe join our little bunch down there.

Lucius McCordle: Oh, I'm sure. Did you make tea and biscuits for him, too? What's his name?

Sarsfield: Go ahead, talk smart at me. But lissen, I ain't tellin' you his name just now, until we gets a deal.

Lucius: A deal? You must be crazy. Look, Sarsfield. You're talking about someone escaping and taking this note to General Grant up at Petersburg. How the hell is that going to happen? Anyone who escapes here gets shot or caught by the dogs and sent back the same day.

Sarsfield grinned again in his peculiarly spiteful way.

Escapin' would be easy, if I's the one doin' it. All you got to do is convince your goddam court martial that the smart thing is to let me get that letter from this scared boy who has it now. Once I get loose I know how to get word to Grant. Wouldn't take more than a day.

Lucius and Jed both shook their heads.

Lucius: You think we're going to go to that Court Martial President and say one of the six Raider leaders has got to be let go, and double quick, so he can escape from this prison and get a secret message to General Grant? He would laugh his head off. Soldiers hear lots of escape plans, but this one's enough to make anyone go wild as a turkey trapped in a fox cage.

Even if we convinced them there IS a letter, would they think you're the man to take it out of here? They'll say no one with brains would trust a crooked cobbler to try patchin' things up for General Grant.

Sarsfield shook his head slowly, but held his conniving grin.

You two maybe think I'm dumb, he said. But you see, I been in a court once or twice myself. Been in jail, too. Heard people talk how the law works. Someone charged with a crime kin sometimes get off if he be a witness against someone who's done worse.

And I can say lots of things about Curtis and Collins that will make them look pretty bad. I think this is called 'witness for the persecution,' or sump'n like that.

Sure. Like Muir, Sarsfield is willing to snitch on others to save his own neck. Well, if all six do that, they'll put some humor into the trial. So much for honor among thieves.

Lucius said, You mean witness for the prosecution. It's an interesting notion, but a judge—or a court martial presiding officer—wouldn't be very likely to deal with an accused ringleader. Like you. Remember, these jurymen are Sergeants, and Sergeants are hard as nails on privates in trouble. And you are in big trouble; we don't need to remind you.

Sarsfield decided to play his next card. Okay, look, he said. I have half that letter right here, inside my fancy shirt.

Simmons blurted: You have HALF a letter? Right on you, right now?

Well, Lucius thought, *my fellow defense counsel seems truly surprised. It looks as if Sarsfield didn't mention this letter to Jed after all.*

Sarsfield: Yep. I have half the letter. See how smart I am? This boy who had it, he give it to me and I tore it in two. Half he keeps, half I keep. Ain't no good to anyone unless we bring the two parts together. But then, it's a real whapper.

Jed Simmons: Don't you mean a 'whopper?' Like a whopping big fib?

Sarsfield: Naw…you know what I mean. You just don't re'lize how smart I am. When they dragged me in here, one a' Key's boys went through my clothes, he did, and he see this piece of paper with writing on it. He couldn't make no sense of it—like I knew he wouldn't—prob'ly signs with an X. So when I said it was just a scrap I picked up to write a letter home on, he let me keep it. The bastard even said, good, it'll be your last letter to ennybudy.

So where is that…letter? Lucius asked.

Waal, with my hands in this damned stock, ain't enny way I can reach it. So get it yourself, in this here pocket under my coat…no, the other side.

Lucius reached carefully under Sarsfield's Zouave jacket and into a small pocket handsewn just above Sarsfield's beltline.

Yeah, now you got it, Sarsfield said. But it's no good until you get the rest of it, and I ain't yet said where.

Lucius pulled out, from Sarsfield's pocket, a wrinkled three-cornered piece of paper ripped from what had once been a rectangular sheet. He held it up in the hazy sunlight and squinted at it. His own eyesight was suffering some from the poor food since his capture.

Along the top, Lucius read the carefully hand-written words, *Headquarters Army of Northern Virginia,* followed by: *General J. A. Early, Cold Spring, Va. Rout or destroy the Union Army and Washington DC...Attack it and burn it if you...*

There was no date and no signature on the fragment.

Jed cleared his throat, while Lucius whistled softly.

Now having his lawyers' attention, Sarsfield spoke quickly.

Lissen here. When you two find out who has the other half of this letter—and he shows it to you—you will goddammed for sure believe what this letter means. And when you do, it'll be your job to convince the court it's real.

Lucius scratched his chin, starting to grasp what this was all about.

He now spoke carefully: We're both rather new here in the Stockade, and only know a few people. So who could it be? Are you saying it's one of the Sergeants out here?

I ain't sayin' anything yet, Sarsfield pouted. 'Fore I tell yuh, you've gotta agree to my deal.

Your deal? Lucius asked. You're not exactly in a position to make ANY deal.

Well, I ain't sayin' who has the other half of this letter from Lee to Early, unless I get a big promise from you two, Sarsfield answered.

He can't really believe he can hold us to any bargain. And yet....

Slowly, Lucius folded the paper scrap—what Sarsfield claimed was half a letter—and carefully shoved it into his shirt.

Then he looked at Sarsfield and asked,

Well, so what's your deal?

Sarsfield screwed up his face, in another contorted and crafty grin.

Sergeant McCordle, you gotta give me back this half of the letter you just took, so I keep it until you get the other half. Then, you gotta promise me that if I'm convicted, you'll bust your gut talkin' the court into letting me try a one-man escape, takin' that letter—both halves—with me.

Your oath, Sarsfield continued, that's what I want, like a fellow Irishman. That you make it the goddammdest try of your life, even if you get your head blown' off tryin' it.

Jed Simmons looked away, saying, in a low voice:

I want no part of any deal like that. Sarsfield, you never told me about that letter when you did my shoes and you know what? I'm wondering whether you didn't scribble out the whole thing.

Sarsfield answered in a mock petulant way. What a shitty thing to say! Sure, I been around lawyers, but you think I can write in a nice hand like that? And spell that good? Sargint, I wish instead of fixin' yer goddammed shoes I had sewed some sandburs into 'em.

Lucius interrupted: Sarsfield, I'll offer a different deal that you won't like. Either you tell me who has the rest of that letter, or we leave you on your own. We'll just tell the Court you need different counsel, or you can defend yourself.

Sarsfield shook his head. Waal now. You ain't going to talk so tough when I tell you who has the other half of that letter.

Lucius was now beginning to put things together in his own mind. *Things have gone far enough. I'm going to make a wild guess:*

Stop humbugging me, Sarsfield. You got that from Harry Nickels, didn't you?

Sarsfield's face fell, but he recovered quickly. Okay, so you figgered it out. Or Mosby told you, huh? Wa-al, yes, Sergeant McCordle, it's your own chum, Corporal Harry Nickels.

Lucius shook his head, pulled his sweaty kepi off his head, wiped his matted hair and then his growing whiskers with the other hand. It was an odd time to wish he hadn't lost his folding razor and ability to shave.

By dang, why don't I just keep that letter, until I can see if it matches something Harry has? But no, I made a sorry deal with this man, and I can't back down now.

Sarsfield pressed on:

See what this means, you dumb lawyer? You tell me to go to hell and I tell the court that Nickels and I share this letter. AND that he showed it to all the Irish, the men you call Raiders. Know what the court martial boys will think then? That Nickels is one of the Raiders, a close chum of one of the chiefs, namely me. And if they decide to make us swing, he will too.

Now…Sergeant McCordle…you want to think again about my deal?

Chapter 12.
3 p.m., Friday, July 1, 1864

Lucius squatted down on his haunches and tried to think. *So Harry Nickels has half of a secret letter that General Robert E. Lee is supposed to have sent to General Jubal Early? But if he does, how did he get it? We were both captured at Cold Harbor; where in the world would he have found it? And Sarsfield knew that Nickels and I were chums? Harry seems to have a big mouth and a smaller brain than I thought..*

And what else has Harry Nickels been up to that I don't know about? He obviously got mixed up some way with Sarsfield and maybe other Raiders as well. That's why he was rounded up yesterday, but still lucky enough not to have someone offer witness against him. But ... damn! What do I do now? Make a deal with Sarsfield? Harry is in real trouble—they might go round him up again. Or would they? They already made gang members run a gauntlet, including him; wouldn't that be punishment enough?

Lucius McCordle walked away from John Sarsfield in the stocks and from Jed Simmons, who had turned aside as if ignoring the whole thing.

Sarsfield grimaced from his arms being held at an upward angle. He was tiring. His words came out in strained grunts.

Lucius scratched his now-bearded chin, turned back to Sarsfield and said in low tone:

Well, Private Sarsfield, I'll go part way. Here, I'll put this half of the letter back in your pocket. Which Lucius did.

Lucius continued:

I could make the argument that having the letter means you were working hard for the Union cause. Then, for that reason, your punishment should be less than execution.

In return, you simply say nothing about Nickels, regardless of what he says as a witness.

Sarsfield grimaced. You're cheap, Sergeant. A cheap Irishman, but I've seen 'em before. All right, I have your oath that you treat me different than the other five head Irish. And, yeah, I got my half of the letter, now. Jest get me out of these stocks so I can see it again.

Lucius summoned the guard to take Sarsfield away, while Jed looked at his fellow lawyer in disbelief.

Jed Simmons, now in bad humor, cursed the weather.

Christ, Iowa never gets this hot. That sun is frying us like flapjacks in a fast and hard bake.

Then Jed straightened up and scratched his left arm.

Now, let's see if I have this straight, Lucius, he said. Sarsfield claims that your friend...Nickels, he said? Did I ever see him... is supposed to have the other half of this so-called secret letter? A command from Lee to Early to just hitch up and go assault Washington?

And besides: Nickels never said anything to you about it? Even though the two of you came into this place together? You sleep in the same hut? And you're old chums?

Jed shook his head.

Sounds awful fishy, if you ask me.

An uncomfortable Lucius had trouble answering. *It DOES sound fishy.*

Jed, maybe this is all tommyrot. But suppose it's the square truth? It would mean thousands of Rebels sashaying

3 P.M., Friday, July 1, 1864

through the mountains and the Valley and General Grant hasn't got the word. Most of us think the whole Union Army is down there south of Richmond. They needed those boys to take Petersburg and then Richmond itself.

If this is all so, Washington could be hit at any day now. With almost nobody there to fight back.

Well, shoot, Lucius, Jed said. We don't get any news here, so what do we know? We're as ignorant as sheep in a shit shack.

Oh yeah? How about the new prisoners, Lucius answered. Every day they pour in from Grant's army. Right among us, you know, like the other Sergeants in the Court Martial. You heard any of them jabber about this?

No, Jed answered. You have a point. An attack on Washington would be on everyone's tongue. That is, IF they knew about it…and, IF it was really in the works.

Well, that's the thing, Lucius said. If Sarsfield is right, it's all secret and nobody is guessing it. So someone captured, say, a couple days ago and arriving here today wouldn't know a damned thing about it.

The way armies move, Lucius added, it would take Jubal Early at least three weeks to get from Cold Harbor to Maryland and Washington, wouldn't it?

Jed shrugged. I'm from Iowa. I don't know Virginia that well.

Well, I saw a map of Virginia once or twice, Lucius said. Early would have to go west to the Shenandoah Valley and whip the Union divisions there. Which, I should add, Early might or might not do.

Jed fussed with his cap, reached under his stained tunic, now missing some buttons, and scratched his once-ample but now thinning belly.

Dammit, Lucius. Smart aleck criminals like Sarsfield always try to throw you off the track. I remember defending a man accused of murdering a whore. He tried to save his skin—sort of like Sarsfield here—by claiming the Madam had killed the prostitute, to keep her from yelling around town how the House was paying the Police Chief.

That case had the whole town fired up, because the murdered woman had been well liked before she bedecked and bedizened herself. Folks assumed the Madam was paying the police, and my witness claimed to have seen some silver change hands.

So did it work?

Well, the prosecutor didn't know what to do about it, Jed said. They talked to my client and finally decided he was bluffing. Didn't really know anything.

And?

Jed sighed. And, my client finally gave up. He pleaded guilty and got life at hard work. He was lucky he didn't get his neck stretched.

Now it was Lucius' turn to sigh.

So where does this leave us, here and now?

Well, if we think there's anything to this crazy letter, we're on the spot, aren't we? I'll admit, Lucius, it would be hard as hell even for a Sarsfield to think that one up. But then even if we think this IS a secret order from Lee, how in the name of all creation would we get word to Grant?

Lucius shook his head.

I don't know, at least not yet, but here's the conundrum: As prisoners, do we or don't we owe our army something? Prisoners are expected to try escaping, aren't they? And they aren't supposed to say anything that will help the enemy's cause. Right?

Well...yes, I guess, to all three questions, Jed answered. But you and I both know that prisoners on both sides like to jabber. Happens all the time. What a war! Both sides speak the same language and worship the same God, so it's easy to interrogate prisoners. And for soldiers to understand what the surrendering boy blabbers about with his hands up, hoping what he knows will save his hide.

But now here we are, with information that our side can use...maybe needs bad. If one of us tried to escape, we'd almost sure get shot trying. Everybody's talking tunnels, and nobody gets out through one. And if you DO get out of here and into this consarned Georgia countryside, how do you eat and stay alive? Not to mention try to reach General Grant. By the way, do we really know where he is?

Lucius scratched his itching jaw.

I dunno. Maybe near Petersburg?

Could be, Jed said, but even Petersburg must be five hundred miles from here, across the Carolinas, and nothing but Johnny Rebs in between. Including kids and old folks who would run a pitchfork through us and brag about it.

Jed, think of it this way, Lucius answered. Some day, if we live, we'll be back home. Suppose word gets out that we knew about a secret command from Rebel headquarters and didn't even TRY to do anything about it? Especially if Washington DOES get attacked and, for Christ's sake, even captured. Now THAT could get US court-martialed, couldn't it?

Jed, now squatting, traced a meaningless doodle on the tramped-over ground. Unlike the dirt inside the main stockade, this soil was not contaminated with human waste.

Well, you have a point there... Jed's voice trailed off, and then he continued: If this were a case in a real court, or a real court martial, we would take this up with the judge or, in an army court martial, with the court president. Good old What's His Name Blanchard.

Lucius asked: But should we get him mixed up in this quite yet? He hates my guts. I need to find Harry Nickels and see if he really has the rest of this letter—or whatever it is. And see what it looks like, and how the blazes he got it.

Jed shook his head.

Lucius, between that letter and your old fracas with this Blanchard, we've got one hell of a mare's nest here. Right now, I doubt it's smart for you to go back in that stockade before the trial is over.

Why?

Someone might recognize you, as a lawyer defending these Raiders. Think you'd live long after that?

Well...I thought about that, but wouldn't most agree with having a defense for these thugs? Some might even sympathize with a lawyer burdened with this job. Besides, there'll be many men coming and going for this trial, however long it takes. So maybe I'm taking a risk, but...

Jed interrupted:

How about having Nickels sent out here? Just tell the guards we need him as a witness?

That might work, but what are the chances he would bring his half of that letter...IF he has it, at all? No, I'd rather get to him inside, because he may have stashed it somewhere and not on his body, like Sarsfield did. We've got to see it, and by just showing up and surprising him, there's less chance he'll do something else with it...whatever that might be.

Lucius pulled out his pocket watch, one of the few personal possessions he hadn't lost.

It's nearly 5 o'clock, he said. I've got about 4 hours to find Harry.

Jed looked up and pointed toward the southwestern sky.

Look there, Lucius, buzzards. Must be five or six, maybe more. See how they bend their heads down? They're looking straight at the dead house.

They're always circling up there, Jed. They're the only creatures that know the real future in this place.

Yep. Any idea how many dead boys they hauled out today?

No...that's one of the advantages of being out here, where we don't see those stacks of stiff arms and legs and jaws hanging open. And bloated bellies, when they lay there a full day or more.

Jed looked back to Lucius.

Don't get yourself killed, now. Those buzzards have enough meat. Besides, I'd hate to defend these bastards by myself.

Oh, don't fret. If I get killed, they'd find another Sergeant to take my place. He grinned. And share your glory when you get them all acquitted!

Jed was not amused.

You know as well as I, Lucius, these filthy creatures will all get the noose. Maybe some of their followers, too. And after the hanging, they'll probably skip burying and let the buzzards at them. In fact, that's more of a certainty than whether this letter is real or a bunch of humbuggery from one of the most cussed men to ever pull on a pair of Union pants.

Lucius now rued his weak joke.

Yes, it could be a trick. But that half letter...there's just enough to it to make me want to check up on it. Even though we see no date, no signature and we can't be sure of the message. And I doubt Sarsfield could write that well.

Just remember, Lucius, Sarsfield played cat and mouse with us. Told first about the letter, but not who had it. Frankly, that smart cuss tricked you into making a deal—well, sort of a deal—with him. You were a sucker, man, to make any deal at all.

Well, Jed, maybe that's why I never made a big name as a lawyer. Meanwhile, I've got to go into that stinking stockade and find Harry Nickels.

Chapter 13.
5 p.m., Friday, July 1, 1864

Lieutenant Horatio Granbury, the Confederate prison guard officer, wouldn't let Lucius into the stockade without clearance from Court President Blanchard.

So, much against his wishes, Lucius had to see his old antagonist, the Wisconsin (or Missouri) judge and politician and Colonel-turned-Sergeant. He decided he would tell Blanchard only that he needed to find a witness or two for the defense. Which he did, as briefly as he could.

Blanchard removed his wide-brimmed but now floppy, hat, held it in his left hand and folded his arms, in such a way that he could wave the hat slowly back and forth, fanning himself. He tipped his head back and looked down his nose toward Lucius. This took some doing, because Lucius was slightly taller than the Court President.

Just like he would do back in Wisconsin, with people he held in contempt or wanted to intimidate, like defense attorneys.

Nope, Blanchard said. We're putting out a call from the pigeon roost up here, atop the North Gate, tomorrow morning. Anyone wants to be a witness, one way or another, just come to the Gate when the trial starts. They'll show up, you can be sure.

Lucius answered quickly, saying Sergeant...

But Blanchard cut him off.

I AM COURT PRESIDENT BLANCHARD to you, Counselor, and don't forget it! Now what the hell do you want to know?

So he wants to go formal. Okay, I can play that way, too.

Very well. Mr. Court President, I must counter that the call for witnesses will bring forth many on the prosecution side. But I must submit that there will be a considerable sense of intimidation among anyone testifying for the defense. So therefore, I cannot discharge my responsibilities adequately, as a defense attorney, unless I am allowed to actively seek out witnesses for the defense.

Blanchard rubbed his chin. Now that he had Lucius talking deferentially (in spite of that rather bothersome and sarcastic undertone) the Court President would play along, but still keep this loathsome lawyer off balance.

You know, McCordle, I remember you, and I can't say it gives me a great deal of pleasure. You were a miserable Copperhead Democrat, weren't you? And after I tried to give you some nice, friendly, professional counsel, you went cackling to that blasted Copperhead editor and got him to libel me about every flumdiddle notion under the sun.

Yes, McCordle, I spotted you right away when I got here; I'm blessed with one hell of a good memory, and don't you forget it. And you know something? I never did think you were any great shakes as a lawyer. But here, I figured you were just the right cocklehead to defend these birds, so I told Wirz to horse collar you and the fellow who's been chumming with you. Then, I'll be damned if you didn't VOLUNTEER for the job, even quicker than I figured.

And if you think I'm looking for some revenge—by Gawd, McCordle, you would be so dammed right! And if you don't like it, by all means, go take your complaint to Captain Wirz. I'm sure he would respond to you in a most solicitous and gracious way.

In other words, my good Copperhead lawyer, I've got you over a goddammed big barrel.

5 P.M., FRIDAY, JULY 1, 1864

So here we are: a Goliath, a dragon, a nemesis. Been after me ever since that stuff in the Times. The sonofabitch—that's what he is—blames me for all his problems. I wonder how much he paid, and who he paid, to get back into the army in Missouri, even as a sergeant.

Lucius abandoned all sense of rank and decorum and asked: Just when did you enlist in that Missouri regiment as a sergeant?

What the hell...what does that matter? And careful how you address me. This is impertinence!

Lucius persisted. Because, my dear Colonel turned Sergeant, if you want to be vengeful, let me tell you that you're going after the wrong man. First of all, I was named orderly sergeant in my first enlistment, back in '62. I ask you again: When did you become a sergeant? It has to be after I got my rank, because you were a Colonel then...and, I dare say lost that rank for reasons I have yet to hear you explain. So, Mr. Court President, I outrank you!

Lucius was now fuming and not finished with his tirade.

And just what can you do to me, Mr. Blanchard or whatever the hell your title is these days, that this godforsaken place can't do by itself? Kick me off this trial? Fine! Go ahead!

But let me warn you...when you talk revenge, you'd best remember I'm the only one in this goddamned hell hole who knows your background, and your pine-shingle courtroom oratory. Well, Harry Nickels probably does too, but he's too nice a fellow to hurt you. But me? I'm not a nice fellow, that is, when I don't want to be, which you know from our unhappy past!

Blanchard took all of this without expression. He pulled out a mangled cigar he had gotten from somewhere, bit the end off, lit it, and blew a hefty ring. Lucius turned and started walking away.

Lucius! Blanchard said loudly—but in a different voice. Lucius stopped and turned half around.

In his well-practiced way, the Colonel-turned Sergeant-turned Court President changed his manner in the interest of regaining advantage.

Look, Lucius, this place is getting to all of us. So I threatened you. Just wanted to keep you on your toes. Testing you. See if you've got balls enough, to see this trial through. We won't get anywhere with you and I braying like jackasses at each other, now will we?

Now, I do have some advice for you, young man...well, younger than me. You want to go in the stockade? You won't be too popular, looking for someone to speak in favor of these skunks. Wasn't many hours ago, they were a hot-headed howling mob, thirsty for blood.

Lucius shrugged; his challenge to his nemesis had worked—for the moment.

I may have to beller at them a few times, he said to Blanchard. Rowdy boys don't fool around much with me.

That so? Blanchard answered, his testiness back. We'll see, won't we? And I couldn't be happier that it's your job, my Copperhead friend!

Now that he had regained advantage with this reminder, Blanchard relaxed his heavy frame. He dropped his thick hands and clasped them loosely together, knuckles up, just under his beltline. His eyes softened under their heavy, bushy lids.

He again became affable, convivial—even sympathetic. He could switch moods in a wink.

5 p.m., Friday, July 1, 1864

Boy, I tell you, McCordle. You've got one whangdoodle of a case on your hands here.

By the way. How did your lawyer career go after I left Coulee City? Ever try defending six guilty men at the same time? No? Well, I haven't seen it done, either. Now and then someone tries and someone defends a pair, maybe a trio. But six? Makes it tough, I'll allow.

Now, then ...you're willing to risk your neck inside that stockade? Waal, I'll sign for you because that rebel guard Lieutenant has to keep his behind out of trouble. Just be sure you're back by dark.

Just how do you deal with a chameleon like this man? What I said to him would have ruined my career back in Coulee City. But see what he did? He changed his tune—and still put us right back where we were a half hour ago, with him on top.

When the guard opened the North gate, Lucius walked into the stockade and quickly became even more nauseated than the first time. With the scorching July sun beginning to descend and the evening air becoming deathly still, the miasma of thick, smelly, smoke from the cooking fires hovered above the slope north of the sink, wafting up every possible fetid odor of demoralized, distressed, and decaying humanity. Down at the sink, a gaggle of men pulled up what was left of their pants after leaving the latrines.

With more than 20,000 men here, that's not many at the latrines. Hundreds of Others are relieving themselves right now...but where? Anywhere they fancy, that's where!

Among the scores of bleary-eyed, pathetic young men milling around the north entrance were a few pugnacious sorts. They stood with hands on hips, stalking back and forth as if expecting the trial to be done and over with by now.

Raiders still on the loose? No; scaredy-cats of last week who are now daring to look and act tough.

One recognized Lucius McCordle as he walked slowly from the gate:

Hey, Sergeant, ain't that trial over yet? When do we get to hang those bastards?

Lucius shrugged and walked on into the milling crowd.

Trial starts soon, he muttered.

Not everyone was on his feet. The excitement of the Raider roundup may have kept some of the sickly, starving men alive and erect for a time. By this evening, though, scores of the weak, emaciated men had taken to their crude shelters and lay on the same rotten blankets, straw, or plain ground as before, in the groaning, whimpering stupor that signals impending death.

On the ground was the moaning, dirt-covered form of a man hardly 19 years old, too weakened from starvation and disease to stand and walk. Another equally filthy man squatted next to the prostrate man, talking to him softly.

Lucius fought off the urge to stop and take charge; he remembered a few days earlier, helping a delirious man write a letter. Now, his own mission couldn't wait. He stepped over a crumpled man's feet and through what passed for a row between shelters.

He made straight for the shebang that he and Harry Nickels inhabited for their first few days. He slowed his steps, not wanting to surprise the fellow. *A wrong word might put Harry to flight after seeing the comrade he had deserted. At least, in my mind, it WAS a desertion and Lord only knows what else.*

At first, Lucius saw nothing.

Where is Harry Nickels?

Lucius looked again and saw the lumpy figure stretched out under the remains of their old blanket and a piece of rotten dog-tent. He stepped close to the shelter, reached down and flipped a corner of the canvas away. Harry Nickels, his face bruised and swollen, opened and closed his battered eyes and looked at Lucius without expression.

Harry! Lucius said sharply. Man, you look like you've been dragged through a knot-hole and splattered with mud and shot on the other side!

Harry blinked a few times, and murmured.

Yah, I been… through the mill… all right. A few more… of these hard knocks, and… I'd of been dead as a doornail. And… maybe… better off than I am right now.

You ever get hit… by 20 men… with clubs or knotted ropes? When each one gets a second crack at you? And… no one there… to take your side?

Where the hell were you, Lucius… when I ran that gauntlet? I though we wuz close friends…like two peas in a pod.

Harry's eyelids closed. His head sagged.

Lucius had no answer to this accusation. It reminded him of once, back in Coulee City, when he stood aside while thugs beat up a helpless Black man.

You got any broken legs? Lucius asked. Broken arms? Can you walk?

Oh… my legs ain't broke, Harry said, but my left arm is, like you know. He lifted it, inside a torn and shredded sleeve of a grimy uniform coat that had once been blue. He tried to sit up, then rolled back to rest on his right elbow. The left, broken, one was swollen and obviously painful.

Lucius wasn't sure he had tied the splint right, but decided not to try fixing it now.

You bring... any food, Lucius? I ain't ate anything since you left. I yelled to the next shanty, but... they wouldn't... pay me no mind.

I don't get fed any better, Harry. But they did bring us rations out there, today. Here.

From a pocket Lucius pulled a piece of hard tack and a hunk of sour bacon. He handed it to Harry, who tried to bite into the bread but couldn't.

I can't chew this. My teeth hurt.

Yes, and after a few more weeks of living this way, on the edge of starvation, your teeth will hurt even more, and start falling out of your head.

Maybe it'll help if we soak it up, Lucius said softly. You got any water left here, Harry?

No.

Lucius used one of his two remaining Union dollars to buy a half pail of water. It was briny and smelled bad. He found the stick tripod, started a fire, heated the water to boiling and dumped in the hard tack. He swished it around a few times, eased it out with two sticks and offered it to his unfortunate old friend.

Here, Harry, have some nice, fresh, skillygalee.

Harry ate it slowly. After a few minutes, he sat up and his color improved slightly. Lucius decided to ask his question:

Harry, I've got to know something. What's this about some written orders you found, from one rebel general to another?

Harry eyed Lucius warily, through swollen and reddened eyes.

How'd you find out about that?

A better question, Harry, is why the goddamned hell you didn't tell me when you found it? Or, at least, when you told me a pile of things about those Raiders? Why? What were you hiding?

Lucius, Harry answered, I…well, I didn't know what was on that paper when I seen it layin' there in the dirt. We were all looking for scraps of anything the Rebs might of left, remember? Geez, I need some water. You got any?

Lucius handed him a cup with the leftover hot water, no longer boiling but probably safe to drink.

Remember that morning we went through the Rebel bivouac? Harry said slowly. It wasn't quite light yet. I found two pieces of paper, and stuffed 'em in a pocket. I saw they was blank on one side, so I might be able to use it to write to… somebody. Like my mother.

But damn, I'm hungry enough to set me cussin'. Sure could use some doughnuts and milk gravy.

Anyway, I didn't even look at that letter, not atall, till we got here. Then Sunday night, I think it was, I brought back a pail of water? I went through my pockets. That's when I first saw that piece of paper with the writing on it…

So, Lucius said sharply, why didn't you tell me? What the aitch was going on in your mind? I got to thinking how much you learned about those crooks. So tell me the truth. You DID get mixed up with them, didn't you?

Harry dropped to his back, and then slowly rolled to face Lucius.

Yes, Lucius, you might say I got mixed up with them. But not the way you think. I didn't go rampaging and stealing and clubbing or anything like that. Others think I did, that I was fresh fish they collared quick for their side.

So, Lucius interrupted, is that what happened? You joined their side?

No! Harry answered. One of them sweet-talked me into coming over south of the sink, said he knew I just got here and had stuff he could sell me, better than the sutler. Said he always helped out the new boys and I was dumb enough to believe him.

Was that Sarsfield?

Yeah, like I said before, he was a good cobbler, too, liked to fix shoes. Had some shoe tools.

Anyways, he said he had some good potatoes, that I could have four for a dollar. I reached in my pocket to pull out a greenback, and this here piece of paper came out with it.

Before I knew it, this John grabbed the paper. Looked at it quite a while. Said it looked like something a general wrote. He asked me to read it, and I was dumbstruck. It's in fancy words, like headquarters stuff. It seemed to be orders from one Rebel general to another.

Seemed to be? Lucius asked.

Looked like the real thing, when I read it good. It said something about the Shen'doah valley and raiding Washington.

Well, this John, this Sarsfeel…Harry continued.

Sarsfield is his name, Lucius interrupted. I'm going to defend him at the trial.

What? Harry blurted. No humbug? You're going to defend a sonofabitch murderer like him?

Yes, I am. In fact, I'm defending all six of the Raider chiefs. But then what happened?

Harry then continued. This John, he grabbed the letter back, and quick as a wink, tore it in two. He handed one half to me and said something like keep it but don't lose it.

How did he explain that?

He told me to do what he said, or he'd tell a guard and they'd be on my hind end right quick.

Did it occur to you that the letter might be your ticket out of here?

Yes, Harry said, John tol' me that, but he din't say how, and I don't know yet.

He didn't suggest any plan? Lucius asked.

No, Harry said. But I thought maybe…after this war, it might be worth money. Anyway, this John had sort of a hold on me. But now he's on trial, so I don't have to worry about him, I guess. Unless….you get him off and he comes back in here.

Harry, give me that piece of the letter.

Harry rummaged painfully through his pocket and brought out a torn scrap of paper, badly soiled and smudged. Lucius studied it, trying to remember the other half Sarsfield had shown him.

In the lower right corner, Lucius saw the words …cross the Potomac… …warn the newspapers… and, in the signature corner, R. E. Lee, General.

Lucius exhaled heavily.

It's what Sarsfield said. Signed by General Robert E. Lee. The date, as I remember, is June 13. That's—let's see, today is July 1—more than two weeks later. Damn. Early could be way down the valley now, heading toward Washington, and the city probably doesn't know what he's up to. The outcome of the whole damned war could depend on Grant finding out about this.

―――――

After he returned through the North Gate, to the holding area outside the stockade, Lucius showed Jed the scrap of paper from Harry Nickels.

Looks like it might be a perfect match, Jed. I mean, we can't be sure until we get the other half back from Sarsfield, but it's what Sarsfield said it would be.

Guess so, Jed muttered...but I still have no sense why they tore it in two.

Yeah...maybe that was smart on the part of Sarsfield... and maybe not, Lucius answered. Anyway, I believe Harry when he says he found it on that Rebel campground. But now that we have it, what next?

Jed cleared his throat noisily.

Haven't the faintest damned idea. I s'pose we have to go back to Sarsfield and get both pieces together.

Jed sighed. I still think you were nuts, Lucius, to make any promise at all to that shyster. Me, I'd of kept that piece of paper and made no deals with him. But...then, you're the one Blanchard put in charge of the defense, so it's your game now.

Lucius exploded.

Dang it, Jed! Are you with me on this, or not? I'm in this goddam mess up to my neck, wondering what the hell to do next, and you're still hounding me about that promise I made to Sarsfield. When he said Harry Nickels had the other half, he had me by the balls! So that's done! I had to do it to keep Harry from the noose. So quit pitching horse manure at me!

Jed Simmons was silent for a moment, before answering carefully.

Lucius, when you were gone, I thought seriously about asking Blanchard to be replaced. Frankly, the only thing that kept me from doing it was not wanting to betray a fellow counsel.

Maybe, Lucius thought, *and maybe also simply not wanting to go back into that filthy stockade.*

5 P.M., FRIDAY, JULY 1, 1864

I really doubted your boy Nickels would have the other half, Jed said, because without that you've got nothing…no signature, nothing sure. But…now that you have the matching piece, well, that puts a little different slant on this. So, what now? This is maybe like the Crimean War. You know, when the English Light Brigade got the wrong orders, believed them, charged the Russian artillery, and lost 300 men?

Lucius heaved a sigh.

We gotta talk more to Sarsfield, because he still has the other half of this miserable document.

———

Sarsfield was not alone. A few Raider followers were nearby, but too scattered to easily talk—or conspire—with each other.

The Court Martial jury, all 12 members and a handful of alternates, huddled beyond the outer stockade wall in a crude shed, where Court President Blanchard was speaking in his loud, commanding, voice, about rules for the trial.

Lucius and Jed could now talk in low voices with Sarsfield, without being heard by others.

Lucius began:

Well, Sarsfield, you were right. Harry did have the other half of that letter and, yes, it DOES look like it came from General Lee. I have it here.

But I've got to make sure. Hand me your half of that scrap so we can see whether it matches.

With a grunt and an I-told-you-so smirk, Sarsfield reached inside his shirt and produced his torn half of the note. Lucius held the two grubby pieces together, found they indeed did match, and then read through the entire contents:

Headquarters Army of Northern Virginia June 13, 1864
General J. A. Early
Cold Spring, Va.

I would like you to move the II Corps as rapidly as possible to the Shenandoah Valley, so as to rout or destroy the Union Army of General David Hunter, who is desecrating our railroads, killing livestock, burning crops, and thereby threatening our army and nation's food supply. Then work North, down the valley, cross the Potomac, and if feasible drive on Washington DC. Attack it and burn it if you can. But warn all the newspaper men to say nothing about this plan. It must be kept secret until you are across the Potomac and bearing down on the enemy capital.

R. E. Lee General

Well, Lucius said, it DOES look like something from the Confederate Big Man, and it does mention a possible attack on Washington City.

Sarsfield growled.

Hell, McCordle, it ain't 'just possible.' That makes it dammed sure Washington is the target, even I kin read well enough to see that.

Sarsfield, Lucius said, you thought this letter would be your ticket for an escape. But you know damned well that's not possible.

Sarsfield screwed up his face again, in that brutal but conspiratorial grimace.

I told you who had the rest of that letter, Sarsfield grumbled, and in return you promised to do anything possible to get me out of here. You recall that? Or do you have a shyster's memory?

Sarsfield, I said anything possible. But what the hell do you think possible means? That I can give you a ticket to sashay out of here, get on the train, and ride leisurely back to New York?

No, the question is, what is your big plan for an escape? Even if I were to get shot trying to help you do it, I've got to know what you planned.

Sarsfield answered in the same grim tone.

Well, fact is, we don't really need any prisoners to escape to get this letter back to the Union Army.

Lucius lost his patience:

We don't? So what do you suggest? That we go see Captain Wirz, and say, Oh, please, nice Captain, may we telegraph a message to General Grant about how this big bad General Early is going to attack Washington?

Sarsfield was used to sarcasm.

Oh, sure, get smart that way, he answered. You don't know too much, do you Sargint? As a fact, you're closer than you think but too dumb to reck'anize it. To get this letter back to the Union Army, you don't go to Wirz. No, you go to one of his guards.

A rebel guard? How the hell... Lucius shook his head.

Sarsfield's bruised face smirked utter contempt for his defense counsel. He stared without blinking at Lucius, almost forcing the Sergeant to turn away.

Sarsfield sneered. You don't know a goddammed thing about how prison camps work, do you? Well, now, let me explain it to you, McCordle, real simple.

See, there's this Ohio guy—I got to know him good—went south and became a Reb. Now he's a prison guard here, comes inside every now and then. Name's Oliver Thomas. Irish, like me and Collins. And you. Still just a private, and that's one a' the things keeps him mad.

Well, turns out he now hates the South and wants to go back north.

A prison guard?

Sargint, I keep tryin' to tell you, every damn prison has some guards tradin' with pris'ners. Sometimes it's phony, to find out stuff their officers want to know. You gotta be smart, like me, to read their brains and figger out what they're really thinkin'.

You read their brains? Lucius asked.

Well, I can spot the phony ones. I can tell which ones will sell goods or even their souls if the price is right. Collins is good at that, too.

Now Nickels, he didn't even know, when he pulled it out, what this letter was. And when he saw it, he first thought he might use it to buy his parole and get him sent outa the South on an early exchange.

So why didn't he? Lucius asked.

Sargint, I pointed out some hard facts to your boy. I told him that if he went to Captain Wirz with this letter, Wirz would go wild-eyed, take the letter from him and torture him into telling how he got it. Nobody would believe he found it on the ground.

Wirz would think for sure he bought it from some traitor in gray, and he'd want to know who. Everybody would go into crazy fits. But then, when Thomas let on to me he wants out of the Reb army, I told him about this letter, and how it would make him a hero in the Union once he turned himself in.

Lucius asked: So did you show this prison guard—Thomas—the letter?

Sarsfield shook his head in dismay.

Of course not. Remember? If Thomas knew the details he might brag to someone, and get shot quick.

This Thomas, he sees in Atlanta papers how Joobie Early is in the Valley. But the papers don't say nothing about the secret plan to hit Washington, a hundred miles away.

Jed Simmons asked:

How do you know Thomas isn't just looking for a chance to turn you in and get promoted?

Naw, Sarsfield answered, I got him sized up good. Oliver Thomas REALLY wants to desert. Got him a mother and a wife and a daughter, up in Columbus, Ohio. The Confeds don't know all that, cuz he also has a woman in Birmingham but that one don't know his whole life, either.

You see, Thomas asked for a transfer to the infantry at Petersburg. Soon's he's there, he'll volunteer for picket duty and walk right over to the Yankee lines, get himself captured. Then he'll show them this letter and get sent back to Ohio. Or so he thinks.

Lucius asked:

This how you let yourself get captured, Sarsfield?

Mebbe, mebbe not. But now you're thinkin', for the first time. And you see, it just might work.

Well now, tell me, Lucius asked, how this guard would get out of here carrying a torn letter with General Lee's signature?

Nobody would see that letter, Sargint. See, I'm a cobbler by trade. I fixed this Thomas boy's old shoes so's he can stick that letter in the sole. I smudged my work up with mud so nobuddy kin see it.

Lucius rubbed his chin.

I don't know. That's the old Nathan Hale trick, and it got him hanged. Did you spell all of this out to Harry Nickels?

Nope, 'cuz I wasn't exactly sure then whether I would try escapin' with Thomas or not. I knew there was a notion to round up us Irish, so I had to figger out a coupla different plans.

Nobody's got my connections with guards, even Mosby and Curtis. Fact is, I did those boys a lot of good and they din't help me, so I'm good and ready to testify against them.

Lucius shook his head.

Look, man, that works only if the prosecution is short on witnesses. And they've got a whole henhouse cackling against you.

No matter. You just get Wirz to send me out of here, I don't give a damn how or where. An' 'f yuh don't, my boys inside won't let you sleep for fear of your neck getting' slit open.

I'll worry about my own neck, Lucius answered. You're asking us to join a scheme to get this Thomas out, and then get you acquitted and put on parole? You want us to make a full moon, too?

Just as I figgered, Sarsfield muttered. Bastards, both of you.

5 P.M., FRIDAY, JULY 1, 1864

Lucius shrugged and asked:

Do any of the other top Raiders, like Curtis or Collins, know about this letter?

Hell, no. Just me and Nickels and Thomas, who ain't seen it yet but who'll give his left arm to take it with him when he gets transferred.

Oh Lordy. This is July 1 and the letter, is dated June 13. That's 18 days ago! But…surely Grant knows by now that Jubal Early is northwest somewhere. And knowing that means the Shenandoah Valley, wouldn't Grant suspect Early might head for Washington? The way one General can read another General's mind? Or is Grant completely in the dark?

Headquarters Armies of the United States
City Point, July 1 1864—11:30 p.m. (received 9 a.m. 2d)

Maj. Gen. H. W. Halleck Chief of Staff:

…Ewells corps has returned here…
U. S. Grant
Lieutenant General [8]

---

8 *WOTR Series 1, Vol. 37, Part II, p.3. Grant apparently either did not know, or preferred to ignore the fact, that Early now had command of the major portion of Ewell's corps.*

Chapter 14.
9 p.m., Friday, July 1, 1864

The Court Martial conferees met in their slapped-together wooden shed behind the oak and pine trees to the west of the stockade's outer wall, uphill from the cookhouse whose odor was only slightly less disgusting than the stink inside the stockade proper. A long shadow from the setting sun cast a funereal pallor over the entire wretched body of humanity within and around this walled purgatory.

The tacit question for the conferees was whether the timing of death for a few dishonorable ones could be advanced according to their demonstrated degrees of personal evil—in the interest of prolonging death and discomfort for the other thirty thousand.

Lucius McCordle and Jed Simmons walked slowly toward the gathering, where Court President Blanchard was telling the others in dull tones how he would run the trial.

Following Blanchard's monologue, the two defense attorneys told him about the letter—and how Harry Nickels acquired it.

Blanchard reacted with jaw-dropping disbelief.

He thundered:

Jeezus, what goddammed kind of flummery are you two nincompoops up to now? First you have to go inside the stockade to find defense witnesses. Now, you come to me with the purest bunch of hogwash I've heard in all my years in the courts of Wisconsin and Missouri.

What is it about you two? You think I've got cow manure between my ears instead of brains? If you had a letter in your hands, something I could look at, that'd be one thing. But to tell me...Say, Simmons—that's your name, isn't it—have YOU seen this letter?

Without waiting for Jed to answer, Lucius carefully pulled the two torn halves of the letter from his pocket, held them together high, about three feet from Blanchard's face.

Blanchard was unimpressed.

What the hell...you expect me to look at these scraps in this light? You had to wait for the sun to go down, so I could read this scrum by candlelight?

Well, Lucius began, we had to recover these pieces from two different persons. One was Sarsfield, the accused Raider in stocks over there. The other was from a man inside the stockade.

Lucius felt no need to mention Harry Nickels by name. Not yet, anyway.

Blanchard exploded.

See here, McCordle, I once thought you were maybe a smart young lawyer. But this, now, is the kind of pettifoggery nonsense no Wisconsin OR Missouri judge would tolerate for a second. I've got half a mind to kick you out of the court martial proceedings and get someone else, you bringing in a wild cockamamie tale like this.... Except, I'd be doing you too goddamned much of a favor...

Lucius had enough...again.

Oh settle down, Mr. Court President. If you'll stop and read this carefully, you'll see this just might be something momentous.

Jed Simmons, without much conviction, tried to back up Lucius.

Now Sergeant Blanchard...

The Court President cut him off immediately.

Listen, you two. We're about to start a trial—tomorrow—of some men who will most likely end up swinging from a timber, and I'll be goddammed if I'm going to get us sidetracked with a wild story about a letter I can't make out—not in this light, anyway—that's supposed to be from one Confederate general to another. Just what kind of a mutton-headed dummox do you two think I am?

Blanchard's tirade boomed across the area. The entire Court Martial Jury, the prisoners in their shackles, the guards, the Regulator men, and a pair of Confederate officers went silent and listened. Lieutenant Granbury took a few slow steps toward the group of Sergeants.

Faces of some jurymen remained impassive, a few showed wariness, and some beamed with pure amusement at this latest burst from the Court President. This was as close to entertainment as anything that had happened since the roundup of the accused Raiders.

Lucius looked around cautiously, wondering whether the guards had overheard any mention of the Lee-to-Early letter. He waited until the Court President had spent his wrath. Then Lucius held his hands up in his most conciliatory way and said:

Allow me to suggest this, Court President Blanchard. Send a guard to bring Corporal Harry Nickels in. He can verify my version of things.

Blanchard, his fists now doubled and resting on his hips, cocked his head to one side and peered quizzically, first to Jed and, then to Lucius. He wagged his head from side to side, straightened, and spoke slowly.

By Gawd, I'll hand it to you two for not giving up. Here we are, wallowing in the swill of prisoners trying other prisoners, and you want to bring still another hog to the puddle.

Lucius interrupted, abandoning all pretense of court protocol:

Look, Blanchard, if Corporal Nickels' story isn't convincing, I'll ask to be relieved from the defense counsel position. But I swear the potential importance of that document is so great—so potentially critical to the Union cause—that I believe it would be folly to ignore it.

Blanchard took a few steps away, then slowly turned and came back to the group, saying:

Okay, you go back in to go get—what's his name? Nickels? But I'm promising you two. If he doesn't sound believable, I WILL replace the both of you and you can go back and live in the muck with the rest while this trial goes on.

Now, meantime, McCordle, you keep these goddammed pieces of paper. Or burn them, I don't give a damn which. Just tell the Guard you're after more defense witnesses, they'll believe that.

Lieutenant Granbury wouldn't send a Confederate guard into the stockade at this time of day. It would have taken a whole squad, which he didn't have to spare. So he told Sergeant McCordle to go in alone to find his witness, or witnesses—not now, but tomorrow morning.

Lucius wondered: *How much did Lieutenant Granbury hear? And what difference would it make if he heard it all?*

Chapter 15.
6 a.m., Saturday, July 2, 1864

This time, Lucius found Harry Nickels quickly—not in their shebang but tottering to the latrine in the sink area at the bottom of the stockade valley. This was just north of where the Raider chieftains had kept their relatively well-furnished huts. Today, those huts were in shambles. All the Raider possessions—clothing, food, candy, watches, trinkets, extra shoes—had been looted by prisoners who no longer feared to go up that once-dangerous southern slope.

Harry, I've got to take you out to the trial, Lucius said.

Harry Nickels didn't respond. He continued on his errand. He found a relatively bare piece of ground, dug up some dirt with his fingers, rubbed it over his hands, and wiped them on what remained of his ragged trousers. He was, like most prisoners, teeming with infectious organisms that he did not understand. Filth was considered a problem only if worse than that of everybody else—and Harry's wasn't.

Yeah, I've been expecting to see you, Harry mumbled. But what happens to me now, Lucius? Am I going to be charged anyway? I ran that gauntlet once. I gotta do that again?

Oh, Christ. I didn't get any promises from Blanchard about what happens to Nickels after we get him back out with the other prisoners. I may have to do some quick-time talking to save Harry's hide.

Lucius answered Harry slowly. Look, old friend. I'll try my dammed best to keep you from being charged with anything. I'm here to bring you out as a witness for the defense.

Holy hell. I made a promise like that to Sarsfield, and I probably can't come through on that one, either. I'd better be square and true with Harry, and right now.

Harry, my job is a thousand times harder than you might expect. You'll never guess who the Court President is for this trial. Remember Judge Mahlon Blanchard from Coulee City? And all the stuff in the papers claiming he stole company rations and payroll money?

Well, the army court-martialed him or threatened him with a court-martial, I'm not sure. However it was, he resigned his army commission and went down the river to St. Louis. Looks like he practiced some law in Missouri and re-enlisted there.

Now, he shows up here as a Sergeant and—you won't believe this—Captain Wirz picked him to be Court President!

Naturally, he has it in for me. Remember? I made the mistake of telling a crazy Copperhead editor about Blanchard's scheme to be a circuit judge. Sewall, the editor, had fun in print with that, even made wisecracks about Blanchard's being a fast man with the ladies.

Well, if all this comes to mind...

Harry interrupted.

That's enough, Lucius...I 'member the Blanchard story and why you never got commissioned. It was the talk of the company.

Lucius... Harry continued slowly, his head drooping... don't you think maybe you and me, we're under a spell of some kind? A curse, or a hex, I mean?

Oh, hell. Maybe so, Harry. But if there's a curse, it's fallen over thirty thousand men here. A hundred or so are dying today, another fifty or hundred will croak tomorrow and...

Lucius, I think I'm going to die, along with them.

You can't, Harry. You're part of a little drama, now, with a chance to help get something to General Grant to help him finish off Lee's army.

Well…maybe it will help, but I don't yet see how. Anyway, if you'll help me stand up, I'll go out where you say. And I'll be happy to tell old Judge Blanchard how and where I found that letter.

Let's do that, Harry. But don't call that bastard Judge. He wants to be addressed as Mr. Court President, so be sure to use those words when you address him. He'd probably like to forget his past, much as I would mine.

Harry Nickels so far hadn't tried to rise. He frowned, partly in physical pain and partly in a different kind of discomfort.

Lucius, he mumbled, I don't know if I'll make it many more days, but with all the stuff here…I'm bothered about somethin' I ain't never told you.

It's about Maryanne Callander. Monstrous pretty, ain't she? Yeah, you wanted me to tell you about my times with her, and I brushed you off. Din't think it was any of your business. But if you ever git out of here and back to her and marry her…or did she tell you this? That she can't never have no babies?

Lucius looked at Harry without responding. *No, Maryanne never said this…nor had I asked.*

See, we was planning to get married, and, well, we spent time together, and, you know how these things go…and, well, she got pregnant, and…she said she couldn't face the Reverend or anybody, and she knew this phony doctor from St. Louis…she went to him and he fixed her so the baby wouldn't be born. But he hurt her so bad she couldn't have any more babies and…

Lucius wasn't ready for one more revelation, especially about Maryanne. But he couldn't stop Harry now—nor did he really want to.

...and that was when she and me quit seeing each other, Harry continued, and decided not to get married...

A disturbed Lucius interrupted. Your choice or hers?

Both, I suppose...that's when she got interested in the slavery thing, and getting escaped ones up to Canada. I guess...anyway, it seemed to me...doing that put her back in peace with herself. That all happened, Lucius, some time before you two got together and all these other things...

And even though you didn't ask me this, Lucius, I give you my word, I tell you no lies.

———

Court President Mahlon Blanchard waited impatiently for the return of Lucius and Harry Nickels. He ordered Jed Simmons, and the two prosecuting attorneys—Warrick Breck, and Delano Richman, the skinny, sharp-featured little Quartermaster Sergeant from Illinois—to stay near.

Lucius half-carried Harry to the gathering, out of earshot of Lieutenant Horatio Granbury and his sorry squad of ill-clothed, unhealthy and semi-literate guards. Blanchard fixed his stare on Harry Nickels as Lucius carefully eased his beaten, sickly friend to a broken packing box that served as a rude chair.

So you are Corporal Nickels? Blanchard said. Your Sergeant—or should I say attorney—says you can attest to the origin of a document that he deems of some significance.

Blanchard's folded arms told all that the document would most likely have *no* significance in the trial.

6 A.M., SATURDAY, JULY 2, 1864

Lucius started to speak, but the Court President held up his hand.

First of all, McCordle, hand me those shreds of paper your attorney calls a letter…yeah, …now, Corporal Nickels, tell us what this alleged document is.

What's this about calling me Nickels' attorney? Damn! He's leaving it open for Breck to charge Harry with being a Raider after all! Now this is vengeance, changing Harry from witness to defendant! Without even waiting for Breck to think that one up!

Harry looked up. Yes, your Honor, I found a piece of paper on the ground, at an army camping place, after some Rebels, maybe thousands of them, had moved out. It was only part light, in the morning, and when I seen it blank on one side, I just thought it…

Blanchard thrust his heavy hand out, interrupting but in a softer voice.

Well, Corporal, this isn't exactly a County Court House, so you can forego saying Your Honor. I'm the Court President.

Anyway, I need to read these pieces of paper, and now that it's daylight so a person can see… Blanchard shifted his gaze accusingly at Lucius McCordle. …I'm going to finally read what it says.

He tilted his large head back, held the two pieces of the letter together in front of him, and tilted them up to catch the rays of the early morning sun. With his left index finger as a pointer, he slowly went through the letter and attempted to read it word by word, line by line. He read, aloud but very slowly, the words that said:

Then work North, down the valley, cross the Potomac, and if feasible drive on Washington D.C. Attack it and burn it if you can. But warn all the newspaper men to say nothing about this plan. It must be kept secret until you are across the Potomac and bearing down on the enemy capital.

While Blanchard read slowly from the torn letter, Warrick Breck shifted uneasily and said in his high-pitched voice:

Court President Blanchard, I must object to the introduction of any such document as irrelevant to…

Blanchard's heavy lower lip pushed up against his cushiony mustache, as he turned and glared at Breck.

Sergeant Breck, he fumed, I'll thank you to hold your objections until I decide what the hell these two scraps of paper are all about. At this point, neither you NOR I know what in Jeezus name is going on here. But just remember that I, AND NOBODY BUT ME will determine whether this paper is relevant to the proceedings about to begin here!

Blanchard shook his massive head. Damn! He added. One more crazy thing like this and we'll have one for the theatre. Say! Maybe that's the way out of this place. Get up a show so blithering funny the Rebels will want to put us on the train and stage it all over the South!

Breck clamped his thin jaws together and stared straight ahead. His long, stooped frame sagged a bit more.

Blanchard returned his gaze to the letter. Goddam, he muttered. Need a table to put this on…which we don't have right here.

Well, he said, it was certainly written out by a scribe who knew what he was doing.. Better than many a court document I've seen, and, I must say, as good as much that comes out of our own War Department.

Yes, he should know about U.S. War Department documents. With all his shenanigans, he's seen plenty of them.

Blanchard looked up as if in thought and said, Now, Sergeant Breck, you may review this strange piece of paper.

Blanchard impatiently drummed his fingers on the crate, while he waited for Warrick Breck to read through the two mangled pieces.

Now, Corporal, tell us in detail, Blanchard said to Harry, how you came into possession of this piece of paper? Or, I should say now, *pieces.*

Well, let me see…, Harry began, …we were captured June third, it was, and the Rebs moved us around from one place to another, and then one morning—was it the 14th, Lucius?—we was marched through a trampled field at the edge of some woods where it looked like a million Rebels had been. We all was looking for things to pick up, and I seen this piece of paper. It was half dark and I saw writing on one side, but the other side was blank so I figgered I could use it to write a few lines home on it, some time.

Blanchard eyed Harry without blinking.

That was the 14th, you say? And now when did you say you first really looked at it?

Harry looked down, rubbed his forehead with his right hand, and then dropped that hand to hold his sore left arm. It wasn't healing right.

I…I…guess I forgot about it. Didn't go through my pockets till we reached the stockade here…

Blanchard: So you want us to believe you had it…where… in that same shirt pocket for, let's see, about 10 days…before you even looked at it?

Harry Nickels: Yes…that's right…isn't it? I…I wonder if I…

Lucius McCordle: We were on the move all that time, weren't we, Harry? No real time or chance to…

Blanchard: Goddammit McCordle, DON'T MAKE UP WORDS for this man!

Warrick Breck: Mr. Court President, I must object. We are about to try a bunch of thieves and murderers, and his so-called 'letter' is an obvious hoax planted by the accused to distract the Court Martial.

Blanchard: Your response to that, Sergeant McCordle?

McCordle: Mr. Court President, I believe anyone familiar with military correspondence will insist that this letter is genuine, and...

Breck: I object to that, your Hon...Mr. Court President. For example, who here knows what General Lee's signature looks like?

Blanchard: Sergeant McCordle?

McCordle: Well...I can't claim to have seen it before...

Well, this may be the end of the story of the letter from General Lee...

Simmons: As a matter of fact, Court President Blanchard...and this may surprise everyone...I CAN vouch for the authenticity of General Lee's signature.

All eyes turned sharply to Jed Simmons.

Blanchard: (Stuffily) You really can? Please, then, explain this to the Court...to all of us, Sergeant Simmons. This, I can't wait to hear!

Simmons: Well, my father has a law practice in Dubuque—that's in Iowa—and he often had cases in Burlington, a short boat ride down the Mississippi. He knew Charlie Mason, a famous lawyer, in that town. Great man, Mason is, he ended up as chief justice of the Iowa Territorial Supreme Court.

Blanchard: Come, now, I know Justice Charlie, too. Good man...Democrat, sort of, but opposes slavery, favors the union. But what's that got to do with...

Simmons: Well, Charles Mason was first in his class at West Point 30 years ago, something every lawyer in the territory knew. Second in that same class was Robert E. Lee—no, I'm not fooling. These two were good friends, and sent each other many letters, back and forth…

Blanchard: M.m.m…yaa…ss, I see. So how does that pertain to this alleged letter?

Simmons: Well, my father over the years had many a meal, and some whisky now and then, with Mr. Mason. The Justice liked to talk about his West Point days, and his fondest memory was his old chum Robert E. Lee, who hadn't made general yet.

Back in 1861, we heard that Lee was heading up the Confederate Army in Virginia. Pa and I happened to be in Burlington one day—went down from Dubuque on a packet boat—and met up with Mr. Mason. My brothers and I were either in the militia or about to join, and we were curious about what kind of general the Union was up against. Mason had worked hard to avoid war, and Pater—Pa—respected him for that.

We ate in a place near the railroad station, and Justice Mason, with great pride, showed us some letters from General Lee, over the years. I read through several and couldn't help noticing the particular sweep of his letter R and the E. and the curious L in his last name that looks more like a small letter d. And I say that this message we have here, from the famous General, is authentic.

Oh man. All of this is news to me. Up to now I knew only that Jed was from Dubuque, a few hours down river from Coulee City. It's going to be hard now for Blanchard or anyone to claim this letter is a hoax, even though I was almost hoping the letter WOULD be proven a humbug.

Blanchard: Well…well… Sergeant Breck, you may now state your views about this document.

Breck: I've had my say already. Sergeant Richman, why don't you put it in the prosecution's words?

Richman: (Straightening up his slight, thin build and holding his sharp chin high) Mr. Court President, the prosecution formally submits its objection to any further consideration of this purported 'document.' It seems patently obvious that it is counterfeit, even though the honorable Sergeant Simmons has just testified as to its authenticity. It nevertheless is readily apparent to a careful observer that the characteristic signature of the famed General Lee has been carefully reproduced by some unknown but highly talented calligrapher residing somewhere in this place of confinement.

With those words, this tiny sliver of a man draped a curtain of courtly formality over a squalid pit of human chaos, torment and degradation. In as damnable a human purgatory as the earth had ever seen, the lawyer had spoken as if all were robed and bewigged barristers in the high courts of the empire.

Lucius wondered whether to congratulate Richman for bringing courtly decorum to this cesspool, or to simply laugh out loud.

Even Mr. Court President gaped in sheer awe at Richman's delivery. The man's small face and dark eyes glistened over his sharp chin as he blushed with satisfaction.

Blanchard asked: Your response, Counselor Simmons?

Simmons answered: I stand by what I said. I say it's a message from General Robert E. Lee to General Jubal Early.

Blanchard looked down, thoughtfully. In a stalling style borrowed from Abraham Lincoln, he told a yarn.

Well, boys, this reminds me of a case back in Wisconsin—before your time, McCordle—when a timberjack sued a railroad company to honor an easement. The timberjack claimed he had a paper with the notarized signature of a previous landowner, declaring the trail meandered back to the timberjack's land where he wanted to cut big oak trees for railroad ties.

Problem was, the notary lawyer was dead, the seal was badly smudged, and the signature was an X because the signer, also dead now, had been illiterate. So to prove the signature legitimate, the timberjack's lawyer brought in a writing expert who claimed the X was same as the X the man had put on his will.

Well, the railroad lawyer then showed this witness a few other X'es—you might call him a real X-PERT…heh, heh… and asked him to pick the ones that were authentic, that is, from the hand of the dead landowner. The expert pointed to one and said 'this one, here, is authentic.'

This put a big smile on the railroad lawyer's face. He brought in a different witness who testified under oath that the X that the expert called authentic was, in fact, a mark made by a foot from a dead chicken, with ink on it.

I had to bang my gavel a dozen times to quiet the courtroom down, everyone was laughing so hard.

Simmons: So, I presume the railroad attorney won the case?

Blanchard: Not exactly. The timberjack's lawyer asked for a continuance, and next day brought in another witness, woman in her eighties, who remembered the trail being used throughout her life, up to 5 or 6 years ago.

A pause.

Well, that's a thumping good yarn, Lucius said.

Might as well humor the old goat.

Then, still genial, Blanchard added:

Now, gentlemen, let's talk this over like the good thoughtful men we all are. Let's assume for starters this letter really IS from General Lee to General Early. What do you suggest we do about it? If anything? Or is there anything we CAN do?

Breck: Whatever these ragged pieces of paper are, it's out of our hands. We've got the trial of the century here, and a need for justice. I say, forget about this so-called letter, and worry about today. The sooner we start, the better.

McCordle: Sergeant Simmons and I have gone over these arguments. The Union may be in peril they don't yet see. Now we're Union soldiers, aren't we? Even though we are prisoners, isn't it also our duty to help General Grant and the Union cause—any way we can?

Breck: That's the clincher, McCordle. There's no way on God's earth we *can* help. Everyone knows that. This letter, even if it's real, which I still doubt, is out of date. Whatever's happened has happened. If Early is going to attack Washington, he's already there...

Simmons: Not so fast, Sergeant Breck. We hear rumors and taunting from the guards every day, don't we? Still like to brag about how we Feds got slaughtered at Cold Harbor, don't they? If Early was heading for Washington already, they'd be bragging about it. You heard anyone mention that?

Breck: Well, no...but I haven't heard anyone talk about the sun setting in the east, either, and that's just as likely as this damned letter being real.

Blanchard: Now, boys, let's say for the moment that this goddammed letter is what McCordle and Simmons claim. How in hell's name would we get word to Grant, or the War Department in Washington? Now me, I've been there....

You damned right he's been there. That's when the Army got fed up with his shenanigans with payroll and rations.

…and I say the one to reach is General Halleck. 'Old Brains,' they call him. He's Chief of Staff. Met him myself. Cantankerous cuss, but knows his onions.

We'd have to get a telegram to him, and I sure as hell don't see a way to do that.

Breck: (Sarcastically) Yeah, I suppose McCordle would have us mosey down to the railroad station, put a gun to the telegraph operator's head, and order him to wire a message directly to Union headquarters in Washington. I'm sure he would oblige…

McCordle: Think that's impossible? Suppose there's a big breakout here, and 40 or 50 of us storm that station…

Breck: Oh, don't be stupid. We'd all be shot before we got there. You haven't seen those cannons on the southwest hill? One surge of our boys toward the stockade wall, and tons of grapeshot would slaughter us all before we got 10 feet from these walls.

McCordle: Maybe, maybe not. Yes, there would be some of us killed, perhaps most. But some would make it…

Blanchard: McCordle, suppose somehow a ragtag bunch of half-dead prisoners did make it to the station and the telegraph keys. Do you know Morse code? No? Well, then, let's suppose you DID know. Now who the hell do you think would receive any message you sent? IT WOULD BE LEE OR RICHMOND, GODDAMMIT! There wouldn't be any telegraph lines from here to Washington, don't you know that?

McCordle: Well, listen to this. There's a different plan already hatched. It involves a clever escape and a rebel prison guard who wants to desert.

Blanchard: What? An escape involving a guard? Listen, I know all about dumb guards, but if there's one who's that cockeyed, he wouldn't have the brains to make an escape work. So this idea sounds hatched from rotten eggs. Careful, McCordle. I've wondered all along whether you were touched in the head.

McCordle: Well, you may wonder more when I tell you the rest. This isn't my idea. It comes from one of the Raider chieftains.

Breck: Aw, talk about humbuggery. You can't be serious…which one?

McCordle: Sarsfield. He's been playing up to this one guard, trading stuff with him, knows a lot about him. Claims that boy wants to escape. The idea is for him and Sarsfield to escape together…

Blanchard: Oh, shit! Any more hogs we can run into this wallow? The more I hear, the more I think this whole thing is loopy as hell. You've got a shifty criminal mind there, dreaming up every possible way to wiggle out of this place with his hide in one piece.

I tell you this: Whatever that piece of paper is, it isn't going to make any difference in this trial. I expect to sentence some boys to dangle from a rope. Now, I'm not *entirely* sure of that, of course; it's up to those 12 Sergeants in the jury panel.

So boys, whip your backsides into shape for the trial. It starts at 1:30 this afternoon. And right now it's…let's see… about 9 o'clock. Either get some rest or work out your opening statements. You've got, say, three hours, with time to eat whatever they bring on the slop wagon, when it rolls by.

———

As soon as they stepped aside, Lucius said quietly to Jed:

Jed …I have to hand it to you. That was a gift from heaven, your knowing General Lee's signature. Whatever Breck and Richman say, Blanchard now seems to believe that letter is authentic.

Jed Simmons was in no mood to be commended.

He straightened up and cocked his head.

Lucius…I need to tell you a couple of things. Breck and Richman were half asleep. If they were good lawyers—probably never were—at least one of them would have said that if this letter is introduced into the proceedings I'd have to be sworn as a witness to testify under oath about that signature.

You see, Lucius, I DO know Lee's signature. What I said about the meeting with Justice Mason in Burlington, Iowa was correct. But the signature on that letter? Not from Lee. It was probably written by the General's scribe, because it flows like the rest of the letter, and a General wouldn't be likely to do the letter with his own hand, on ink and paper. That's why they have clerks.

I truly suspect the letter is what it says it is. But signed by the General himself? Not if I remember that signature as well as I'm sure I do.

So, Lucius, thank your stars the Almighty allotted Breck and Richman a thin stock of brains. And you…you were so damned eager to hear me say what I did that you didn't try to guess how those other two think.

But even so, Lucius persisted, wouldn't the General want his own signature on the letter, so Jubal Early would know it and trust it?

Ordinarily, sure, a General would sign it. But, if he was sick, or in bed, he might just dictate the letter. Lee and Early probably talked this over before, and the letter was just Lee's way of putting everything in writing.

What I did there, Lucius, was tell a fib, one that would get me disbarred back in Iowa, if I tried it with a judge there. I did it because the way it's written in that perfect script, and the kind of language used, I'm quite convinced it's a real letter. But for whatever reason, I think in this case the General had his aide write R.E. Lee at the end.

Lucius started to speak, but Jed raised his heavy hand:

Lucius, the fact is, I agree with Breck and Richman, thick-headed as they are. I told that fib to give you some credibility—at terrible risk to my own. But on the other hand, that letter has no goddamned bearing on this trial. Yes, I think it's real and, yes, it's a worry how we do anything with it. But it isn't worth a fart in a whirlwind as defense for these Raiders.

Now an aroused Jed bellowed:

Look here, man! We haven't talked at all about how we defend these apes...and the trial begins in three hours, more or less! What are you going to say in your opening statement? Let's forget this cussed Lee-to-Early thing!

Lucius walked a few steps and turned toward Jed. He looked down, then, up, and talked quietly for several minutes.

Yes, Lucius said, let's talk about the six Raider chieftains. Take Collins. He has this bizarre story about 'helping' a youngster in earlier life. Is this any help in a trial?

Then we have Curtis, a tough, ornery fellow. Scary, except that now he's kinda beaten up like the others. Claims to be a sailor, and makes you wonder if Curtis is his real name. I heard him answer to 'Rickson,' so maybe he goes by different names. These bounty jumpers, which is what they are, have probably gone by all sorts of different names. Usually Irish names. Rickson could be anything. Curtis is proud of being Irish, and thinks this whole trial is a way of getting back at people from his country.

Delaney, he had a laboring job in Pennsylvania. Tried to tell us he's a shoe maker, but I figure he was just trying to copy Sarsfield and get a job that might parole him.

Delaney's the toughest of these birds, in my mind. Has comets for eyes. Says he ain't afraid to die, and the quicker they get to it, the better.

Then there's this little guy, Sullivan. From a New York infantry company. He's been a tent mate of Collins—Mosby, they call him?–and I think they did a lot of things together. He's got different names, too. Seems to answer to John, Cary, Terry…hard telling what else. Another tough little customer. I think he learned his criminal ways in the slum neighborhoods of New York. And I know this sounds crazy, but I heard someone yell at him with the same name I heard for Curtis. It was 'Rickson,' so I don't know what that's all about. I'm guessing these boys are mostly hiding their real names.

Jed nodded.

They may not want to embarrass folks back home. So… suppose we argue that these men are not guilty because they are insane?

Lucius: The insanity defense?

Jed: Yep. Used mostly when a man shoots his wife's lover. Ever hear of Congressman Daniel Sickles? He learned that Philip Key—whose old man wrote the Star Spangled Banner, by the way—was sleeping with Sickles' young wife. Sickles took his gun and shot Key, not far from the White House. He had a good lawyer, Edwin Stanton, who argued Sickles was temporarily insane.

Stanton got the jury to go along with that insanity plea, but not because they believed it.

You see, most people believe a husband has a right to kill a man who has cuckolded him. It's an unwritten law, and this insanity plea is a way to make it respectable.

Lucius: So might the insanity plea work here? At least keep these men from getting hung?

Jed: Not likely. Even though Stanton was smart enough to become Lincoln's Secretary of War, remember? Anyway, like I said, about the only time the insanity plea gets used is when jury men think the murder victim was a son of a bitch who deserved it. Here, Lucius, the jury believes—quite accurately in my opinion—that the sons of bitches are the ones on trial.

Lucius shifted topics.

Okay, what about proof? Breck and Richman have to prove, beyond a reasonable doubt, that EACH ONE of these men is guilty of the crime. And what is the crime? Robbery? Murder? Assault? Simple thievery?

Jed: All those things, and maybe more, like unnatural acts.

Lucius: Oh? And what man would testify to those?

Jed: Good question. Probably none.

Lucius: Anyway, they have to prove guilt beyond a reasonable doubt. But do any of us know what the hell a reasonable doubt is?

Jed: My older brother, he went to Yale law school, and he says reasonable doubt isn't really much help to defendants.

It's a big help to the jury, though. Say you're on a jury and you take your religion very seriously. I mean, you're certain that if you send an innocent man to the gallows, you'll go straight to hell.

So we have this reasonable doubt business. No matter how strong the evidence seems, it is always possible to get it wrong. So you won't go to hell if you convict someone believing there is no REASONABLE doubt he was guilty. So the rule does wonders for the juryman who has a conscience.

Lucius: But does it help the accused?

Jed: I doubt it. Most defendants would stand a better chance if the rule simply said the jury had to be absolutely sure. Then, few men in good conscience would send anyone to their death when all they have is someone who claims to have seen the act—maybe by moonlight.

Lucius: Conscience? You think any of the jury people here will have any conscience problems hanging these Raider leaders? I think not. What worries me is that the reasonable doubt rule will work AGAINST us.

Jed: How do you mean?

Lucius: Something my old teacher Eldon Ashton said. They won't admit it, but the fact is, they'll expect us to prove INNOCENCE beyond a reasonable doubt. The burden of proof will be on US, not the prosecution.

Jed: Frankly, Lucius, I would hardly blame them for thinking that way. My old man always said, just see that his rights are protected, and that he's not punished too harshly. But try to get someone off when you KNOW he is guilty? Most unethical, Pa would say.

Lucius: But murder calls for hanging, Jed. So if we are certain these men are murderers, and instigated others to commit murder...then what? We don't defend them at all?

Jed: Only if we want to get into that insanity defense, which I don't think has the chance of a snowball on a red-hot stove. In my mind, our job is to make sure Breck and

Richman bring out testimony that really shows they committed murder and robbery.

Lucius: And suppose they don't? Suppose every boy who comes out here gives us second-hand testimony? All hearsay. Then what? Would you still be convinced they're guilty?

Jed: Look, Lucius. Life here is so abominable, that ending these hourly raiding parties is the one thing that might gratify a few thousand wretched men. If the sight of these animals swinging in the breeze can provide that satisfaction, that quieting, that ability to sleep through a muggy night with nothing more to worry about than the rain and the stink and the bugs and tomorrow's rations—well, I think these poor bastards, all thirty thousand of them, deserve that much.

Lucius: Well, at long last, Jed, I guess we don't agree. I think the people who created the conditions in this stockade, share much of the guilt. Just like the stupid officers who created training camps that killed more men than die on battlefields, like a government that won't allow prisoners to be exchanged—they as well as Confederate prison commanders are to blame for the way we live here. Our soldiers didn't learn how to take care of themselves in the militia camps, so how can they figure out how to live here? They've been trained like animals, so they act like animals!

Jed: Lucius, whatever you do, don't try that one in your opening OR closing statements. They won't cotton to it. They'll figure—as I do—that survival under difficult conditions requires MORE man-to-man compassion, NOT LESS.

Well, that's my view, Lucius. Now, what about the letter from Lee to Early?

Lucius: Yes, what about it? Right now, I don't have the faintest idea. Maybe I'll think of something in the next hour or two.

Chapter 16.
1:30 p.m., Saturday, July 2, 1864

It's a mortal hot day, the juryman said, as the sweltering Georgia sun burned through the putrid haze hanging over the stockade on this windless afternoon.

The sergeant and his 11 co-jurymen sweated profusely in the stifling heat. They shuffled under the open shed roof just outside the stockade. Most still wore their Union Blue, with sergeant stripes large and bright on tunics still not frayed, shredded, or fouled from the 24-hour-per-day wear they would endure after a few weeks in the putrid stockade.

They eased their bottoms down on crude seats, either half-rotted wooden boxes with heavy nail heads protruding, or rough, splintered boards teetering on unevenly sawed blocks of wood. They sat in a semi-circle facing a pair of rickety table-high benches.

To one side was the Court President's bench, which until yesterday had been a storage shelf for beans and sweet potatoes. Someone had knocked out enough of the lower center cubicles for the Court President's feet. This was as close to court furniture as could be provided, yet superior to any other fixtures in the area.

Beside this bench sat Corporal Gilbert Daniel, at a table of two short pieces of flat board over empty ammunition boxes. Daniel had two pens, an inkwell, and three pencils from Captain Wirz' office, ready to transcribe as best he could.

Facing the Court President's bench, and at a right angle to the jurymen, were Warrick Breck and Delano Richman for the prosecution, and Lucius McCordle and Jed Simmons for the defense.

To the left of Lucius and Jed sat the six accused ringleaders of the Raiders—Curtis, Collins, Delaney, Muir, Sarsfield and Sullivan. They sat on the ground, each with a 24-pound steel ball clamped to an ankle by a short chain. The length of the chain was determined by the man's height, allowing him to walk only by leaning over and carrying the ball in a stooped position, too awkward for more than one slow step at a time. If the wearer was so foolish as to demonstrate his ability to move easily and quickly in spite of this impediment, guards would simply add a second ball to the other ankle. Or shorten the chain. Or both.

Behind the six ringleaders sat some 20 other stockade prisoners, all of them thought by the captors to be followers of the Raider chiefs. Each wore a ball and chain, but lighter than those of the leading six. Most, like the ringleaders, bore scars and bruises gained during the violent capture.

Court President Mahlon C. Blanchard rose from his rickety chair and strode before the jurymen, with his back to the prisoners. He hooked his thumbs on his belt, spread his feet, and cleared his throat.

We are about to begin the trial of more than two dozen accused prisoners in Camp Sumter, he said. I am authorized to convene this court by Captain Henry Wirz, commandant of this stockade. Corporal Gilbert Daniel, who used to write for papers, will keep a complete record of the trial. His notes will go by fast courier to Richmond for approval of any sentences I may impose.

I am told by Captain Wirz that the Confederate States of America, in this peculiar case, may even share the transcript, or the gist of it, with the Federal authorities in Washington. How they might do that, is up to them.

As you may know, we are without the U.S. Army Courts Martial Manual, and have access to only a few law books of the State of Georgia. So our deliberations will be more informal, but we will proceed as best we can like a Civil Court.

I shall rule quickly and fairly on the admissibility of evidence, and on whether any new charges or specifications offered by witnesses will be considered by the jury.

The Court President cleared his throat again, stepped to one side, and continued:

In view of the brief time since apprehension of the accused prisoners, it has not been possible for the prosecuting attorneys to write out a detailed statement of charges for each individual. We shall allow each witness to specify charges against defendants, specifications which may not have been stated earlier.

A sullen murmur rippled through the hapless group of defendants, as Blanchard continued:

Prosecuting Attorneys Breck and Richman, however they may divide the task, will now state the principal charges.

With that, and a throat-clearing harrumph, the Court President strode back to his bench.

Sergeant Warrick Breck, for the prosecution, stretched his bent frame to his fullest height. His rounded, humped back flowed in almost parallel curvature with his large, hooked nose. His receding chin hid under a well-trimmed graying beard reaching from one ear to the other. Watching him, Lucius assumed he had access to both a razor and a mirror—or the help of a barber. Chaotic as things were in the Andersonville stockade, barber services were available—for those who had money to pay for them. Warrick Breck had obviously, in his brief time in Camp Sumter, kept his money from being stolen.

Thank you, Mr. Court President, he said slowly, nodding toward Blanchard and then turning toward the jury panel as he spoke.

You members of the jury have a historic duty to perform here. So far as any one knows, this is the first time in the history of our nation—if not the history of man—that a community of imprisoned soldiers has taken it upon itself to formally charge and try members of its community for such vile crimes of assault, robbery, and murder. Oh, I am sure there have been kangaroo courts, perhaps in the Crimean War that sought to…

Court President Blanchard cut him off.

Sergeant Breck, we are not here for a history lesson. We are here for a trial. State the charges.

Mosby Collins grinned. A murmur sifted through the jury panel of 12, now sweating and almost as uncomfortable in the afternoon heat as the accused men sitting on the wood blocks or sprawling on the somewhat cooler earth.

Breck: Yes, Mr. Court President. The prosecution is charging the six men in the two front rows, as principals and as fomenters, of willful assault on various other prisoners, of theft of an immense amount of private property from other prisoners, and of outright murder of other prisoners. The other men are charged as accomplices.

Court President Blanchard: The defendants have heard the charges. Each shall now stand, give his name, and state how he pleads, guilty or not guilty to these charges.

Collins, all six feet of him, struggled to his feet, putting his left foot on the 24-pound ball chained to his right ankle. This gave him a profile, he thought, something like George Washington standing with a foot on the gunwale of a boat crossing the Delaware. Collins, however, had to put all his weight on his right leg, because the ball wobbled under the other. So instead of appearing Washingtonian, he looked more like a befuddled drunkard as he spoke.

I ain't guilty of nothing. I ain't stole from nobody, I ain't kilt nobody, I wuz just a good trader.

Blanchard rapped on his bench with the carpenter's hammer he was given to serve as a gavel and addressed Collins sternly:

Private—what's your name? Mosby—answer guilty or not guilty.

Not guilty, Collins aka Mosby mumbled and dropped himself to the ground, the heavy ball smacking the opposite ankle as he moved his feet. He'd had enough of the slivery block of wood.

Curtis Rickson, Blanchard called.

Charles Curtis slowly but confidently rose, showing no effects of the buck-and-gag treatment of a day and a half earlier. Unlike Collins, he kept both feet solidly on the ground. He shifted his left, unshackled leg to one side, folded his arms and presented an imposing figure to the court.

How do you plead?

My name is Charles Curtis. Some call me Rickson. I plead Not Guilty! He said this loudly, and slowly sank back to his block of wood.

The remaining four Raider leaders responded much the same way as Curtis.

Then the Court President turned to the 12 sitting behind the six leaders.

All you others. Arise and address the Court, one at a time. State your names and units, and how you plead—slowly enough so that the Court Clerk, Corporal Daniel, can enter it into the record.

Murmurs rippled through this bedraggled group, as several anxiously looked left and right. At the left rear corner of these huddled miserables, a short, squat man whose uncovered head showed blond but filthy hair, stood and shouted:

Private Elias Welch, New York Infantry. Not Guilty!

The next 11 responded similarly, all pleading innocence. The last one to plead was Harry Nickels, his pathetic plea nearly causing Lucius to lose his composure.

Court President Blanchard: The Prosecution will now state its case.

Warrick Breck stood again, his bent body now swaying slightly, in crude rhythm with the cadence of his words.

Mr. Court President, and members of the Jury Panel, the prosecution shall demonstrate by abundant testimony and other evidence, that the six leaders and their accomplices have committed the most heinous crimes imaginable inside these stockade walls. Just imagine. Some thirty thousand brave, courageous men, still proud in their blue Union uniforms but captured after heroically fighting their Confederate enemy (Breck had intended to say despicable, dastardly foe, but thought better of such phrasing after noting the guards in gray nearby) have entered this godforsaken stockade, hoping to keep body and soul together until they would be exchanged as honorable prisoners of war. They came here, expecting their fellow unfortunates to be banded together in like purpose, all for one and one for all, to preserve themselves and make the best of the most desperate circumstances.

1:30 P.M., SATURDAY, JULY 2, 1864

But, instead, what do these heroic men meet when they first enter this miserable stockade? These six hooligans and their 13 accomplices (Breck waved toward the leaders) have contrived continuously, with cunning and force, to engage in forceful pilferage of the most private possessions of these unfortunate heroic arrivals. They have forcefully stolen everything imaginable—money, food, watches, tools, blankets, tent pieces, cooking utensils without which survival is impossible. If a new arrival should successfully ward off the first attack, he and anyone who helps him would be visited in the dark of a moonless night by a mob of these creatures, to have his entire shelter knocked over, his possessions taken, and his head bashed in. Many, many, a prisoner has died from these assaults! And since you jurymen are new to this stockade, you may till now have been innocent of the knowledge that these depraved men have not hesitated—not one bit!—to steal whatever they wish from the pockets of sick and dying men, who should deserve only the most humane succor and comfort that fellow men can provide.

Oh, men of the jury, for many months have these vultures preyed on this camp, employing the most dastardly methods they have learned in the schools of crime in Pennsylvania, New York, and everywhere else these rum-loving Irish congregate.

In their nefarious methods, these vile beings—to call them human is impossible—have negated the argument, which the defense will no doubt offer, that they took possessions simply to stay alive. Stay alive? These abominable creatures have prospered! Their shelters are no longer shanties or shebangs but have become the most comfortable, even luxurious, abodes. Why, these hoodlums were able, with their purloined materials, to construct a tent for dining and revelry that in appearance and trappings would rival the lavish pavilions of the richest Arabian Desert Kingdoms!

In summary, this is a band of murderous criminals, whose guilt, individually and collectively, will be made abundantly clear in the coming hours and days of this trial. Gentlemen, the survival and well-being of our thousands of gallant Yankee soldiers are at stake here, and we shall leave no doubt this is so!

Warrick Breck then sat on his box, and the Court President called on Lucius McCordle to make his statement for the Defense. Lucius, his arm pits wet with sweat in the stifling afternoon heat, sipped slowly and deliberately from a tin cup of water, drained it, and carefully placed it near his feet. He walked before the panel, rubbed his bewhiskered chin with his left hand and began speaking slowly.

Gentlemen of the jury panel, the Defense agrees wholeheartedly with one of the first things the attorney for the prosecution has said. This IS a godforsaken stockade. It is a place of unparalleled filth. There is not room for 2,000 prisoners inside these decrepit walls, not to mention a dozen times that many who are now here. And with hundreds more arriving each day! Most of you have been here less than a week, and have perhaps spent no more than a few hours on the other side of these high walls. Two or three, I understand, of you newly-arrived Sergeants have been so fortunate as to not yet step inside the stockade at all.

But even if you haven't seen the horror inside, you can smell it right now, can't you? Have your nostrils ever been assaulted by such a hodgepodge of smoke from rotted wood and foul, burned pork, all mixed in with that horrendous aroma of human excrement spread over 10 or 15 acres where each man has maybe one or two square yards for himself?

1:30 P.M., SATURDAY, JULY 2, 1864

Where the only drinking water you can depend on is from a well that you or someone else dug farther up the hill from that filthy creek whose water is contaminated by sewage from the cookhouse and guard troops before it ever gets into the stockade?

Many will contend that these conditions simply push men over the edge, tempting them to do anything for personal survival. No, the defense does not condone killing your fellow prisoner—but it is our contention that no direct evidence for murder by the accused men here exists. Oh, rumors abound in this sordid place! And men do die—sometimes a hundred in a single day! They die of disease. Of starvation. And, yes, from fights in the far north end of the stockade, where the accused are never seen. You may hear many a man say everyone knows these accused soldiers murdered a particular person. But gentlemen, remember that it is your duty to judge guilt or innocence according to strict evidence. It will be asked whether any particular witness actually saw a murder committed, and I will tell you right now that no truthful witness will be able to make that claim.

Now, to say that many men die every day in this place is not to minimize the seriousness of the charge of murder. No! Outright murder of one's fellow man—one's fellow soldier—is more monstrous in proportion to the degree of squalor and hopelessness of an environment that cannot be escaped. But we do, and will, contend that the unconscionable daily loss of life from infection, sickness, and melancholy leads easily to the suspicion that some other prisoner is responsible for these deaths. Yes, gentlemen, many people are responsible for the wholesale death of young men in this stinking place, but we ask you, resist the temptation to make scapegoats of a group of men who are called Raiders. Known by this unholy name, these men have been adjudged guilty in the minds of hundreds, perhaps thousands, of prisoners here in Camp Sumter.

Gentlemen, there are many RESPONSIBLE parties for the death and human chaos in this prison. These include, first, a series of blunders in military decisions by Union commanders.

We are not making accusations of General Grant or the Army of the Potomac. We are talking about the origin of conditions of this stockade, one aspect of which is the swelling population that stems directly from a series of unfortunate military actions that...

Blanchard did not bang his crude gavel; he tapped it rapidly, in a staccato much like a pileated woodpecker in its morning hunt for weevils under the bark of a rotting cypress tree in swampy woods beyond the stockade. Privately, he fully agreed with the opinion that General Grant was one of numerous field officers who had made monumental blunders, especially at Cold Harbor. Mahlon Blanchard, he assured himself, would have avoided such miscues, had he been given his proper rank of Brigadier and a field command instead of being forced to resign his commission over a trivial question of how and when soldiers were paid. And what may have happened to missing rations.

Sergeant McCordle, Blanchard said, you will not be allowed to introduce any parties not in this camp—including, of course, the Union OR Confederate armies—as culpable parties in this case. The conditions in the stockade may be argued as mitigating factors, but not in any manner intended to cast guilt upon the parties outside these confines.

Lucius took a thoughtful step to one side, scratched again at his itchy bearded chin, and continued.

What we shall demonstrate is that much of the alleged criminal behavior on the part of the named defendants was, in fact, a way of defending themselves against a hostile prison population. We shall show by testimony that these six accused men, called 'ringleaders' by the prosecution, were assigned by the prison commandant, Captain Henry Wirz, to a small patch of ground on the slope of the south end of the stockade, beyond the creek and so-called 'sink,' where they quickly became known as 'The Irish Hooligans,' and were subject to attacks by the far more numerous population of Irish-hating....

Objection! shouted Warrick Breck. The Celtic background of these defendants is totally irrelevant to this trial! The argument of self-defense is specious and only confuses the question of whether the defendants did or did not attack, steal, plunder and murder!

Objection sustained, Court President Blanchard said.

Sergeant McCordle, whether or not you can demonstrate that the defendants were slandered on account of their nation of origin, you will NOT present such evidence as a rationale for violent behavior against those who slandered, unless you have evidence that such slander was accompanied by violent physical attack on the accused. The jurymen will disregard Sergeant McCordle's references to the background of the defendants.

Having succeeded in having the question of bias aired—with the help of Sergeant Breck—Lucius withdrew the statement. Then he continued:

We shall establish the fact that on the average, at least 70 men in this camp die every day, from disease, malnutrition, infection, and mistreatment from others not being tried here.

Breck was on his feet again:

Mr. Court President, to move these proceedings along, the prosecution will stipulate that dozens of men in this camp die daily. Further reference to this point is unneeded.

Blanchard: Corporal Daniel, let the transcript show that the prosecution stipulates as stated, that dozens of men in this camp die daily.

Lucius McCordle: The Prosecution may well bring forth witnesses who will claim that certain prisoners died at the hands of the defendants. Gentlemen of the jury panel, this stockade like any prison is rife with rumor. On any given day there are scores of rumors buzzing among these 30,000 hapless souls like a swarm of angry bees. I urge you to be most wary of the danger of hearsay evidence, and to accept only that testimony based on direct, first-hand seeing.

The conditions inside this despicable stockade are partly, although certainly not entirely, a result of the unfortunate tendency of confined soldiers to regress to an animal existence. As well-trained leaders of soldiers in a vast army, all of you Sergeants in the jury panel know the importance of, and difficulty in achieving, habits of sanitation and personal hygiene among soldiers in camp. These men are most vulnerable to the type of sickness and body malaise that results from failure to accomplish body functions away from places of shelter, rest, and eating.

We shall show you that the defendants have in fact aided numerous prisoners who were in ill health when they arrived at Camp Sumter but have survived thanks to the help they received from members of the accused group.

Identify the men who received such aid, you will ask. Yes! We will show you that food, clothing, and shelter materials were given by the accused group to several Colored prisoners

1:30 P.M., SATURDAY, JULY 2, 1864

who were located—by the Camp Sumter guards, not of their own accord—in the south end of the stockade, not far from the shebangs of the accused. We shall offer this aid as evidence, jurymen, that the accused had good intentions. They gave help to perhaps the most vulnerable prisoners in the entire stockade, vulnerable because they were former slaves who had good reason to fear for their very lives when captured.

Lucius paused a moment, raised his voice and spoke slowly, to make what he hoped would be a telling point:

In providing this aid, the accused reached out to help men whose status—as human beings—is at the very heart of the cause that brought us into this horrible war.

Another murmur went through the accused group; a few jurymen shook their heads. Warrick Breck fingered his receding chin thoughtfully then put his hand out to quiet Delano Richman who was about to urge an objection. Breck, knowing the prejudices of at least half the Union soldiers, did not believe this last argument would carry much weight with the jurymen. Better to just let it go, he thought.

Now, Lucius began speaking in a low bass, as if he were sharing, confidentially, an important secret. As he continued, his voice rose to a loud tenor so as to be heard around the entire area.

Finally, jurymen, we will introduce evidence that at least some members of the accused were taking steps to aid the Union cause in this Great War. This evidence will be the finding, within this stockade, of a secret letter from General Robert E. Lee, ordering General Jubal Early to attack Washington City—which may be about to occur within days!

Lucius had not completed this sentence before Warrick Breck was on his feet spluttering objection, while Court

President Blanchard banged his hammer on his bench and shouted Objection Sustained!

With his peripheral vision, Lucius saw three guards, including Lieutenant Granbury, open their mouths in awe and wonder. The Lieutenant turned and headed quickly toward Captain Wirz' headquarters building to the Southwest.

Counsel for both the Prosecution and the Defense will approach the bench! the Court President shouted. When Lucius McCordle and Warrick Breck stood before him, Blanchard was livid.

Goddammit, McCordle, what…the…hell are you doing? You know goddam well that letter is bogus and, even if it isn't, it sure as hell is no secret now. Have you gone out of your dim-witted mind entirely?

Lucius stayed calm.

Sergeant Blanchard, he began, looking at Blanchard directly, as if daring him to once again demand the Court President label. This morning, we wondered how to get the word of this letter to General Grant.

Then, again, he lowered his voice to a hushed level.

Don't you see, all of you? Lieutenant Granbury has already run to Wirz. The guards know about it, and this letter will probably be confiscated. And mark my word, it will be the rumor within hours inside the stockade and among the entire guard unit here. Gentlemen! The rumor mill will turn so rapidly that soldiers in gray all over this part of Georgia will know it within 24 hours.

Lucius was now on fire: This is our best chance! The Confederate Army, and the guard detail here, has any number of men waiting for a chance to desert. And a Reb with information like this has the perfect intelligence to make him valuable to the Yanks!

Court President Blanchard tugged at an earlobe with one hand, and held the other up to restrain Breck. He, too, spoke now in a low voice.

Yeah…I see how your twisted mind works, McCordle. You think you're so all-fired right, but you've got one hell of a problem. If they come to confiscate that letter…probably on their way now…you just might get your neck stretched for having it in the first place. You'll have to tell where you got it, and then they'll go after your boy…what's his name? Nickels, you said?

Lucius shrugged. I may have to say I found it myself. I'll take that chance. Let's see what happens.

Chapter 17.
5:30 p.m., Saturday, July 2, 1864

Captain Henry Wirz was in equal measure dumbfounded, infuriated, and worried.

He doubted Lieutenant Granbury's excited report that a defense attorney—Captain Wirz had already forgotten the name—had a secret letter from General Robert E. Lee, to General Jubal Early. For an attack on Washington, of all things! *Ach scheiße*! It was exactly the kind of preposterous thing that he feared might come out of this trial.

He was beside himself with consternation and rage. He had gone out on a limb with General Winder, advising him strongly to let this trial take place, and the General had cleared it with Richmond. Some of his junior officers—not Granbury, but others—had thought it better to simply round up these Raider thugs and shoot them. Or, more simply, have the soldiers spot the Raiders and pick them off with well-placed shots from the pigeon roosts. Wirz had rejected that kind of summary justice, but not for the inhumanness of it. Rather, it might set off the very kind of riot and attempt at mass breakout that he had feared ever since these *idiotisch* Confederate commanders started sending him thousands of Yankees that his stockade couldn't possibly accommodate. *Pferd-Scheiße!*

Then he had to worry, because if somebody in the stockade did in fact have a secret command letter from General Lee, the consequences could be catastrophic for a division or more of the dwindling Confederate Army. It was enough to put Captain Wirz in a sweat. He had to get his hands on this paper, whatever it was, as soon as possible. If Lieutenant Granbury had heard about this letter, so had all others in and around the North Gate enclosure. *Verdammen!*

He ordered Lieutenant Granbury to send two dozen additional guards to the court martial area, on the double quick, to prevent anyone passing in or out of the stockade, or to or from the court martial shed. Then, once the area was sealed, he, Captain Wirz, would go in and force the man now in possession of that letter to hand it over.

The Court President was still in his heated tirade before the four Sergeant-attorneys when Lieutenant Granbury and a squad of armed guards—aroused with curiosity—suddenly appeared and surrounded the entire group of jurymen, counselors, and accused prisoners.

Lieutenant Granbury was formal but direct: Sergeant Blanchard—I believe that's your name—we are here to confiscate the letter referred to a short time ago by this other Sergeant. He pointed to Lucius.

Captain Wirz appeared, almost breathless, behind Granbury, and his accent was thicker than ever.

Now what is this about a letter from General Lee? The G from Wirz sounded more like a Ch. And his wh was a v.

Court President Blanchard had prepared himself for this eventuality.

Yes, Captain Wirz…sir…the counsel for the defense has happened upon a shredded document—a doubtful object, I may add—that is purported to be a letter originating from the high command of the Army of Northern Virginia.

Blanchard, fully mindful of his previous rank as a Colonel (a rank he would still have, he reminded himself, were it not for this confounded McCordle putting a hateful soldier on the witness stand back in Coulee City) found it difficult yet tactically necessary to treat this Captain and his Germanic accent with such respect. He hoped to get out of Andersonville Prison in one piece, and offending the Captain who had assigned him to such a responsible position would not help achieve that end.

There was, to Blanchard, something odd, almost grotesque about a court martial made up of prison inmates. On the other hand, judicial oddities were nothing new to this legal man with his mixed past. He found it quite possible even to revel in this predicament and the freedom it gave him to rule as he wished, unfettered by the usual codes of jurisprudence.

But right now he had to comply with the Commandant.

So give me this letter, right now! Captain Wirz demanded.

Blanchard simply nodded toward Lucius McCordle who, without hesitation, pulled the two ripped, triangular pieces of paper from amidst the thin pack of notes he was carrying and handed them to the Captain.

Wirz looked at the two pieces and tried to connect them, but looked puzzled. Lucius fit the shreds together on the Court President's bench, and read through the brief letter aloud. As loudly as he could, in fact. With his peripheral vision, he satisfied himself that two Confederate Guards were getting a good earful.

How you came by having this letter? the Captain asked.

Lucius beckoned Harry Nickels, now chained to a 12-pound ball (half the size of the Raider chiefs) in the back of the prisoner group. Harry arose painfully, now somewhat stronger as a result of the double ration he had consumed this morning as an unwilling witness and vaguely accused Raider gang member. Once more, Harry poured out the story of his finding the letter, not recognizing it until he was in the stockade, and its being torn and shared briefly with the accused Raider Sarsfield.

Like Blanchard, Breck and Richman earlier, Captain Wirz did not know what to make of either Harry Nickel's tale or these scraps of paper. He asked Lieutenant Granbury to read through them. Granbury did so, aloud, as Lucius had done earlier. Two guards looked at each other, both now having heard the full contents of this mystery document twice, in clear language.

While Captain Wirz hoped to play down the importance of this letter, his fluster and excitement now had exactly the opposite result. The two guards hearing the readings by Sergeant McCordle and Lieutenant Granbury were thoroughly convinced this was something big—so big the outcome of the war might depend on it.

News about the letter would now sweep the entire compound. These Confederate guards were ready to act on an old principle of rumor, namely, that the urge to gain personal advantage by divulging a state secret is often in direct proportion to the state's need to protect it.

———

Privates Josiah Marsh and Oliver Thomas had enlisted in the Confederate Army for very different reasons. Josh, as Marsh was known, was the slightly deformed son of a leather-maker in Charleston. Customers included farmers along the Carolina coast and—more recently—the Confederate Army's stables of cavalry and caisson horses. Josh was a firm believer of the views of the legendary South Carolina Senator John Calhoun, repeated often by his father: Slavery was a sacred institution and the underpinning of the South's great traditions and gentlemanly manners.

5:30 p.m., Saturday, July 2, 1864

Josh remembered April, 1861, when as a 17-year-old he heard Confederate guns firing on the Yankee's Fort Sumter in Charleston Harbor. General P.G.T. Beauregard, who ordered the cannonading, became an instant hero to Josh and his friends.

A Confederate doctor rejected Josh as a cripple when he first tried to enlist. However, as the Army became unable to replace its losses to disease, Union assaults, and desertions, men like Josh were taken in and given noncombat roles. He became a guard of prisoners, first on trains and later at Andersonville.

The healthier Oliver Thomas was born in Ohio, but when he was 10 his father left his wife, took his son to Birmingham and landed a comfortable job in the Postal Service. Young Ollie, as his mother called him, returned every summer to her place in Columbus. When he was 18, he was smitten by a young woman who worked alongside his mother in an Ohio garment factory. The relationship led to the woman's pregnancy, a daughter, and a promise from Ollie for support. Then a letter from Ollie's father brought him back to Birmingham for a modest city government job. There, he married a young woman who knew nothing of his background, or child, in Ohio.

He joined the Confederate army at his father's insistence, took a bullet in his left arm at Fredericksburg, and after partial recovery was sent to Andersonville as a prison guard. Bad news came quickly. His father died from a broken neck when his horse tripped and fell. Next, Ollie heard rumors about his young wife's carrying on with other Soldiers in Gray in Birmingham. He decided to desert and go back to Ohio. He would rejoin his girl friend and their daughter, both of whom were now living with his mother. This, he decided, was where his home should be and the Union

Army was where he really belonged. His mother would be pleased. He knew of other soldiers who had changed sides, and considered the switch entirely proper, if not noble.

But also dangerous; one slip and he would be a goner.

Shortly after arriving at Andersonville, he requested a transfer to an infantry brigade at Petersburg, in Virginia where the bulk of both Lee's and Grant's armies now faced each other. His stated reason was true to the Confederate cause: His wound had healed and he wanted to get back to the battlefield to join his brothers in arms. Privately, his plan was simple: Get sent to Petersburg, desert to Federal troops, and get assigned to an Ohio regiment. At some point, he would no doubt go on furlough to visit his girl, their child, and his mother. And, finally, marry the young woman.

Ollie like other guards dealt on the sly with the tough Raider gang, trading them fresh vegetables and coffee for precious Union greenbacks and other stolen items like watches and jewelry. John Sarsfield was his favorite prisoner; they even talked in muffled tones about how the two might escape together. Sarsfield told him a few days ago—just before the roundup—about the letter that Captain Wirz had just now confiscated. Sarsfield didn't show Ollie the letter, but Ollie nevertheless agreed to help Sarsfield escape when he deserted, in return for getting the letter to take to the Union side. It wasn't a good bargain because getting caught would mean a quick court martial and a firing squad. Or the noose, he wasn't sure which.

Now, though, things were coming together for Oliver Thomas in a way he could hardly believe. His orders for transfer had been given to him yesterday, and he was to get on the train for Virginia tomorrow morning.

Furthermore, with the infamous letter now in Captain Wirz' hands, Ollie could forget about any promises he made to Sarsfield. He was on his own, with valuable knowledge and no need to sneak out. Today was the 2nd of July; he would leave on the train tomorrow the 3rd, and by the 5th he might be near enough to Union lines to cross over with his hands high. His *knowledge* of the secret orders, he reasoned, would be of value enough to the Union side.

On this, his last night at Camp Sumter, he relaxed with his friend Josh Marsh, who sat on the next cot with his stiff leg stretched out. Josh wished his comrade well in his next assignment:

That's real bravery on your part, Ollie. I mean, this is a stink hole and all, but asking to go to Petersburg? Friend, you've been in battle and got shot once. You want to go back to real fighting, do you?

Well, you know, Ollie answered with rather smug confidence, in a way there's fighting here. You've seen those brawls in the stockade. Men die here, lots of them.

Shure—lots of boys die in this place. But it ain't the same, Ollie. You get in that battle at Petersburg, and your first job is to shoot some Yankee right in the face. Can you do that? Did you really shoot anyone up at Fredericksburg?

Can't see it as no big thing…hell, Josh, I shot a man here. Dead. One shot.

You did? What? Someone try to jump you, to get your gun?

Nope. A Yankee who leaned over the deadline. They've been warned we'd shoot them on sight if they did that, so I did what I was told. Wasn't nothing to it.

This was a lie, intended to lay to rest any suspicions Josh might have about Ollie's being a deserter. If Ollie was known for killing a Union prisoner, it would be unthinkable for him to desert to the Union army

Holy Goobers—you really did that? I've shot that way once or twice, but only to scare someone. I mean, everyone talks of that, but I din't think we really killed anyone that way...

Boy, this gets me a-thinkin, Ollie...if you shot a Yankee prisoner...you wouldn't want to walk inside that stockade alone, would you?

Well...in fact, I go in a lot.

What Ollie kept to himself was that when he was in the stockade, he was never far from the South Gate and the better-than-average huts of the Raider Gang. But now that Josh mentioned it, Ollie Thomas decided he wouldn't want his future Union captors to know about his Andersonville stockade service, especially the idea of his shooting a prisoner. He would simply tell them that he had served all the while in, say, the garrison at Petersburg. And hope the truth never surfaced.

But if he did that, how could he make them believe he knew about the secret letter from Lee to Early? Oh, Lordy! He would have to concoct a different story about where that letter was found. Well, he would think of something and, anyway, whatever he thought up would be no more unbelievable than the truth.

And, maybe, the truth would be the best after all. Yes, that's it! He would say that he WAS a guard at Andersonville, and the gross inhumanity of the place—including orders to shoot prisoners who touched the deadline—was so revolting that he simply had to escape before they court-martialed him for refusing orders. That, plus the accurate story of family in Ohio, should make him entirely credible. So be it! He couldn't wait for tomorrow, to get on the train.

Chapter 18.
6 a.m., Sunday, July 3, 1864

Private Oliver Thomas and a handful of other Confederate soldiers quick-stepped from the stockade barracks to the Andersonville depot. He watched slaves unload food supplies, meager as they were, for the stockade and garrison. The same boxcar a week ago carted a load of cattle and pigs to Johnston's army defending Atlanta.

Another such car disgorged 40 Federal soldiers, all captured in recent days from Sherman's forces bearing down on Johnston. Ollie and others in Gray boarded this same car which, after taking on water and wood fuel, headed for Macon.

On this 40-mile run, soldiers grumbled about the grim outlook for the Confederate cause, especially near Atlanta.

Hell of a big battle up thayer at Kenesaw Mountain. Man, I heard them Yankees took a licking, way they always does.

Mebbe so, but Johnston keeps movin' back, case you ain't heard.

Think they can hold the Mountain?

Bet y'all they does!

Listen, you two. Sherman's getting closer and closer to Atlanta. Them Yankees has three men to our one. And if they can't grow enough in Boston and Penns'vania, they ship in more from Ireland.

Think they'll take Atlanta?

Silence.

Ollie Thomas made some calculations. His orders were for Petersburg, but that was probably a two-day trip up through the Carolinas, The rickety rail system required repeated transfers, some on different gauge rails. By that time his valuable knowledge about a secret assault on Washington would certainly be old news. Maybe it was already. So why not go straight to Atlanta, join the Confederate forces there, and then desert to Sherman's army, maybe tomorrow? Surely, Sherman would be in telegraph contact with Grant, and Ollie would be rewarded for that critical intelligence.

Macon depot roiled in massive confusion. Cars loaded with critical supplies sat on the sidings. Bags of flour, coffee and beans, crates of uniforms and shoes, and a few boxes of munitions filled these cars, which wouldn't move until a working locomotive engine could be found to pull them. Soldiers and civilians milled around the platform, their faces lined and mouths pinched tight with raw anxiety. The entire mood was about battle, death, and—for civilians—chances for escape to Savannah or the Carolinas.

A depot agent shouted in his practiced monotone that the next train was about to leave for Atlanta. The train would haul as much food, ordinance and soldiers as it could pull.

Ollie approached a Major and showed him his orders, a hand-written scrawl signed by one of General Winder's staff officers, sending him to the Army of Northern Virginia.

Sir, Ollie said, I reckon I could do more good joining General Johnston up on the Chattahoochee, and help keep those damn Yankees from getting into Atlanta.

The Major looked at Ollie as if he'd lost his mind, then squinted at the orders, shrugged, and scribbled a change to Johnston's division.

Yep, they can use you up there, Soldier, the Major said gruffly. Climb into that car, there, he said, pointing to one carrying hay for cavalry horses. There'll be a couple others with you, just out of the hospital and ready to go back to their units.

When the train squealed into Atlanta, smoke from the fighting at Kenesaw Mountain to the northwest hung gloomily in the air. Pandemonium reigned, making Macon of a few hours ago seem calm by comparison.

Merchantmen trying to empty their stores futilely shoved their goods into broken wagons. Their horses and mules had already been commandeered by Johnston's army. Long lines of women, children and aged men, a few with rickety buggies pulled by mules too lame for the army, others with two-wheel hand-drawn carts and still others simply carrying or dragging bags, streamed toward the southeast. Some had escaped Marietta just ahead of Sherman's marauding troops, filing in a piteous column through the middle of Atlanta and deepening the despair overtaking the entire city.

An armed marshal with the conscript guard yelled at Ollie to show his papers. Ollie pulled out his wrinkled and amended orders. The marshal grunted and ushered him to a gathering point where three captured deserters were watched by another armed man in civilian dress, but wearing a huge badge on his chest.

Ah, another that tried to skedaddle?

Nah, this boy ain't no skulker. He has papers, changed for Johnston's army, up from down Macon way.

The home guard man was marginally literate and couldn't understand the sheet Ollie carried. He grinned humorlessly through yellow, broken teeth. The fact that Ollie had his pack and shelter half strapped to his back didn't impress the marshal. Skulkers often kept their uniforms and military gear, just to bluff people. But since the marshal thought this one was okay, the home guard man motioned Ollie to stay with the others.

This ragtag group of four soldiers then marched northwest, under close watch by the same broken-toothed home guardsman and his ancient flintlock musket. As they neared the smoke and booming cannons, they met a stream of ambulance wagons and wounded soldiers in their painful trek toward Atlanta. Many had crude crutches and bandages around heads, limbs or torsos.

Ollie yelled at three heavily swathed men on a donkey cart:

What y'all hear from up at Marietta?

One man offered a doleful reply:

Ever' division is falling back. Big fight at Smyrna today. Johnston's goin' to make a stand at Nickajack Creek.

By afternoon, they reached a Confederate encampment southeast of the Nickajack. It was a brigade in reserve today but, ragtag as it was, poised for tomorrow's battle. A war-weary Sergeant looked at Ollie's once-changed orders and hesitated.

Surrounding the Sergeant and Ollie, a group of veteran, grizzled riflemen, bone weary from earlier fighting and rearward marching, watched this new arrival with tired disdain.

Whose Corps y'all from, boy? the Sergeant asked Ollie.

Ollie told him the truth—up to a point.

Guard duty at Camp Sumter, waiting for my wound to heal.

Oh, yeah? So they thought y'all were fixed and shipped y'all up here?

Thinking quickly—but without noticing that the Sergeant was talking in a pronounced hills dialect—Ollie answered:

Yep. That's about it. They said General Johnston needed good men, so here I am.

He immediately regretted the obvious arrogance of this fib.

6 A.M., Sunday, July 3, 1864

The Sergeant scowled. He sat on the bullet box for a long moment, his stare fixed on Ollie, before he responded in his hills drawl, now deliberately exaggerated.

M'boy, y'all got me to noticin' here that y'all's a' talkin' pow'full Dixie, but y'all ain't exactly whistling it. What I mean is, y'all's a talkin' Yankee talk, way it sounds to me. Just where'd y'all grow up, anyhow?

Ollie wagged his head quickly, as if to shake off the red color crawling up from his neck. He had to think fast: How much to admit, without too much?

Yeah, everyone at Camp Sumter said the same thing, he said. See, I was born a little north of the Kentucky border, but Pa and the family hated Yankee country.

So after I did the 7th grade, he moved us to Birmingham. Many people say I never quite got over that Northern way of a'talkin'.

Those last words aren't my way of a talkin' at all, Ollie thought.

The Sergeant relaxed his scowl, and chewed the inside of his mouth. He looked down and away, then up again. Should he send this one to the Captain, or maybe a Lieutenant, for some grilling? But no, the Captain was with the regiment officers, talking about tomorrow's battle formation. This was no time to bother him about a doubtful transfer with a Yankee twang who sounded a little too eager.

Okay, soldier, we'll put y'all to the test in the morning. Now, get out to the earthworks and use your diggin' muscles. After that, find the quartermaster and git your weapon and gear. Then we'll send you out with the pickets at sunup.

That way, the Sergeant figured, the other pickets will watch him, too, as well as the Yankees down below the mountain.

Chapter 19.
9 a.m., Sunday, July 3, 1864

Nearly a hundred stockade prisoners lined up near the North Gate early in the morning, hoping for a chance to testify against the Raiders. Sergeant Leroy Key questioned each one briefly, deciding which ones would be most believable. Within a half hour, he sent some three dozen in to the trial.

Sergeant Breck, the prosecuting attorney, lined them up in the order he would call them, but kept them in the enclosure, where they would not be privy to the Court Martial proceedings outside.

The first witness was a slightly built, thin-faced fellow, barely 18. His freckled skin showed red from too much exposure to the punishing summer sun. He walked with a limp to the witness chair, a dilapidated crate, in a shuffle that drew attention to his odd black pants that clearly came from no army quartermaster. His tattered shirt lacked a sleeve on the left side, leaving his left arm uncovered and showing the same dangerous sunburn as his face and neck. He tried to straighten his badly fitting and torn Hardee hat. No one suggested he remove it.

Corporal Gilbert Daniel, the man assigned to transcribe the trial, administered the witness' oath.

Sergeant Breck began:

Soldier, state your name, rank and unit to the jurymen.

Private Simon Welch, Indiana Infantry.

Breck: Private Welch, do you recognize any of the accused men here?

Welch: Yup. At least four of them.

Breck: Can you point them out and name them?

Welch: Yup, I can...that's Captain Mosby there, and Cary Sullivan...and Sarsfeel...and that one, I think his name is Andy Munn. And...oh yes, Rickson there.

Breck: Before these men were captured, do you remember seeing any of them steal, or rob, or kill?

Lucius McCordle rose immediately. Objection. That question is leading the witness.

As if he expected that objection, Court President Blanchard rapped his table with his hammer before McCordle had spoken the last word.

Objection overruled, he intoned evenly. We're here to find out what witnesses saw or heard, and we have limited time. The witness will answer the question.

Lucius sat down, resigned. *Not surprising. Blanchard is punishing me as much as hurrying things along. Well, that quickly sets the tone for how a trial with a pre-determined outcome will proceed.*

Welch: Did I see any stealing or killing? Oh, they do it all the time. Why, just last week, Mosby...or was it that other big guy, Rickson...and about twenty others came by at night and knocked over my shanty and took one of my blankets, and...

Breck: Did they hurt you or anyone else?

Welch: Yup. They killed a boy over on the next row. They had clubs, and shovels, and yelled and laughed like they were having a big party, and...

Breck: Did you know that boy they killed?

Welch: Well, yup...name was Dexter Temple, from Vermont, I think...nice fellow. Helped me find wood to cook with once.

Breck: Did you try to stop these Raiders from stealing and killing?

Welch: I yelled at them to stop, and my partner Johnny Shepson, he tripped one of them and you shoulda seen that big ruffian fall on his face! But no, I din't do too much cuz everyone knows you can get kilt trying to fend them off if you do it too hard. I ain't as big as most of them Raiders.

Breck: Your witness, Sergeant McCordle.

Lucius McCordle stood up slowly and walked toward Private Welch.

McCordle: Private Welch, you said the Raiders came by one night. Do you remember about what time of night that might have been? Say, before midnight, maybe, or early in the morning?

Welch: I ain't got no watch or clock with big hands Sergeant, but I can tell you it was after dark, dark like a stack of black cats and…

McCordle: So can you tell me exactly which of these men (points to the Raider chieftains) took your blanket?

Welch: 'Course not, I mean not exactly which one. They came in a big bunch, way they do ever time. But I knew they took my blanket 'cause it was gone after that and I cou'nt never find it again.

McCordle: So how did you know this big bunch, as you call it, was these accused men, here?

Welch: Why, next day, Johnny Shepson, he told me it was Mosby and his Raiders. He knew them well.

McCordle: So….you are saying that you don't recall, specifically, any of these men here?

Welch: No one specific, 'f that's what you mean, I seen a whole bunch of them and I knew it was them. Ever'body did.

McCordle: You said these men (pointing again to the accused prisoners) killed a boy, I think you called Dexter…in the next row, you said.

Welch: Yup. Dexter Temple, nice guy.

McCordle: So you saw one of these accused men kill this prisoner named Dexter?

Breck: Objection! The witness has already said he doesn't recall specific persons! This is browbeating!

McCordle: Mr. Court President, what we want the jurymen to appreciate is that charges as serious as murder require positive identification of the accused, and I'm simply trying to establish, for certain, whether this witness is able to do that!

Blanchard (tapping his hammer): The jurymen are intelligent fellows who can tell what this witness can establish and what he can't. Let's quit inching along like hands on rusty watches. Sergeant McCordle, you have any further questions for this witness?

McCordle: No more questions.

Breck: Wait a minute, Private Welch. I have one more direct question. Can you name anyone who might be able to more specifically name who did the killing?

McCordle: Objection! This is simply asking for speculation to add to guesswork! If the prosecution has more witnesses, let them come in and be questioned, one at a time!

Mahlon Blanchard tapped his hammer again and motioned the two contesting attorneys, Lucius McCordle and Warrick Breck, to come to his bench. His heavy face scowled with irritation.

Listen, you two, Blanchard growled. Where the hell do you think you are? Arguing a case before the goddam Supreme Court? Now look. We're trying these men on multiple charges of thievery, mayhem and murder—and we don't have the time or patience to act as if this is a marble-walled castle in London, before a bunch of judges with powdered wigs over their goddammed heads.

9 A.M., SUNDAY, JULY 3, 1864

We're going to move this trial along. There are maybe 20,000 men in that damnable stockade who will tear our guts out if 10 days go by and we've only heard 10 witnesses.

Sergeant Breck, bring in your next witness and get to the point as goddam quick as you can. If you're going to prove murder, you'll need a helluva lot better witness than this joker you just had on the stand. And McCordle and Simmons keep your questions short and quit screeching away like you've got a crooked pin under your bung hole. You two got that straight?

Breck asked for a five minute recess, which the Court President granted with a grunt.

The chained prisoners in the center of the court area stirred, some standing and some sprawled uncomfortably on the ground. Willie Collins wound his nervous fingers around sprigs of grass and tore them up by the roots. The sweat lines under his armpits had spread noticeably during the past hour.

Breck's next witness was a taller man with a coarse frame, his sagging shirt telling of a once-heavier body that had thinned noticeably during his weeks in the stockade. He spoke his name, Corporal Edward Jussen, Michigan artillery, clearly and confidently.

Breck skipped the preliminaries:

Corporal Jussen, before today, and before the roundup, what was the last time you saw one or more of the men in the prisoner group here?

Jussen: About a week since. Late one night. I heard them singin' down there. Then the singing stopped. That's when you look out, they're prob'ly on the prowl. So I nudged my tent mate...

Breck: And who is your tent mate?

Jussen: Fulton Martin, another Michigan boy.

Breck: Okay, you nudged Private Martin and...

Jussen: He's a Corporal, like me.

Breck: Right. Then what?

Jussen: I heared these voices, I know 'em. It's Rickson and two or three of his gang.

Breck: And how did you know it was Rickson?

Jussen: I know his voice. I heard him say, clear as a bell, here's these Michigan boys...Let's clean 'em out,' somethin' like that...

Breck: And then?

Jussen: I said, loud as I could, Not one step farther this way, Rickson. And he says, Kiss my arse, sojer; you ain't got nothin' we need anyhow.' And so they went by us.

Breck: What did they do then?

Jussen: They went past and jumped a shebang just a few feet from us. Some Massachusetts boys, I think. Those boys yelled, I heard clubbing and one boy screams and swears and says he's been hit, and another says they took his potatoes and his watch. And then I hear fighting and men start running ever' which way.

Breck: Did you take any action at that time?

Jussen: Damn right I did. I said to my chum Martin, I says, let's go and we went and jumped the backs of two of those Raiders and knocked one of 'em asprawling on the ground. Then something hit me on the head and I saw stars and fell to my knees.

Breck: You were hit on the head. Do you have a scar or bruise or something there?

Jussen: Sure do. Here.

Jussen removed his cap, leaned forward and showed a heavy lump, still matted with blood, under the hair above his left ear.

Breck: Now you said earlier you recognized Rickson when the group came by. Do you know for sure he was in the fight at the other shebang?

Jussen: No doubt about it. I knew his voice, and he's big, and I knew it was him swearing at me. Fact is, it was his back I jumped on in the fight. If it weren't him that hit me, must have been one of his gang.

Breck: Then what happened?

Jussen: Then I hears Rickson say, Let's go, boys! And the bunch of them grabbed up the stuff and run off back toward the South slope.

Breck: Did you then talk to the Massachusetts boys who had just been attacked?

Jussen: Much as I could. One of them had a bashed-in head and his hand was cut off, clean, like you'd shave the end off a turnip with a case knife. Blood was pouring out like it was a tube. Other boys crowded and someone took a rag and wound it round the boy's wrist stump. Next morning they took him to the hospital, and he died that night. Bled to death.

At this moment, Charles Curtis struggled to his feet, pointed his finger at Jussen and yelled, Goddammit, now I know the night you mean, and that weren't me! Some call me Rickson, but by God, that's Sullivan he's talking about, not me! I wasn't even north of the sink that night! I heard all about that Boston boy getting his head bashed in and his hand cut! Prob'ly was Mosby!

Warrick Breck turned slowly toward the shouting, gesticulating Curtis, then back toward Blanchard and said:

Will the Court President please have the guards remove that man from the area? I'm questioning Private Jussen, not him. If Sergeant McCordle wants to swear him as a witness, then…

Blanchard tapped his hammer slowly, until Curtis quieted. A brief lull fell over the court area. Blanchard folded his hands thoughtfully, then unfolded them and scratched his whiskered chin.

You know, I'm going to make an unusual ruling here. We aren't going to get anywhere if we try to follow all the niceties of a court martial in Washington City. We have more than… what? More than a dozen accused of all sorts of mischief that we haven't specified for each one? And six accused of murder and various other acts that would be criminal anywhere.

So I'm going to allow any one of the accused to object when his name is mentioned. But he can't just stand up and yell. He's got to hold his hand up and wait for me to recognize him. Then he states his name and, in simple words, why he objects. And it has to be short. If you just start yelling without being recognized by me, I'll have you taken out of here.

Warrick Breck dropped his shoulders and hands and exhaled, shrinking like a wind bag that suddenly lost its air. Mr. Court President, he said I would like to ask for another recess.

Fine. Five minutes, Blanchard answered briskly. You lawyers step over here.

Lucius McCordle, Jed Simmons, Warrick Breck and Delano Richman had hardly reached Mahlon Blanchard's bench, when the Court President launched another tirade.

There must be a hundred Union soldiers who want to testify, he thundered, maybe a THOUSAND, if they weren't so goddammed scared they'd get their throats cut afterwards. But we won't get a dozen to testify, the way you farts are diddling away, playing trial lawyers! Shit, who are you trying to show off for? This won't get you any business back home!

Now listen, and get this through your thick skulls. Captain Wirz and General Winder want to put this Raider business to an end with a short and sweet trial, and I'm going to goddammed well see that's what we do. So: We're going to let these witnesses come in and sit here in threes. They'll talk one at a time, and they'll hear what each other says and that's just fine.

That will be less work for you two, and that ought to be dandy. I'm running this trial, and that's how it's going to be! So…back to business. Let the court come to order!

Corporal Jussen came back to the box and Sergeant Breck said, immediately, Your witness, Sergeant McCordle.

Jed Simmons handled this cross-examination, starting with:

Corporal Jussen, how long have you been in this stockade?

Jussen: Since the first week of March, got captured near Richmond. I'm a horseman, one of the best in Kilpatrick's cavalry. If old Jud had been smarter and less a braggart, we wouldn't have got cut off and surrounded…

Simmons: So they brought you to this prison and you got here, when, exactly?

Jussen: March 20th. They first sent me and a hundred others to Belle Isle at Richmond and then shipped us down here…

Simmons: And where did you set up your Shebang?

Jussen: North side of the sink, near the Sutler shack.

Simmons: I see. Now you said you recognized a Raider, I think you called him, named Rickson? Is that right?

Jussen: Yeah, that's right.

Simmons: Now would you point him out, please, even if you have to walk over to him.

Jussen: (Rising and pointing directly toward the diminutive John Sullivan). That's him. Goes by Rickson.

Sullivan protested: Rickson ain't my name! That's him, there!

He pointed toward Curtis, a much larger and more muscular man.

At this point, Warrick Breck thought Simmons was simply trying to show the witness so confused he couldn't accurately identify any single raider. But that was not Simmons' strategy.

Simmons: Now, Corporal Jussen, do you still insist that the man you pointed to calls himself Rickson?

Jussen: Damn right. He introduced himself....he said sure enough that was his name.

Simmons: You started to say he introduced himself to you?

Jussen: Well, yeah...I mean first time I saw him he said that was his name...and he never said no differ'nt after that.

Simmons: (Repeats) He never said no differ'nt after that you say?

Jussen: Yah.

Simmons: So you had talks with him?

Jussen: (Starting to see where the questioning is going) Well...a few.

Simmons: About how many is a few?

Jussen: Oh, maybe three or four...maybe a half dozen times.

Simmons: And what did you talk about?

Jussen now looked flustered, and Simmons continued the questioning, to the point where Jussen said:

See, this Rickson...or Sullivan or Cary, or whatever he's called...after we had all those talks, he wanted me to work with him, the way he put it.

Breck: Objection! This is an attempt to discredit Corporal Jussen as a witness, simply because he had conversations with a man who is now accused of murder.

Court President Blanchard (impatiently): All right, Sergeant Simmons, where are you trying to go with this, before I shut you up for wasting time.

Jed Simmons showed no sign of being intimidated by the former Colonel-turned-Sergeant-turned-Court President.

Sergeant Blanchard, Jed said, I ask you as Court President to allow me to continue showing there was simply a falling out between the witness and defendant Sullivan, who the witness thought was named Rickson.

Court President Blanchard heaved a sigh, paused and said bluntly:

Objection sustained! I don't want these jurymen to give a damn whether witnesses did or did not have a falling out with one or more of the defendants! Lots of talk goes on in a stockade! Move to a different line of questions, or excuse this witness!

Jed Simmons stared directly at Blanchard for a moment, then shrugged and said, No more questions.

Lucius and Jed looked at each other without expression. Discrediting witnesses with evidence pointing to attempted retaliation wasn't going to work here.

―――

Ruling out one line of questioning still did not satisfy the Court President. He called a recess. He watched Breck and Richman leave, in the direction of the latrine, with Simmons following them, and Lucius McCordle now alone. The Court President then walked over to Lucius and abruptly said:

McCordle, I'm giving you an ultimatum.

McCordle: Wha.a...You can't talk to me without Breck and Simmons here...

Blanchard: Oh, don't give me a spasm with your nasty look, you Copperhead skunk. Yes, that's what you are, and don't argue with me. Maybe you think I don't sound like a judge? Not right now I don't, and I'll tell you why.

McCordle, this trial is going to have one outcome and one outcome only. At least six men are going to hang, and you're going to quit acting as if you can get one or more of them acquitted, or somehow saved from the noose.

Don't you have any blithering sense at all? Wirz and Winder are doing everyone a big favor in this stockade by setting up this court martial, and they know these six need to have their necks stretched and by god I'm going to help them do it. So forget trying to save them, you damned Copperhead!

Lucius blanched, then steeled and fired back:

Blanchard, you are so goddammed far out of line...

Blanchard held up his hand.

Forget the tough talk, he said, and I'll tell you something useful. This war is going to end some day and even if it doesn't, Wirz and Winder will make sure people like me... and you, if you have any brains at all...will get paroled out of here and sent somewhere else, maybe Savannah. That's to save OUR necks, don't you see? I'll end up back in Missouri and have either another judgeship or a very good law practice, and I can even do you some good...if you play it smart.

Now maybe you think you can send in a complaint on me? To whom? And on what grounds? This trial is not according to Federal Army regulations, never was, never will be. And don't think for a minute you can some day go back to a transcript.

Here, Blanchard pushed his heavy face up close to Lucius and growled: Because there won't BE any transcript! Wirz and I will see to that, as soon as Winder decides to go ahead with the hanging.

Lucius now lost his composure, and good sense as well, saying:

Blanchard…you horse's hind end…it will be my word against yours, if ever both of us get back to the Union army and by god…

Blanchard didn't give an inch.

And by god, what? Go ahead, threaten me. I'll give you a warning that will trump any threat your lame brain can think up. This Corporal Nickels, he's a friend of yours, isn't he? Goes back to your boyhood in Coulee City, doesn't he? Well, he's in limbo right now, but how would you like it if I declare him a defendant? I can do that, you know. And with the right directions to the jurymen, he just might end up on whatever gallows they construct inside the prison.

They're so bloodthirsty now, with the Raiders in shackles here, they'll salivate over the chance to choke the life out of the defense attorney's best friend!

Blanchard breathed heavily:

What say you to that?

Lucius answered, I…can't believe even you would…

Wouldn't what? Blanchard answered. That I wouldn't think of getting you all bollixed up? Shit, man, all you have to do is back off this heavy defense stuff. Your pal Simmons, I notice, wouldn't mind that a bit, would he? If I've got the right sense of him, and I'm sure I have, he figured from the start your defense was a lost cause.

So think of it this way; I want justice to happen, and I've just had a litle chat with you to help you see reason.

With that, Court President and one-time Judge Mahlon Blanchard turned and walked off. If anybody else in the area heard what was said between these two men, they showed no sign of acknowledging it.

Lucius was staggered by what he had just heard. *Yes, I've heard lots of stories about crooked judges, but I can hardly believe this one even after getting it straight from the horse's mouth. Except...I'm talking about the wrong end of the horse.*

So what now?

Chapter 20.
2 p.m., July 3, 1864

Delano Richman and Warrick Breck were quite aware of the heated talk between McCordle and Blanchard, but couldn't hear the words.

The Court President had no intention of telling them about it. He was confident they would be happy to move the trial along toward the outcome everyone expected.

In fact, Richman and Breck had enough sense of professionalism to wonder about the effectiveness of their various maneuvers, small and large, just as they would have in courts back home. At the moment, they wondered whether objecting to Simmons' questioning of Corporal Jussen had been a mistake.

Richman said to Breck:

Maybe we should have let Simmons get that testimony about conversations between a witness and the Raiders.

Then we could have gone back on direct examination, and asked what they talked about. Did Rickson or Sullivan mention planning a raid? That way we could show *intent*, in a way we haven't done so far. The way things are going, McCordle and Simmons can argue that all the injuries were simply from fights. And fights are going on all the time, often over trivial things.

Warrick Breck took this idea a step further:

Say, here's a way to show intent, he said. Let's get some man who damn well DID spend time with the Raiders… like this Nickels, sitting with the Raiders. He's a friend of McCordle and told us about being with Sarsfield—about that letter, I mean—even though he wasn't here but a few days before the roundup. Should we make him a witness? And get him to say he heard bragging about what they'd done, and what they intend to do next?

Richman peered at the hapless little crowd of men trudging under guard to the Confederate latrine. Each accused man was trying to carry a heavy steel ball, and for those who had to bend down to carry it, the walk was grueling.

Harry Nickels was the rearmost man in this sorry column. His chain was long enough to allow carrying the steel ball without stooping over. But it was still hard work. He had only one good arm, the left one totally useless.

Richman wasn't sure about Harry Nickels:

Well...first of all, is he a defendant here, or not? Remember, he was let back into the stockade the day of the roundup. Ran the gauntlet, didn't he?

He doesn't know whether he's fish or foul right now, if he's thinking at all. Looks sick enough to croak any day. Even so, he might well turn on Sarsfield to save his own neck. But would he say he and Sarsfield, and maybe others, talked about plans to rob or steal? Or even to kill? We don't know that.

Breck: Maybe we can get him aside and find out.

Richman: Not easy. You're not going to get him separated from that bunch now, and Blanchard probably wouldn't allow it anyhow.

Breck: Well, my good companion lawyer, we can simply call Nickels to testify. He's a hostile witness, you might say, but why not give it a try? The way I see it, McCordle isn't very likely to object. And, I've a feeling Blanchard wouldn't listen to his objection anyway.

Richman: Hmm. Well, then, what about Blanchard's rule that witnesses now testify in threes?

Breck: Fine. We'll make Nickels the third one, as soon as we get back in session.

Chapter 21.
4 A.M., Monday, July 4, 1864

Private Oliver Thomas tried not to look enthusiastic about being thrown into battle so quickly. This was no longer unusual, even for fresh transfers, in the chaos before Sherman's advancing army. Groups of Confederate volunteers from the countryside around Marietta and Atlanta, including aging men and youths from the fields, trickled into General Joseph Johnston's army. Some came voluntarily, some reluctantly after being caught and brought in at gunpoint by the Home Guard. Many had, or were issued, squirrel rifles and old smooth-bore muskets, all in a desperate attempt to keep the hated Sherman and his marauding Yankee forces from overwhelming Atlanta.

Yesterday, Johnston had abandoned Marietta. He fell back to the Chattahoochee River, trying to protect the vital railroad that Atlanta depended upon for food from the scattered farmlands of the South. But Johnston was unable to hold wherever he dug in; after each brief defensive exchange, with few exceptions, he would move back one more time.

Private Oliver Thomas faced the day with only two or three hours of sleep and an almost empty stomach. On the two train rides the previous day, his food amounted to one slim piece of bacon, a small potato, and a handful of beans when he reached the encampment. After that, he and hundreds of others took to shovels and built earthworks, for his new company's defensive position.

It was midnight before he found a place to bed down, with only his half dog-tent piece for shelter. Shortly after the early bugle call this morning, he found the quartermaster wagon, where a lethargic corporal reached into a pile of dirty infantry rifles, some taken from captured Yankees and some from dead and wounded Confederates. The corporal handed Ollie a gun and a cartridge pack.

It was daylight before he would see the weapon, a dirty and battered but usable English-made Enfield rifle, common on both sides of the war. It was superior to the smooth-bore muskets Ollie knew from Camp Sumter and his fighting at Fredericksburg.

When the bugler sounded the fall-in call, Ollie had hardly looked at the weapon, let alone become familiar with it. As his column trudged toward the line of earthworks, he tried to remember the loading procedure: *bite the end off a paper cartridge, pour the powder down the barrel, insert the cartridge and paper, carefully but quickly pull out the ramrod, jam ball and paper down the barrel, replace the rod, half-cock, insert the percussion cap...cock, aim and fire.* A good rifleman could go through this entire procedure three times a minute, even in battle. Ollie would be lucky to do it once in that time.

A battle shaped up around Nickajack Creek, Ruff's Mill and Concord Road, where Ollie would find himself today. His only instructions were ten minutes of shouting to him and the other new men by the same Sergeant who had grilled him the previous afternoon. The once-vaunted discipline of the Army of the Confederacy was crumbling among the demoralized aggregation of soldiers in gray and butternut.

Fix bayonets, a Lieutenant screamed.

Holy Jesus, how do you reload in a hurry without slicing your hand on that bayonet?

Ollie then learned how battle can juice one up to where sheer energy almost overcomes fear—even when one's excitement comes from seeing the chance to cross over to the other side.

His company fell back from Nickajack Creek as long lines of Union infantry appeared on the northwest side and

4 A.M., MONDAY, JULY 4, 1864

explosions from Union artillery fell closer and closer. His heart pounded, as the Lieutenant shouted:

Skirmishers! Check your loads and take to the line!

Ollie sweated and went through the loading sequence quickly. *Good. Did it in about half a minute, even with that bayonet attached, and nobody wondered if I was slow.*

Three hundred yards in front, a thick blue line of soldiers advanced at double-quick.

Fire at will!

Ollie aimed slightly over the Union line and fired. He reloaded and fired again, still high…and again, and again. He was shooting in harmless rhythm. Smoke poured from both the Union and Confederate lines as rifles cracked and cannons quieted. A soldier 10 feet to his right slumped and fell, his rifle clattering to the ground.

Fall back!

Ollie welcomed the order to retreat…not that he intended to. Smoke now rolled heavily over the line. Other soldiers yelled, some screamed and, dimly through the rolling smoke, Ollie saw two more fall, including a youth on his immediate left. All others were now back of the line of earthworks. Ollie let out a convincing scream of his own and slumped over his rifle on the earth pile before him—low enough not to be hit by fire from the advancing blue line.

Ollie couldn't have been happier; the first Union battle flag he saw after his willing capture was the 81st Ohio Infantry. When he told his capturing soldiers he had important intelligence, they sent him to a regimental staff officer, a Major who listened patiently to Ollie's story about a June 13 letter from Lee to Early.

The Major was unimpressed:

Huh. That was a month ago. Early went up to the valley. The papers are full of it. Know anything important? Any new units joining Johnston?

Ollie had nothing more to tell except the confusion of yesterday at the two railroad depots: He knew of no big troop movements at either place, and the Major noted this on his pad. Ollie added that his mother and wife (this much was not quite the truth) and daughter (this was true) lived in Columbus Ohio. The officer waved him back to the guards, who put him in line with dozens of other prisoners and marched them toward a prison compound. Billowing clouds of thick smoke hung over the burning town of Smyrna, darkening the northern horizon and mixing in with the acrid fumes from cannons and rifles.

The famously secret letter had done Oliver Thomas little good, except for driving him to leave the Rebel ranks when he did. And, for that, he was thankful.

He was happy that he had gone over to the Union side on Independence Day. He was not, however, part of any celebration. He accurately thought it unwise to show too much pleasure among other Confederates who were not as willing captives as he. But then, he had little reason for pleasure, anyway. Instead of sending him to Ohio, the Major regarded him as just one more prisoner of war. Possibly, even, a traitor who had eventually lost his nerve.

The next day, he was on a train to a prison at Elmira, New York, where conditions would be nearly as bad as at Andersonville. For Ollie, even worse; there he would not be a guard, but a prisoner. Until, maybe, he could sign an oath of loyalty to the Union, if someone at Elmira would give him the opportunity. He had no idea of his chances; maybe his Ohio accent would help.

He hoped so.

Chapter 22.
8 a.m., Monday, July 4, 1864

Court President Mahlon Blanchard today chose to show his warmer and more amiable side, the alternate persona he mastered when sitting on cases in Coulee County Court back during happier days. Men on the Court-Martial panel noticed his pleasant mood, and wondered: Was he simply enjoying full rations this morning from the cook house just down the hill from this shed where he and the Court Martial people spent their nights?

No. It was the day—July 4—solidly imprinted in his memory of better years. On those Days of Remembrance of 1776 he would stand proudly on a bunting-decorated bandstand in the center of Coulee City. It was a glorious setting, nestled in a verdant valley amid the lush grain fields and the oaks, maples and hickories of the gentle hillsides. His oratory would flow in rich timbre about the heroism of American men and the national fortitude that had made this Great Nation a reality.

There was nothing unusual or hypocritical about these speeches. Mercurial as he was, Mahlon Blanchard passionately believed everything he said then and believed it today. He also believed with equal fervor that his own value to the Union was sorely compromised by lesser humans. There were those too persnickety about paperwork for such things as army rations, supplies, and payrolls. And there were overzealous lawyers best described as weasels…like Lucius McCordle.

So, July 4th always made Mahlon Blanchard feel good and today was no exception. His booming voice opened the court proceedings without waiting for Clerk Daniel to call it to order. The Court President was so moved by the day's historic significance, and so inspired by his own voice, that he overlooked the potential danger of irritating the Confederate camp commandant and his staff. He bellowed:

Fellow Union soldiers, let us begin this historic day by singing the *Star Spangled Banner*! Oh,h, say, can you see-e-e-ee!..

A surprised group of waiting witnesses, prosecuting and defense attorneys, and defendants let him go through the first line solo. It was a stunning vocal performance, especially so from being utterly unexpected. Once belted out, the richness of his deep baritone was infectious. First, the witness group fresh from the stockade joined in, then the handful of attorneys.

It finally occurred to the sorry crowd of defendants that a highly energetic musical show of patriotism, however imperfect its tonal quality, could not hurt their cause and just might help it.

One by one, these wretched creatures struggled to their feet. Their rusty voices were timid and lackluster at first, then louder and louder, eventually reaching an impressive if discordant level of total cacophony. The otherwise abrasive brogues of Collins, Curtis and Sarsfield, for a time, almost rose above even the throaty tones of the Court President. Only at the larynx-straining falsetto *...and the rockets' red glare...* did Blanchard's trained professional voice again rise above all others.

It was a massive and stirring flow of adrenalin, perhaps anticipating what a century later would be a regular passion for huge crowds at athletic contests. It overcame the entire assemblage. Even a few Confederate guards hummed along, remembering a day when the famous creation of Francis Scott Key was at least as well known in the South as Dixie was in 1864. Lieutenant Granbury silently noted all of this, but except for a faint grin showed no sign of approval or disapproval.

Blanchard did not go beyond the first stanza. He considered doing the *Battle Hymn of the Republic*, but quickly thought better of that. While the Confederate military men tolerated the *Star Spangled Banner*, they would certainly have been infuriated by the Yankee's most stirring marching song. Instead, the Court President delivered a most ingratiating statement.

Let the court transcript show, he said, that all present here at Camp Sumter on July 4, 1864, sang out with impressive vocal ability, and that the Court hopes this richness and clarity of voice will carry over to all who testify or otherwise address the court on this historic day. All in the court, including defendants, are to be congratulated on their fine vocal performance. The guards will ensure the ready availability of freshly boiled coffee to keep all these voices in such fine fettle!

The four attorneys—Lucius McCordle and Jed Simmons for the defense, Warrick Breck and Delano Richman for the prosecution—were equally dumfounded by this pronouncement. *Would it be grounds for a mistrial? Well, that's an absurd question simply because there can obviously be no appeal of whatever comes out of this misbegotten trial, one way or another.*

Whatever happened would be final, no doubt on that.

The defendants looked questioningly at each other. Some whispered in muffled tones, wondering whether this expansive show of jurist good humor and patriotic feeling somehow improved their chances of surviving this trial. Others feared that the inspired singing of Francis Scott Key's creation was more likely an omen—like the heavy roll of military drums just before the gallows platform falls away beneath men with their necks in nooses.

Blanchard spoke again, quickly:

Let the proceedings resume! Sergeant Breck, bring in your first three witnesses!

With that, the Court President took his seat, folded his arms, and regarded the court area with the same benign judicial countenance.

He had established a strange and clearly extra-judicial procedure yesterday, and this was how it would work: Three witnesses sitting on a splintered plank supported by two empty powder kegs, would all answer the same question and thus be free to modify or elaborate on their recollections after hearing what the others had just said.

These men gave their names quickly:

Private Frank Eckert, 17th Ohio.

Corporal Chauncey Quimby, 7th Pennsylvania.

Private Jonathan Walker, 4th Massachusetts.

Sergeant Warrick Breck, adjusting to this unusual way of doing things, said:

Starting with Private Eckert, would each of you tell the Court Martial panel of any occurrences of robbery, assault, or murder you may have seen that involved any one or more of the defendants.

Lucius McCordle looked at Jed Simmons, who shrugged and spread his hands open in futility. Neither raised any objection. This was how things would proceed now.

Eckert, a small, round-faced man of about 30 years, gave a highly explicit account:

I been here since the first week of May, and I seen three of these Raiders (he pointed to Collins, Delaney, and Muir)

8 a.m., Monday, July 4, 1864

rob and kick and take everything this one man had. I remember it all.

About a week after I come here, that one (now pointing to Delaney) and three of his gang come running up the east side of the stockade. That one (still pointing to Delaney) was yelling that somebody had stolen something from him. He says, There's the guy, and points to two sickly boys from New York just a few shanties from me. He kicked this one boy, and when the boy started to get up, Delaney swings his foot and trips the boy, then takes his club and hits the boy on the head four or five times. While he's doing this the other two are kicking the other boy until he's knocked out, then they strip his shirt from him and pull his pants off and scoop up stuff in the shanty.

Eckert was now in full vocal stride and mixed tense.

Delaney hits the same fella again and again, he said. Someone up the line yells and then Delaney and the other two takes off at a dead run back to the South end. I go to see the man they hit and I tell you, his head looked like corn meal mush with red paint spilled over it. Two or three of us tried to fix him up but it was no use. He died in no time.

Warrick Breck nodded, pointed to the second witness, and asked:

Corporal Quimby, what can you tell the court?

Quimby once had a larger-than-average girth but recently lost so much weight that his uniform, or what remained of it, hung loosely from his wide frame.

Wull, whot I kin say is even worse. See that one there, the big guy Mosby? I watched him shove a club into a boy's gut so hard the poor man puked all over. And then Mosby hit him again and said it was for messing up his club!

The poor fella was laying there on the ground, squirmin' around like a sickly hawg, and Mosby and two-three of his boys then tore up his shanty and took ever'thing they could find. Just like what he (nodding toward Eckert) just said. Then they turned and laughed at me and ran back to the south side.

But they din't go all the way. One of 'em turned back and said I better not tell the Regulators if I knew whot was good for me.

Warrick Breck asked: About what time of day was this?

Oh, I suppose around eight or so, in the evenin'. They was long shadows, but still enough light so's I could see he was one a' the same ones that did the clubbin' and stealing.

Jonathan Walker, the third and final witness in this trio, said he watched a gang of five or six led by little Cary (meaning Sullivan) run down and club a man until he fell unconscious and bleeding like a stuck hawg.

Then they looked around and said that's what happens to boys who get in our way, Walker concluded.

Warrick Breck: Your witnesses, Sergeant McCordle.

This time, Lucius decided to ask a few questions: What time of day was this? (Hardly daylight) Which defendant said that? (That one, Cary, if I got his name right.) Who was the man you said they hit? (Don't know, Indiana boy, I think.) The questions led to no answers useful to the defense, so Lucius quickly ended his cross-examination.

Breck then called the next three by name:

Corporal Harry Nickels, Private Horatio Wendorf and Abel Jenkinson, step to the witness bench.

Lucius McCordle and Jed Simmons looked at each in shock. The *prosecution* was calling Harry Nickels, who was sitting with the accused accomplices?

Lucius was on his feet, unsure of whether what he was about to say would help, or hurt, Harry Nickels. His disastrous run-in with the Court President yesterday made his uncertainty worse.

Mr. Court President, we wish for a stipulation, Lucius said, and added:

Corporal Nickels is sitting with a group of men who are alleged to be accomplices of the six in front, and therefore appears to be treated by the court as a defendant. No defendant may be required to testify against himself.

Therefore, may we conclude that his appearance as a witness means he is not to be regarded as a defendant?

The Court President was well aware of his earlier threat to Lucius McCordle that Harry Nickels might well be a defendant, subject to execution if convicted. Now, since that threat had finally put a stop to all the ranting by McCordle, the Court President had no further need for this young man. In fact, he presumed correctly that, in keeping with his genial manner of this July 4th, it would be in his interest to show some magnanimity toward the hapless Nickels. Especially if it might turn out that the alleged letter was the real thing, after all.

In the same soft, almost grandfatherly manner that he had adopted for the day, Court President Blanchard cleared his throat and said:

Corporal…Nickels, is it?.. Soldier, you don't have to testify if you don't wish to.

However, Blanchard continued, it's my duty to advise you that, since you are being called as a hostile witness about your contacts with the defendants, anything you say might possibly be used against you, and lead to your becoming charged as one of the Raiders.

Harry Nickels, who was now halfway between where he had been sitting and the witness bench, looked pitifully at Lucius and answered:

It's okay, your honor, I'm willing to testify and I don't care who calls me, because I have some things to say that might help the court.

Still the compassionate judge, Blanchard thought a moment and said.

Well, I understand what you say, but have you talked this over with your attorneys? No? Well, I'll tell you what. We're going to take a five-minute recess here, so you can confer with Sergeants McCordle and Simmons. Okay, adjourn for five minutes. Well, make it ten and take just enough time for that coffee I asked for and a latrine break.

Lucius pulled Harry aside and rasped at him:

Harry, do you know what the hell you are doing? They're going to get you so tied up they'll make you look like Sarsfield's right hand man. That could put you in the gallows, goddammit! Don't you see that?

Harry shook his head.

Nope. Fact is, I was going to volunteer to testify anyway, but I didn't think I had to bring it up with you. I hate those sonsabitches and I'm going to do my little bit to make sure they all swing. Look at this arm of mine! If it hadn't been for my being seen on the South side of the sink, this wou'nt of happened.

Lucius argued in vain.

Harry, if you really want to testify, let US call you and question you first. That way, we control where this is all going. You're walking into one hell of a bear trap by sitting there with a couple of others who are aching to get everyone like you hanged!

Harry Nickels hesitated, but finally said:

Lucius, I know what you're sayin', but by god I'm going to go ahead this way. And I tell you why. Ain't you noticed that ol' Judge Blanchard is a changed man today? He's in a good mood, dammit. Hell, he's sounding like the wonderful judge who used to give those nice talks around town. Always spoke nice to you on the street, or if you ran into him at the store or hitching post. He'll watch out for me, just you wait! After a pause, Harry added: Remember, Lucius, your problems with this Judge are yours, not mine!

Further arguing by Lucius and Jed did no good. Harry's mind was made up. Did he know what he was doing? Well, Lucius had to admit that the Court President *who was a sonofabitch just yesterday* did seem a totally different person today.

When the trial resumed, the Court President announced:

As we all know, Corporal Nickels, you have been kept out here since you came in with that curious letter that you and some others think is a genuine note from General Lee to Early. Now, let me point out that you ran the gauntlet once, and were not here when the prosecuting attorneys specified charges, so that means you are *not* a defendant in these proceedings.

Lucius found one of his ends accomplished: Harry Nickels would not be hanged. Now, two problems were left: the Lee-to-Early letter, and Lucius' deal with John Sarsfield.

Defense of the Raider gang at this point was almost secondary for Lucius McCordle.

Chapter 23.
<u>11 a.m., Monday, July 4, 1864</u>

Harry Nickels walked slowly to the witness bench and took the seat on the right, as if he wanted to be third. A badly injured and half-starved man with no friends in the stockade, he struggled silently for courage.

The first two witnesses told of familiar, brutal events.

Private Floyd Evans pointed directly to Delaney and spoke:

Came to our shebang in broad daylight, Delaney did. Asked if we didn't want to have our shanty pertected from all the gangs in the place. When we said no, he said, well, that means you got no pertection, so don't blame us. Then he and two, three others ripped the top off our tent, grabbed our haversacks, pushed me and August down so hard it broke August's leg and ran off with near everything we had. Everything worth anything. I run after them and Delaney stopped, turned and come down on my head with a club. Then he laughed and the others laughed with him and they trotted back to their side of the sink. I still got the bruise and scar, right here.

He tipped his head to show the welt. Warrick Breck motioned to him, to turn his head so it could be seen by the panel.

Private Wesley Salisbury's tale differed from all others heard up to this point:

I heard this one (pointing to Muir) talking to a guard, and saying this certain boy was a trouble maker and ought to be done in. The guard asked him who, and this Raider chief (pointing again to Muir) said Carl Pelzer. I reckanized it, 'cuz I thought I knew who this Carl was. Michigan boy, not far from our hut and so sick he din't have many days left.

It wasn't long after that, maybe a half hour, I see him (pointing again to Muir) telling Carl there was a couple greenbacks between the deadline and the stockade wall. Tells him that money would help him buy some calomel at the sutler's shack, make him feel better. And Carl said he didn't dare go near it because if you touch the deadline, you get shot by those guards in the pigeon roosts. And, n'en, this Raider says no, I fixed it with the guards so this time they won't bother you. Go ahead, this Raider says, and fetch that greenback.

I tried to warn Carl this was a trick, that they's tryin' to put one over on him, but Carl, he's not too smart, sick as he is, and he stumbles his way right over to the deadline and starts to crawl under it and bang! Carl took the lead in his side and he was dead an hour later. And then, it wasn't two minutes after they drug Carl's body away and this Raider (points again to Muir) and two of his boys run over to Carl's hut, rolled up all his stuff in the rotten blanket Carl had. Then they run to the South end again.

A hush fell over the court area.

Private Wesley Salisbury wasn't through. He looked at Warrick Breck and said, Sergeant, could I add something else? What these dirty hounds really did?

Go ahead, Breck said, with an easy nod.

Wesley Salisbury drew in his breath, exhaled, and spoke slowly, saying:

Let me tell you what these goddam creatures really done. It ain't just clubbing and maiming and killing. It ain't just stealin' grub and money...or the watches, belts, tin cups or potatoes.

Know what they really did? Wesley said, looking around at the dirty, bedraggled but petulant defendants. They stole our imagination, Wesley continued. Even yanked out of us our power to think what it's like to be with a woman. They took everything, even our music. Why could they sing so dang well down there? See, they tore the words from our throats, rolled 'em in a blanket and then shook 'em out up the hill south of that sink. They stole our laughter…ain't no one had a good laugh here but you could hear those bastards haw-hawing all the time. The only thing they ain't stole is our religion, simply 'cause they can't. Well, just watch, they'll be crying to Father Whelan purty soon. And by god, I hope he gives them r'ligion, cause they're gonna need it.

Amid a murmur around the court, Curtis bellowed:

That's a bunch of silly hogwash, we din't keep you from singin' or thinkin' about wimmen, did we? Din't we even say where…

Curtis suddenly stopped talking, as if he'd blurted out too much.

Before Court President Blanchard could intercede again, Breck thanked Wesley Salisbury for his words and turned to Harry Nickels.

After the poignant words of Wesley before him, Harry wasn't sure how to start. His lips moved, his mouth opened and he curled his lower lip inside his mouth while pulling his upper, revealing his yellowing and broken teeth under the grotesque and bewhiskered mask of a face that had once been a sparkling specimen of frontier America's manly good looks.

Still no words came. His face twitched. His left hand, dangling uncontrollably from a mangled arm, groped until it finally found and grabbed the little finger of his right.

He pulled on that finger, weakly. Then he moved his right hand, to take control and crack a knuckle of a damaged digit of his left, as if this act might loosen his tightened throat and tongue. He finally spoke, in slow, halting, bursts:

You have heard...and will hear more, I guess...men tell about robbery and murder...and tricking men into taking bullets. If that's all that happened...if that's all these Raiders did...it would be one thing. Wesley just now told about them stealing our minds, I think that's what he meant. But they done even worse and I guess I'm the only one who dares to tell you about it here.

You're gonna wonder why I would say these things...when no one else does. Oh...I been here just long enough to ask fellas...what they write...in letters home...in their diaries. You must know...if you don't, I'm telling you...lotsa men in this hellhole are keeping diaries. It keeps their brains alive and that's the main thing to keep a body alive. No working brain, no body.

Whut Wesley just said is wunnerful poetry that he can put in his book and it will read good. But what I'm goin' to tell you is things ain't nobody going to write...in their diaries or their letters or their home papers.

Court President Mahlon Blanchard shifted his weight slightly, momentarily wondering whether to ask Corporal Nickels to get to the point. Consistent with his amiable persona of the day, he decided against it.

The assemblage quieted, waiting for the Corporal to continue.

Harry pulled again on his left hand, looked at it without focusing, then faced up and directly toward the panel.

Now, what happened when I met this...man Sarsfield? He's sitting right there...you need to know him. He ain't no better...or worse...than the rest...but in my mind he speaks for them all.

I hadn't been here a day...more or less...when this Sarsfield man said...he wanted to git to know me better... he could help me out...come to my hut, he says...I followed him down there...across the sink...I seen his hut, better than most and full of stuff...when we was talking I pulled some papers...out of my shirt and this letter...dropped and Sarsfield picked it up...it was from General Lee to General Early...I didn't know what it really was up to then...just a scrap of paper clean on one side...what I might be able to write on...it got torn in half and he kept half...

I ain't told no one what happened next...Sarsfield said again he wanted to *know* me...and, more he talked... it started to dawn on me what he meant by those words...I asked Father Whelan since then to be sure...what he meant is in the Bible...every God-fearing man here knows the Sodom and Gomorrah story...that's what Sarsfield meant.

How he went about it...he first shows me a couple books he stole somewheres. One was a book full of big words and pictures...about anatomy...full of pictures and drawings to make your eyes bug out...different parts of a human body, men and women...maybe some of you here seen it...Sarsfield says, see what I got to keep boys happy...then he tells me they's women in this stockade...he knew them, he said, and had known them... men were paying him...the women he claimed was working for him...then he says if I joined him I could have time with them...and I could have time, he called it, with young pretty boys, too...

They're whorehouse keepers, that's what they are... but they's making whores out of the whole stockade—a few women and lots of men. They've been buggerin'[9] boys! Hang them all!

Hardly a sound now in the court, only breathing and exhaling. One defendant coughed.

Warrick Breck said, I have no more questions. Sergeant McCordle?

Lucius walked slowly toward the witness bench, entirely uncertain whether to ask the question in his mind, or not. He turned back, leaned over and whispered to Jed Simmons:

Maybe you better handle this. Harry and I are too close.

Murmurs rolled from the stirring crowd of defendants, with the principal six snarling at each other. Sarsfield gazed menacingly at Harry Nickels on the witness bench, who along with the other two witnesses, was studying the rusty Georgia soil at his feet.

Simmons couldn't have been less pleased. There is nothing worse for a lawyer than asking a question in court while having no idea what the answer will be. He hesitated.

Corporal Nickels, did any one of the defendants hurt you in any way? Physically, I mean?

Harry Nickels again rolled his right hand over his left. Several seconds passed. He was sweating hard, even more than the steamy late morning heat would have produced.

No...not me...but he threatened to...if I didn't do my damnedest to help him escape with that letter.

Simmons: And by him, you mean...

Nickels: Sarsfield! And he said Collins would do it too!

Willie Collins was now struggling to his feet and shouting.

Goddammit, I din't bugger nobody! Or claim I would! That's just Sarsfield he's talking about.

---

9   19th century term for sodomizing.

Louder murmurs and mutters now swept through the assemblage. Jed Simmons kept his gaze on Nickels, ignoring the angry outburst of Collins. Court President Blanchard raised his hammer but decided not to tap it, since Collins settled down as quickly as he had risen. The Raider leader had never read a word of William Shakespeare, but his gangster mind finally realized the danger of protesting too much.

And Harry Nickels worried about the danger of saying what, in this culture in this age, was also too much in another sense. A witness to, or victim of, such abuse would be a victim again, in social discourse. Quite simply, he would be shunned.

Jed Simmons looked at Blanchard and said, No more questions, Mr. Court President.

Mahlon Blanchard tapped his hammer gavel lightly and adjourned the trial until the afternoon.

Harry Nickels stood up painfully, looked past Lucius McCordle and said to no one in particular:

Where's Father Whelan? I need to talk with him.

The Priest, always near the assemblage, took Harry's good arm and led him aside, dragging his ball and chain, to where they could talk alone.

The sun dipped low. The western sky reddened and slowly darkened as night fell over the cursed stockade and court martial scene. Jed pulled Lucius aside.

You know, Lucius, now I know why you made so much of that damned letter from Lee to Early. It wasn't you thinking it would do any real good in this world or the world we used to think we lived in.

It was a diversion, Jed continued We thought we had something more important to think about, than deciding how soon to give up this struggle and turn these hideous beasts over to the boys inside with their hangman's nooses. I'll bet that inside this stockade they've tied and untied and retied those nooses a thousand times already, all in anticipation of something you and I know is going to happen and yet we dread it. There's death all around us, maybe 30, 40 or even more dying each day. And yet we dread the deliberate hanging of the worst among us. Why? What's so different about execution?

I'll tell you what it is. Since we got into this war, we've seen nothing but death. Alive one minute, like the soldier in battle, dead the next. Or sick from the measles, suffer a week or two and then die. Or starve to death, like men all around the stockade.

But execution is different. You have healthy men—well, healthiest here—who are alive and breathing, fine one minute then drop from a scaffold and life is suddenly gone. It's so planned and deliberate. Like tying a rock to a puppy's neck and throwing him in the creek. Some people love to watch that sort of thing. Others like me turn away, sickened by snuffing out a life—any life—even though I believe these creatures don't deserve to live.

Listen to those owls back in the woods. The wind must be just right. It blows their hoots toward us, and it blows the stink of this place away from them. Maybe it's right to call them wise old owls.

Lucius shook his head. Owls? Wise? They eat skunks, don't they? Fact is, like Harry told me once, they're dumb as hell and can't smell a thing...which means, by god, they'd get along just fine inside this stockade! Just think...dumb

11 A.M., MONDAY, JULY 4, 1864

and can't smell. Yes, Jed, you're right. We'd be better off as owls. But not for the reason you think.

War Department
July 4, 1864   8 p.m.

His Excellency Governor Curtin (Of Pennsylvania)
...this Department has no accurate information as to the rebel force, but General Grant reports that Early's force has returned to the army in front of him...
H. M. Stanton, Secretary of War[10]

---

10   *Ibid, p. 58.*

City Point (Southern Virginia) 4 p.m.
July 4th 1864
Maj Gen H W Halleck

Chief of Staff City Point, July 4, 1864-4 p.m. (Received 5th)

Maj. Gen. H. W. Halleck, Chief of Staff

...A deserter who came in this morning reports that Early's Corps has not returned here but is off in the valley with the intention of going into Maryland and Washington City...and expects to take the City soon...This...is only the report of a deserter and we have similar authority for (Early's Corps) being here and on the right of Lees Army. We know however that it does not occupy this position...

U.S. Grant   Lt Gen*l*[11]

---

11   *WOTR*, Series 1, Vol. 37 Part II, p. 33.

Chapter 24.
<u>Tuesday, July 5, 1864</u>

Gilbert Daniel struggled with the transcript. This was his first time working a trial alone, without another recorder to check with, to clear up ambiguous statements, or catch things he couldn't hear well. He didn't dare ask the Court President about a doubtful word or phrase—much less one of the attorneys.

He was on his own.

He was reasonably skilled in Pitman shorthand, the system of lines, curves, angles and dots used in most mid-19th century courts. He was tireless, when he was healthy, but now he had stomach cramps and the work of transcribing made them worse. Unlike others here, he couldn't relax at the end of a day's hearing. He had to spend evenings converting his shorthand marks (hen-scratching, others called them) to plain language.

He ordinarily recorded only what was said in formal court session. But here he made a crucial exception: the controversial letter from General Lee to General Early. He faithfully recorded every word uttered by Sergeant Lucius McCordle when he read it for Captain Wirz Saturday afternoon, July 2. It would be in his final transcript, at the correct point in time. If the Court President wanted it struck before it was sent to Richmond, that was his business. Gilbert Daniel had simply followed an old rule: When in doubt, record it. Recorded words can be expunged, but ignored words cannot be re-created; human memory for exact words of even five minutes ago cannot be trusted.

By the evening of the last day of the trial—July 6—he would have the transcript completed. Court President Blanchard could review it and give it to Captain Wirz. Then—it was Daniel's assumption—the transcript would go by some kind of fast courier to Richmond for review and approval.

Captain Henry Wirz' infuriation and frustration hadn't eased a bit. He now had the pieces of a letter General Robert E. Lee had, supposedly, written as secret orders to General Jubal Early. But *Christus*! That letter was dated June 13, nearly three weeks ago! He, Wirz, had heard nothing but vague rumors of one of Lee's Corps in the Shenandoah. Was that General Jubal Early? Was this secret campaign, whatever it was, well known by now? Including the Yankees? Or would he, Wirz, by reporting this crazy letter to anyone, mistakenly put the information in Yankee hands? Or—almost worse— would higher ranking Confederate officers simply consider him a fool for believing something concocted by prisoners in his stockade? *Ach, Ficken!*

The Captain doubted the information, if accurate, was secret any longer. The problem: It WAS secret when it found its way, by some cursed conjuration, into this stockade. Guards probably knew about it—none of them could be trusted—and if it ever reached General Early OR General Lee, it would mean hell for anyone responsible for Camp Sumter. And that would be Captain Henry Wirz.

He had been in tough spots before and had survived most of them with his character intact—although he never thought he deserved this horrible job as commandant of a prison stockade without enough soldiers, equipment, food, or medicine to run it properly. He HAD to inform General Winder.

But...*Ach! That's it! General Winder! Of course! This letter him immediately show and responsibility now his it is!* Thinking for the Captain was always better in the sequential logic of the language he grew up with in Switzerland. General Winder was in Macon right now and would return Thursday, July 7. Captain Wirz would take up this matter with him. Then it would be out of his hands, and happily so.

Lucius searched his mind for a defense stratagem he hadn't tried. Could he save any of these Raiders from the noose? Not likely...but he couldn't shake the urge to try. There was one possibility he mentioned in his opening statement: The African-American soldiers who lived and seemed to survive in relative contentment on the South slope of the stockade area, west but not far from the Raiders' comfortable huts.

Curtis had said the Irish helped the Colored prisoners survive. That sounded absurd, but...would those men verify that, as witnesses? It was worth a try.

Again, Lucius got permission to re-enter the stockade and, this time, he went in the South Gate, crossed the foul sink area, and went straight to the shebangs where the African-American men tried to stay alive.

Ashford Cook, a sergeant in a Colored Infantry company, sat cross-legged under his lean-to shebang that he shared with Jacob Little, a Corporal from Rhode Island. Ashford was carefully and methodically sewing his torn rank stripes back on his faded blue shirt when he saw Lucius McCordle approaching.

Afternoon, Sergeant, Ashford asked easily: What can I do for you?

Lucius hesitated. He had expected dialect, then wanted to kick himself for having that expectation.

I'm a lawyer, trying to defend these men they call The Raiders. Could I ask you a couple of questions?

Depends what you want to know, Ashford said—and then yelled in dialect to Jacob to move aside so Lucius could crawl under the shade of the lean-to.

Afternoon shadows from the stockade poles, a rod to the west, hadn't yet reached this community of huts, and the heat in open sunlight was unbearable. Ashford's companions, from their own shelters, watched Lucius with curiosity.

I'll get right to the point, Lucius said. Do you know Charles Curtis?

Ashford hesitated. Yeah, I know him. Why?

Well, he claims that the Irish, as he calls them, have been looking out for the Colored prisoners here. Is that so?

Huh. I s'pose it depends what you mean by looking out. And who's doing the looking out. It's us, looking out for them. They put us colored troops down here on purpose, you know. A stone's throw from those Irish, as they call themselves.

One night, back a month or more, Ashford continued, four-five of them come over looking smarty at us. But we was ready. I see them, lets out a whistle, and when they gets here they see a line of 12 Colored men standing shoulder to shoulder. So right away, this big man Mosby, he starts talking like we's all friends, got to stick together, talk like that.

Y'know, Sergeant, Ashford said, that Raider man had an interestin' argument. Look at it this way, he tol' me. We Irish are doing to the majority in this hellhole what the majority does to you Colored Folks all the time. Slavery, he said, is just an outlandish case of what the majority always does when its meanness takes over.

This isn't what I had expected or hoped for, but it's very near what Maryanne would have said.

Well, I thought about that, Ashford continued, but still, he didn't fool us none. He was just trying to get on our good side, just to do HIM some good. He said we were Irish, too—jest smoked a little, way he put it. He knew we had a man, Daniel Kelly, Mosby said, who is REALLY Irish. Yeah, we says, plenty Irish slave holders. Where'd he think we got our names? Anyway, seeing us standing tough, they left us alone and have ever since.

Did they play Robin Hood for us? Naw…maybe once they had more beef than they could eat, so they threw some our way. After it was half rotten. That would have been about it.

So you want me to testify? Now, just why should I? Way, I see it, Mosby was right. A few of these big tough fellows made sheep out of thousands of you soldiers. Same way a few slave owners with their guns and whips keep thousands of us weak and easy to push around. But I already said that, didn't I?

Lucius had nothing to say.

The man is absolutely right, and it's taken me years to see it. Why, oh why, Maryanne, didn't I see this when my tortured ideas kept us apart?

But Ashford wasn't through.

Maybe I should testify, he said. Let the court know how real men ain't bothered a bit by those…what's the Irish word…hooligans?

Ashford agreed to come to the court martial tomorrow, and Lucius, a half hour later, decided to do something he had feared to do from the moment he was captured at Cold Harbor in June: Read the letter from Maryanne that had reached him in the middle of May, when the postal wagon finally caught up with his regiment in the Wilderness of Virginia.

He pulled a badly wrinkled, sweat-stained wad of paper from his shirt pocket, where it had rested day and night but untouched by its bearer, who feared looking at words that might torment him more than had his anxiety about keeping them unread. Nevertheless, now sweating more profusely than the oppressive Georgia sun could by itself provoke, his trembling fingers unfolded the letter and he began reading:

Dear Lucius: I find it most difficult to put in words the things that have kept us from a lifetime of marriage. It is even more difficult to say these things to a soldier who, though I pray against it, may need to lay his life down for the sake of ending slavery in our nation.

I must start by assuring you that it was not your decision to serve as attorney for the barrel maker who killed Amos McGurdy. Yes, I was upset with you at the time, but after thinking on it I appreciated your doing it because of professional principle. You say every person no matter how low has the right to counsel and I respected that.

No, Lucius, that is not what has kept us apart. You certainly must remember the next time I saw you, after that trial. It was at the dock near the boarding ramp to the river boat Anna Belle. Remember? I was yelling at two drunken men who tripped Huxton Davis, the other Colored barber who had worked with Amos. Using the most obscene language, they sent Huxton sprawling in the mud. You stood

TUESDAY, JULY 5, 1864

by, Lucius, and did nothing! Even after the drunks yelled back at me for my protests, and called me a Floozy in the vilest terms!

That, Lucius, I'm so sad to say, told me that whatever you might think about principles of fairness and rights of accused people, you were unable to stand up for a man so cruelly treated before your eyes. It is one thing to believe slavery is acceptable; it is even worse when that belief includes denying individual dignity of a person in bondage. You know I lived as a child for a year in Charleston. Even there, accepting slavery as those people do, no man of your position would have stood by as you did to see a person with skin of any color being mistreated the way Huxton was before your eyes.

It tortures me to say these things to you, Lucius, but I hope this letter frees you to live your life with another who shares your chosen beliefs and principles.

So all I can say, Lucius, is adieu. With sorrowful regret, Maryanne.

The words in this crumpled but torturing letter rose to and surrounded Lucius' temple, pressing in as a band of iron so tight his vision dimmed and his head hammered in near-imitation of Gatling Gun staccato.

He crumpled the letter, uncrumpled it, looked at the wadded paper without seeing it, and tore it into shreds usable only for igniting a cooking fire.

Then, Lucius made his decision:

There's no way I can ever return to Maryanne, and no way I can keep any of the six Raider leaders from being hanged.

Have I come through on my so-called 'promise' to Sarsfield? Well, the secret letter is now in Wirz' hands and everyone knows about it, including the Confederates. There is nothing more I can do.

The question is, can I save Harry? Not by anything I can do in the court martial. He will fare better with Jed representing him. Blanchard has me over a barrel; I've confronted him and I came out the loser, as I should have expected. I'm whipped like a dog.

The important thing now is to get word to General Grant or the War Department about General Early. So that's what I'm going to do...or die trying...not for Sarsfield, but for the message.

It's the one honorable thing left for me to try.

Back at the Court Martial shed, Lucius told Jed:

Tomorrow, Sergeant Ashford Cook of the Massachusetts Colored Infantry is going to testify for the defense. Just listen to his testimony. I probably won't be there. Why? Jed, the less you know of my whereabouts, the better.

If I don't return, you make the summary for the defense. Here, take these two sheets of paper. This is what I would have said...or will say if I get back. And If I don't return, you may read it as our closing statement. Trust me. I know what I'm doing.

Simmons stared in puzzled silence. Nothing about this bizarre trial, or the ways of Lucius McCordle, could surprise him now.

Chapter 25.
6 A.M. Wednesday, July 6

Lucius returned to the stockade. Getting clearance was now easy and routine; it would be one more search for witnesses, and no reason for Lieutenant Granbury to doubt what he was doing.

This time, Lucius made no search for witnesses. He went straight to the lineup of sick men, for the hospital, and told the guard (who didn't recognize him) he wanted parole as a nurse for the hospital. Fortunately for his purposes, the guard was impressed by Lucius' size and demeanor and Sergeant's stripes, so he yelled and managed to get the attention of a hospital orderly.

Like the guard, the orderly didn't recognize Lucius or his name; talk of the Court Martial was everywhere, but it was on the other side of the stockade and names of the principals, except for the now-famous Sergeant LeRoy Key and the Raider leaders, were generally unknown, or mistaken. Word was that a hated man called Grigly, probably a Raider himself, was defending the hooligans at the trial. Like the ever-present rumor of prisoner exchange, it was information passed around and accepted even though utterly without foundation.

Lucius immediately impressed the orderly with his familiarity with medications and drugs, without mentioning nostrums that might make trained medical people suspicious. The orderly went to find the chief surgeon. This man gave Lucius—now calling himself Sergeant Luke Maroney—a parole on his own authority. This would ordinarily have been granted only by Captain Wirz, but the decrepit hospital was so woefully understaffed that anyone with this much medical knowledge was one the chief surgeon wanted to grab.

By late that evening, Lucius was in the hospital—a group of tents outside the southeast corner of the stockade—and looking after some of the worst cases of starvation, diarrhea, and disease. Need for such professional help was so compelling he considered staying there to do what he could.

He had, however, a mission that took precedence above all else: Interfere with General Jubal Early's secret plan. *Escape from the stockade, and plant a fake message telling Richmond the secret was out. This might well lead Robert E. Lee to call off Early's plan to attack Washington. A complex plan with many ifs? Yes, but the only one with any chance of success. But...hasn't Captain Wirz already thought of that? Who knows? That man is so panicked, he may not know WHAT to do.*

As night fell, Lucius found his way out to a picket guard and offered him three Federal greenbacks—the last ones Lucius possessed. The guard took them, looked the other way, and Lucius disappeared into the night.

He didn't go far. He waited in a thicket for a short while, crept back in the shadows behind the same guard, and with a quick blow knocked the man unconscious. He took the guard's weapon—one of the few Enfield rifles in the Camp Sumter guard detail—and slung the ammunition and powder pack over his shoulder.

He skirted the guards' tent area and then made for the Anderson railroad station where he assumed he would find the telegraph office. He was correct, but a small train was unloading more prisoners...*would they never stop coming to this cursed place?*...so he waited in the woods until the train left and the station was deserted, except for the lone operator.

A surprised telegraph man turned to see a tall, bewhiskered man in a Yankee uniform, pointing a rifle at his head. Lucius was to the point:

Send this message to Richmond:

The secret of Early's mission is known to Washington, and they have a force of 30,000 waiting for him.

The telegraph operator's face turned white and his voice came in a frantic stutter:

I k-k-kin se-end that message for y'all…but it won't go nowhere. The telegraph line is down from here to Fort Valley, a-a-and we c-c-cain't git no messages through to nobody.

An infuriated and frustrated Lucius McCordle swung the butt of the rifle and knocked the man silly. He tied him, gagged him and stripped off the man's butternut tunic and C.S.A. cap. With these items and the Enfield rifle, he disappeared into the night. Fort Valley, with the closest working telegraph transmitter, was 30 miles or more from here. He had no horse, food, money or water. But he pressed on, guided only by a slivery moon occasionally peeking out behind scudding clouds.

Alone in the wooded area not far from Anderson station, Lucius, the night of Tuesday, July 5, had nothing more than a gun, powder, wads and shot for about 20 rounds. He discarded his Union kepi and shirt with the Sergeant's stripes, and replaced both with those stripped from the telegraph operator.

In the back country near Americus, he approached a slave hut well after dark. The elderly couple eyed him warily. But after hearing his Yankee way of talking, they fed him, offered him overnight shelter (which he politely refused) and pointed out what they thought was the safest route to Fort Valley.

The route they suggested was complicated...cross this creek, turn left at the next fence row...follow the edge of a sweet potato field for the next mile...ask directions again from the next Colored folks in the shacks with the tin roofs but NOT the servants in the Massa's house...and cross the railroad tracks quickly and DON'T follow them because that's where the home guards are watching for skedaddlers. Thanks to trading his Union garb for Rebel shirt and cap, Lucius looked like just one more deserter from the Confederate Army.

Lucius spent the night under pine trees—lost, tired, hungry and thirsty. He didn't find a creek for wash and drink until the following morning.

He would never reach Fort Valley—or any telegraph station where he could force the transmission of his intended message. At a stream crossing on July 6, he mistakenly judged a home guardsman to be simply an elderly gentleman with his mule cart on the way to a country store. He wasn't aware the man followed him, had a musket in his cart, and was signaling a partner farther down the road. Lucius became aware of danger too late, when he saw the reflection from the gun barrel of the partner ahead. He dropped to the ground and took aim at the gleaming metal.

The man behind saw what was happening and, calmly, fired a shot that went straight to the skull of Lucius McCordle, whose own gun fell harmlessly to the ground.

6 A.M. WEDNESDAY, JULY 6

City Point 11:50 p.m.   July 5 1864

Colonel-General Halleck
Washington, D.C.

...We want now to crush out and destroy any force the enemy have sent north. Force enough can be spared from here to do it. I think now there is no doubt but Ewells[12] corps is away from here.

U. S. Grant
Lieutenant-General[13]

---

12   Up to this time, General Grant was still referring to the forces under Early's command as "Ewell's Corps."
13   WOTR, Series 1, Vol. 37, Part II, p. 60.

Chapter 26.
8 a.m., Wednesday, July 6, 1864

A gruff Court President Mahlon Blanchard announced this would be the final day of testimony. He sourly noticed someone missing.

Sergeant Simmons...where is McCordle?

Jed Simmons lied easily and convincingly.

He's down with the runs, Mr. Court President, Jed said. Diarrhea. Pretty bad. Asked me to take over for him.

Blanchard grunted, shrugged, and nodded to Corporal Daniel to call the court to order.

By now, witness statements had fallen into a pattern. Witness after witness—now coming in threes—told of events involving one or more of the six named Raider leaders. None of the alleged followers was ever mentioned by name, at least not by names on which witnesses could agree. A few waved at the entire crowd of thirty or more defendants.

The proceedings were becoming boring, the Raider chieftains were sullen and either apprehensive or simply resigned to their fate. The jurymen were restive.

Sergeant Breck sensed the time to end.

The prosecution rests, he said.

Late in the afternoon, after the latrine and water break, the Court President wiped his dripping face and asked Jed Simmons if he had any further witnesses.

Just one, Mr. Court President. Sergeant Ashford Cook, Massachusetts Colored Infantry.

A murmur went through the defendants. Patrick Delaney smiled wanly; Charles Curtis tensed up and Willie Collins wondered what would happen next.

Jed Simmons: Sergeant Cook, do you know any of the defendants, here?

Cook: Yeah. At least the five or six in the front row.

He named them all.

Simmons led Cook through standard questions: How many Colored soldiers were in his area, their location near the Raiders, and, finally:

Simmons: Did any of these men (gesturing toward the defendants) ever assault the Massachusetts Infantry men in your area?

Cook, avoiding dialect: They wouldn't have dared. They came by one time, they did, and we lined up like a line of big oxes, we did, and dared 'em, come on, we said, and you should have seen those fellas skedaddle back to there own huts.

Chuckling came from the jury men.

Simmons: Did they say, or do anything more…other than skedaddle?

Cook: No…except to say how neat and purty we kept our places…better, they said, than anywhere north of the sink.

Simmons: In your opinion, Sergeant Cook, do you believe that any group of soldiers that stuck together like your group did, would have prevented these men from doing any harm?

It was a most dubious question, a feeble attempt to shift responsibility from the attackers to the victims, but Simmons thought it worth a try—mainly because he had read the closing statement Lucius had prepared.

Cook: Yes, IF they stuck together like we did, these gen'men over there wouldn't have been no problem at all.

Simmons (after hesitating): No more questions. Mr. Court President, the defense rests.

Breck had no cross questions for Ashford Cook.

Instead, Breck began his closing statement immediately.

Gentlemen, Breck said, the testimony speaks for itself. These Raider leaders are six rotten tomatoes, who have spread their rot to several dozen others, and it wouldn't have been long before they infected the entire stockade. Mr. Court President, we must throw out the rot.

All six leaders, Breck concluded, should be judged guilty of capital crimes, the kind of crimes that kill people and kill the souls of men still walking and breathing. They should pay for these crimes with their lives.

Charles Curtis' grin bore an odd combination of malice and apprehension. Willie Collins shook his head but maintained his menacing glare. Andy Muir exhaled through fat, rounded lips. Pat Delaney, John Sarsfield, and Terry/John Sullivan showed no emotion or reaction of any kind. They stared ahead, blank as a slate board.

Jed Simmons apologized for the absence of Defense Attorney Sergeant McCordle and began reading the closing statement Lucius had left him:

We remind the jury panel that this stockade is packed with unfortunate men who are without useful instruction or guidance for living under these conditions. Competition and stealing for the necessities of life is commonplace.

The prosecution has selected certain individuals who are claimed to have seen, or been victims of, egregious acts of misconduct. The transcript will show that few if any witnesses identified specific defendants as having committed the alleged atrocious acts of violence and murder.

Jed then glanced down at the rest of Lucius' script, which said:

> *We also remind the jury panel that fighting and brawling have been, and are, commonplace in this stockade. Altercations occur daily over food, clothing, watches, money and other valuables, and often lead to serious injury or even death. We do not argue that the existence of such chaotic conditions excuses any act of intentional robbery or murder against relatively defenseless individuals. But we do contend that the widespread mayhem around this place, among the many thousands of prisoners here, leaves much room for doubt about the accuracy of any statements about what is often claimed to be precise identification of an alleged culprit.*

Jed ignored those words and decided, instead, to pick up on what Breck had said a few minutes earlier:

The prosecution refers to the defendants as rotten tomatoes, or apples, I forget which, Jed said. Well, let me say a few things about that. We all know the old saying that one spoiled tomato or potato can rot the whole sack or barrel. But gentlemen, remember. The rot inside a barrel or sack can come from the barrel itself! Ever see what happens when you put good spuds in an old barrel or sack that's already moldy? The whole sackful becomes a rotten mess in short order.

Now do any of you doubt this stockade is one big rotten sack? Look what it's doing to all of us! Here we are, talking about taking the lives of tough men who have a reputation for unruly behavior, and what we have in this stockade is a whole sackful of unruly men.

8 A.M., WEDNESDAY, JULY 6, 1864

With this, Jed Simmons returned to the final paragraph in Lucius McCordle's prepared statement:

In summary, members of the jury panel, we contend that the evidence is insufficient for a verdict of capital crimes. You may be convinced that acts of thievery took place and sometimes with attendant force. However, such crimes do not call for capital punishment, that is, for execution of the accused. If any of the defendants are convicted of such crimes as thievery or even assault, the appropriate remedy should be banishment from this stockade, to other prisons for captured Union soldiers.

Jed Simmons concluded, saying: Banishment, we believe, should be the maximum penalty considered after these proceedings.

With that, Jed sat down, and Court President Blanchard instructed the jury panel to consider the evidence carefully and to recommend appropriate punishment for each defendant, according to the severity of the crime committed. He neglected the words Guilty or Not Guilty.

The jury panel deliberated for less than two hours. The defense argument received less than two minutes consideration.

What the hell were they saying about rotten tomatoes? Did you understand that?

Nah. Those defense jackals are crazy as galoots. OF COURSE you get rid of rotten tomatoes if you want any chance of saving the rest of the sack.

Sure. You notice that tall one didn't show up today. Sick, was he? Huh, probably sick of this whole thing, didn't believe what he was saying, so he skedaddled.

On this last point, the juryman didn't realize how close to accuracy he was.

The final vote was taken among 10 jurymen, two having left for the hospital because of severe illness. One had dysentery, the other a leg wound that he earlier thought minor but was now becoming gangrenous. He was facing amputation of that leg without chloroform, and the possibility of further infection that would end his life within the month.

By sundown, the jurymen brought their verdict back to the court area, and Court President Blanchard ordered all to rise. The elected head of the panel stood and stiffly announced:

We find the following six prisoners guilty of the capital crimes of leading and fomenting insurrection and murder.

Blanchard frowned briefly, then shrugged with satisfaction. The term insurrection had not been mentioned at the beginning of the trial or during the proceedings but…well, what difference would it make?

Continuing, the panel head intoned the six names:

Patrick Delaney, Andrew Muir, Terrence Sullivan (whose first name had been variously stated as Terry, Cary, and John), W. R. Rickson (more confusion, since they meant Charles Curtis although some thought that meant Sullivan); Willie Collins, and John Sarsfield.

And what sentence do you recommend for these convicted defendants? the Court President asked.

The panel head cleared his throat.

We recommend death by hanging, for all six.

And for the other defendants?

8 A.M., WEDNESDAY, JULY 6, 1864

We recommend their return to the stockade, through a gauntlet to be formed by the other prisoners.

This, Jed Simmons assumed, would not include Harry Nickels, who quite clearly could not survive another pummeling by gauntlet men with clubs and/or knives of some sort. His assumption was correct. The Court President, continuing in his benign mood, made certain that Harry Nickels would not run the gauntlet.

―――

Here it is, Captain Wirz, the former colonel-now-sergeant-and-prisoner-but-also-Court President said authoritatively, as he handed over the transcript.

Perhaps at some future and...heh, heh...happier day, Blanchard said, we can correspond like gentlemen and discuss some of the interesting legal and philosophic facets of this case.

The camp commander glanced sharply at Blanchard, without replying. He was in no mood to chat about the future, especially with a prisoner even stuffier than General Winder. Ignoring all the pages of testimony, Wirz looked to the end and found the phrase he was looking for:

Verdict: Six Raider Leaders—Collins, Curtis, Rickson, DeLaney, Muir and Sarsfield—found guilty of mass mayhem and murder and sentenced to death by hanging. Captain Wirz yelled for Lieutenant Granbury to review the transcript.

Granbury quickly found something the Captain, with his impatience and poor eyesight had missed: Mention of the secret letter from Lee to Early. Granbury pointed to that section, holding the transcript before Wirz' eyes. The Captain blanched, then with a flash of insight recovered quickly.

Wunderbar! Now General Winder will learn about that *verdammt* letter just by reading the transcript! If he catches it, I shrug; If not, nothing to be upset about. Let them mull it over in Richmond.

———

General Winder returned on schedule, Thursday, July 7. He was in no better mood than Captain Wirz, a man with whom he sympathized, but did little to help. Wirz was always harrying him about more guards, more doctors, more meat, better flour…by gawd, if those fools in Richmond would listen to me and give me decent men, and food for these prisoners…how the hell do they think I can take care of thirty thousand men on 20 acres?

To the General, allowing the prisoners to court martial the trouble-makers wasn't such a bad idea, even though it was without precedent. It was certainly a diversion, and might settle things down, Winder thought. Maybe even prevent a riot or a breakout. This Sergeant from Illinois…what was his name?..had done well organizing those Regulators, and the stockade seemed to be a quieter place.

Not that General Winder ever went inside the stockade. He didn't. And those who criticized him, he thought, were just plain dumb. Why put in danger the life of the one man who keeps fighting to improve this damned place? Here I am, hated like the devil by the prisoners, and detested almost as much by those bastards at Richmond who can't see the importance of a well-run prison camp. The word is out that we don't feed them well, and now those damned Yankees are getting back at Confederate prisoners up there in New York and Chicago.

At 10a.m. Thursday, July 7, General Winder hadn't been at Camp Sumter a half hour before Captain Wirz appeared with a handful of papers: The transcript of The Trial of the Raiders. Winder received his camp commander with his usual grunt, and took the sheaf of papers still reeking from the sweat of Gilbert Daniel's feverish hands.

So do they want us to line up a firing squad?

No, Sir, they will hang them by their necks with ropes.

How many?

Six. The leaders.

Huh. Well, hanging them saves ammunition. Besides, our guards are so goddammed incompetent they probably couldn't hit a man tied to a post 8 feet away. But...only six?

Ringleaders. The others, they will have to run a gauntlet back into the stockade.

Winder looked up, quizzically.

And then they hang the six?

Yes.

Winder rubbed his chin.

Sounds like an exciting day, first a gauntlet running and then a hanging. I thought the whole idea of allowing this trial was to calm things down. Christ, man, there's thirty thousand men in that pen! What if they get so fussed up with the gauntlet and the hanging they charge the two gates?

Ach, I thought of that. I tell the sergeants that the cannons are loaded with grape, and we shoot anyone who bunches at the gate.

Well, Henry, let's hope you're right. Rumors of a hanging are buzzing out in the countryside. Old men, women and kids will be crawling all around the place as soon as we fix a date. Best show they've had in years. Except, if it's inside the stockade, outsiders won't get to see much of it.

And that's going to be next Monday, July 11?

Ja. Not good on Sunday.

General Winder hadn't seen the transcript's inclusion of the fabled Lee-to-Early letter. Wirz decided he couldn't put the responsibility on the General unless he was aware of it.

Wirz reached over Winder's shoulder, flipped a page or two, found the reference to the letter and pointed to it.

General Winder was as startled by this letter as those before him, but his reaction was curiosity rather than consternation:

Well, I'll be gawddammed. Maybe it was a secret, at one time, but not now. It's all over Macon. Early crossed the Potomac into Maryland two days ago and the Yankees in Washington City are scared as hell. Damned good man, that Jubal!

But...dammit, Wirz, it was a secret all through June. How the hell did this letter get into the stockade, for gawd's sake?

Captain Wirz related, briefly, the story of a prisoner who picked up pieces of paper on ground that Early's Corps had recently left.

General Winder drummed his fingers on the table for a moment. What to do? It had been understood initially that the court martial transcript would be sent to Richmond for authorization for whatever punishment the court recommended. But in the past week, things had changed. The hated Yankee General Sherman had taken Kennesaw Mountain and, since then, had overrun Vining's Station and was closing in on Atlanta.

Winder tried to think it through:

If Atlanta falls, Macon won't be far behind and then it's less than 30 miles to Andersonville, where Sherman would probably be eager to recover 30,000 of his troops. Oh, they wouldn't all be fit for

8 A.M., WEDNESDAY, JULY 6, 1864

fighting, but half might and that might be the best part of a Corps in strength.

Well, we won't humbug Richmond with this. They won't give me lumber, meat or decent guards, so why would those dolts give any thought to the hanging of six goons? Their problem now is finding a replacement for that dumbhead Joe Johnston who doesn't have the smarts or guts to defend Atlanta.

Henry, do what you want with this transcript. Then have them go ahead with the hanging. I'll give you a letter authorizing it if you want.

Captain Wirz was worried.

Suppose someone asks later why we didn't tell Richmond?

Easy. I tell them the telegraph was down. Which it is, in fact. I plan to ask for authorization to rebuild it. Maybe tomorrow, maybe next day. And hope we can protect it from our own men.

Andersonville   July 9, 1864

....Believe me, there is very great danger here. Twelve of my reserves deserted last night with arms, and I cannot depend on them....

JNO H. Winder
  Brigadier-General[14]

---

14   *WOTR, Series 2, Vol. 7, p. 451.*

Chapter 27.
<u>The Hanging</u>

Wan, emaciated, and ragged prisoners who hadn't seen usable lumber anywhere in the stockade since their arrival stood transfixed by the mules pulling a well-worn wagon piled with timbers and rudely cut boards. They knew this wasn't for huts or a barracks.

The word was out: The timbers, each one more than 20 feet long, were intended for a crude gallows, to be erected this Monday, July 11, south of the sink and very near the huts of the Colored prisoners. Common and visible as dying was, this lumber would produce death in a way heretofore unseen in the stockade. It would speed six reasonably healthy men to Kingdom Come—together and in full view of thousands of yelling, stomping and taunting prisoners and a huge audience of area Georgians, mostly older men, women and children. Neck-stretching, it was called. The top entertainment of the summer.

So up went the structure, quickly and efficiently, slowed for a short time by professional arguments among three carpenters-turned-soldiers-turned-prisoners.

What? Only two stand posts? Hell, it'll tip over soon's three men climb up there, not to mention six, plus the hangmen and maybe the priest.

Well, Wirz give us these pieces and none more, you try to get more out of him.

Now jest a minit. You ain't gonna have a continuous floor at all?

Don't need none. See? Lemme sketch it in the dirt fer yuh. The main beam at the top will hold it all together, and it's long enough for six nooses. We dig the stand posts into the ground, tamp 'em down…

Jeez, it ain't gonna be steady. You fellas do it. I don' wanna be here when the whole goddam shitteree comes tumbling down. Idea is to hang those bastards, not make us look like fools.

Ain't gonna collapse, or anything. We put angle braces at each top corner, see, like this.

Christ, I hope the priest and hangmen are smart enough to climb down off the damned thing before they drop the planks.

The argument ended when the two stronger and surlier carpenters of the group simply went ahead as they had planned all along. Up went the gallows as a square, inverted U, some 20 feet high, with a 20-foot beam across the top and angle braces at each upper corner. Half-way up each stand post, the workmen nailed heavy wooden cleats to hold one end of each of two planks. The other plank ends butted together in the center and rested on a pair of stacked barrels, with a 10-foot rope attached to the bottom one.

Six rope nooses hung from the top beam, evenly spaced across the 20-foot span. At the ultimate moment, two strong men would yank the rope, causing the barrels to tumble, the planks to collapse, and the condemned men to drop until their bodies took up the slack in their ropes. They would then either die quickly from broken necks or dance on air until strangled to lifelessness.

By 11 a.m., the gallows, such as it was, stood ready for its clients.

———

Some 15,000 prisoners—roughly half the inmates—crowded around the gallows that afternoon. The other half of the prisoners, especially sick and starving ones, saw death as so personally close and inevitable they wanted no part of the spectacle.

I figger bein' gone in a week or two, an' this wou'nt help me git ready fer it, drawled a despondent and bone-thin Michigan man sprawled under his leaky lean-to.

Ya? Doncha think mebbe seein' them bastards stretch their necks would be like a tonic?

Mebbe for you. Not fer me.

Hundreds of local folks—women in gingham, men in tattered work clothes almost as ragged as prisoners, barefoot children in floppy straw hats, a few women in their Sunday finery and a half dozen men of means sporting cravats and puffing expensive cigars gathered in the hill above the south end of the stockade, some atop wagons and carriages, straining for a better look at the coming event. A cluster of Black men and women watched from farther back on the hill while youngsters perched high in the distant trees.

Scores of diary-keepers noted the more memorable moments of the Hanging of the Raiders about 4:30 p.m. Monday, July 11, 1864 at Andersonville Prison.

All the other defendants, except the six Raider leaders, were sent back into the stockade alive, but not exactly unpunished, since their only available route was through another double-lined gauntlet of some 50 club-wielding men on each side, an arrangement that again led to many bashed heads and broken arms and ribs and bruised buttocks and other assorted injuries to all except Harry Nickels who was spared from doing this a second time, owing to the Court President's pleasure in noting that not only had the fickle and bothersome Sergeant McCordle given up on REALLY trying to defend the Raiders but, even better, absented himself from the last day of testimony, leaving it quite agreeable for the Court President to specify that Harry be led in quietly by Sergeant Jed Simmons before sunup that morning in the same state of health he had tolerated during the trial, which meant that he might survive for a while, and then, shortly before 11 o'clock, Captain Wirz led a guard detail and the six condemned Raiders into the stockade, said in his thick Germanic accent that he now washed his hands of this entire affair and asked the Creator to have mercy on their souls after which he and his guard detail did an about-face and marched back out of the stockade, leaving the ensuing proceedings entirely in the hands of the prisoners, soon after which Charles Curtis opined loudly that he did not chose to die this way and accordingly broke the rotted ropes binding his hands, pushed his handlers aside and ran in stumbling stride to the sink area where various prisoners aggrieved by Curtis' previous felonious transgressions joyously ran him down and tackled him in the foul mud, making a scene that led Captain Wirz to believe the long-dreaded breakout was about to begin and therefore it was necessary to yell Fire to the cannon crews, which he did, but was ignored by the artillery Captain who saw the chase was away from the walls and toward the sink and therefore was not a breakout attempt at all, but simply a happy band of Regulators dragging Curtis back toward the gallows while sportingly accommodating his wish for a good drink of water before he should die, all this happening about the same time Willie Collins took a long look at the crude gallows looming up on the South slope and wondered aloud whether they would all be hanged up there and heard Sergeant LeRoy Key's clipped and forever-quoted answer, That's about the size of it, following which three of the condemned six begged for mercy, vowing never to do harm to their fellow prisoners again, while scores of prisoners in the crowd yelled and taunted and urged that the hanging begin, during which time Patrick Delaney sternly advised his fellow prisoners and especially the once-formidable giant but now-weepy Willie Mosby Collins to quit whining and get up there on the scaffold and listen to Father Whelan and face death like a man, which the other four more or less did with some even asking forgiveness from prisoners they may have inconvenienced or even harmed, while all this time Father Whelan continued chanting the sacred words of extreme unction, until Sergeant Key said Time's Up, flour-sack hoods draped over the six heads, Key gave the signal, three strong men yanked the rope, the barrels and planks collapsed, and the six men dropped to the ends of their ropes, although it was really only five since Collins, the heaviest, broke the rotted noose rope, fell to the ground in such a shocked stupor that he wondered whether he was in the next world but then found to his dazed dismay that indeed he was still in the first but only for a minute before he would finally get to the next, information that led him to complain that he was most unjustly being required to die twice, but to no avail since the executioners prodded him back up the rickety ladder where there was now no plank to stand on since the barrels had fallen askew and any attempt to replace them both, or even a single plank, would be most awkward with the other five men in a row dangling and kicking in their death throes so that meant that, See, Willie, what you got to do is stand right here on the cleat, no we'll hold you so you don't fall…well, you will in a few seconds…yeah, this is much stronger rope and now there you go and…yup, now he's swinging with the others.

Leesburg   July 14, 1864

Report of Lieut. Gen. Jubal A. Early, C. S. Army, of operations July 8-14, including the battle of the Monocacy and operations against Washington, D. C.

...On the morning of the 10th I moved toward Washington ...I became satisfied that the assault would be attended with such great sacrifice as would insure the destruction of my whole force....accordingly, after threatening the city all day of the 12th, I retired after night, and have moved to this place in entire good order and without any loss whatever...Washington can never be taken by our troops unless surprised when without a force to defend it...

      Respectfully, J. A. Early
      Lieutenant-General[15]

---

15 WOTR, Series 1, Vol. 37, Part 1, p. 347.

Epilogue

On a cool autumn day in 1869, Maryanne Callander and Aleysha returned to Coulee City after a wearying, dismal train ride from Atlanta through Chattanooga, Nashville, Chicago, Madison and finally to the home town depot. Maryanne worried about making ends meet; Buck Sewall had sold his newspaper and that meant the end of her job there. Her meager savings had paid for the train tickets and losing her job had made the time available for the trip to Georgia.

Next day she checked at the post office where she found a thick envelope addressed to her in a very familiar script: obviously the hand writing of Lucius McCordle. Was this a letter lost for five years, finally found and posted? Such things were known to occur after this civil conflagration that seemed as chaotic at its end as during its middle.

She tore the envelope open and saw the first of several pages in that…oh, so lovingly familiar script. And there was the place and date:

Ossabaw Island, Georgia, October 10, 1869.

Lucius!! He is alive!

My Dearest Maryanne:

I have no satisfactory explanation for why I have not taken a pen in hand and written to you earlier. Such failure is due partly to my own weakness of character, but also to the unhappy circumstances preceding my departure in 1863. Perhaps it was my guilt from failing in both my life with you and in my profession. Now, however, I have finally mustered the courage to tell you about the past five years since I was captured and sent to Andersonville Prison where I failed utterly in an attempt to successfully mount any kind of meaningful defense for a hapless group of hoodlums who, with more inspired counsel, might have escaped the hangman's noose. Yes, they were brutal men, but I have never believed it right to kill criminals, no matter how heinous the crime.

Remember Judge Blanchard? By some cruel twist of fate, that man appeared in Andersonville Prison as judge over the court martial about which I write. My relations with him deteriorated to the point where I found it appropriate to leave the trial and escape the prison July 5, 1864, in a fruitless attempt to inform General Grant about Jubal Early's secret plans, revealed in the trial, to assault Washington

In spite of the full-hearted efforts of enslaved people in Georgia to help me, all of whom risked their lives in doing so, my efforts to get information to General Grant or to connect with General Sherman then were futile. I was seen and shot in the head by a Georgia home guard man, but it was only a scalp wound that left me bleeding although quite able to recover. I convinced these people I was a captain and army lawyer, which impressed them amply. They sent me to a stockade, first at Mellen in Georgia, and when Sherman again approached, to Camp Sorghum in Charleston South Carolina. There I reposed until Sherman's army reached that place in February of 1865. They transferred us to an open field near an insane asylum. It was easy to escape, so I quickly availed myself to Sherman's soldiers. I soon learned that General Sherman had issued an order to make thousands of acres of confiscated land from the Carolinas to Florida available for settlement of freed slave people.

Appreciating the legal problems the resettled people would face, I offered my services as a lawyer to aid these people who have been so oppressed and exploited for so many years. My services were quickly accepted and a short time later Congress created the Freedman's Bureau, with which I am certain you are familiar.

After the Confederacy capitulated in April of that year, I elected to stay on as an agent for this Bureau, and spent my time on Ossabaw and Supelo islands and other places around Savannah, representing these people who, in nearly every case, had been egregiously misled. Each family, in good faith, expected 40 acres and a mule which they would own forever, but they soon learned such was not to be the case. At best, they had to settle for being wage earners (and at pitiful rates!) for the original plantation owners who in most cases successfully petitioned for return of their lands which they had abandoned during the war because of the constant cannonading from Federal gunboats.

Furthermore, troubles of every kind you can imagine rained upon these people who were tasting freedom for the first time. Where would they get lumber for building houses and farm buildings? Schools and churches? Feed grains and hay for their cows and pigs and mules? Machinery for tilling their land and harvesting their crops? The initial enthusiasm of these people turned to dismay and disillusion as one promise after another went unfulfilled. Then human vexations of all manner tore through the fabric of daily lives—courtship and marriage, disputes over property and land, difficulty in working together after being free of Massa's whip.

I did my best to give these people as much legal advice and help as possible, but I could do nothing about the Federal government's failure to provide them with genuine title to property. Yet I continued as best I could until earlier this year, when the Bureau program was discontinued.

I expect to reach Coulee City about a week from now. I don't expect you to welcome me as you might have if I had been in regular and faithful contact with you. I would not be surprised to learn you have a new love, but in any case I wish to see you and Aleysha, who will be about 10 years old now.

There is one thing I should add. I will be accompanied by my daughter Magnolia, now three years old. Her mother, Hibiscus Davis, died shortly after Magnolia's birth, her health diminished greatly by injuries endured during years of whippings from her former Massa at the plantation.

Hoping you will find it convenient to see me again,
With affection,

Lucius

Graves of the six convicted and hanged Raider Chiefs in the cemetery, apart from the thousands of prisoners who died honorably, at the Andersonville National Historic Site.
(Photograph by the author)

Phillip J. Tichenor is a retired Journalism Professor at the University of Minnesota. He is author of *Athena's Forum*, a novel, and is co-author (with Larry A. Jones) of biographical *Civil War P.O.W.: The Life and Death of a Farmer-Lawyer-Soldier*.